FALLEN MESSENGERS BOOK FIVE

HARBINGER

AVA MARIE SALINGER

COPYRIGHT

FALLEN MESSENGERS GLOSSARY

Aerial: An angel or demon who can control wind.

Alchemist: A human who can create new matter or manipulate existing matter into new forms. Emits a scent of powdered iron.

Aqueous: An angel or demon who can control water.

Argent Lake: Home of the Naiads.

Argonaut Agency: Organization responsible for law and order in the supernatural and magical communities. Headquarters in New York. Agents include angels, demons, and magic users.

Astrea Sea: Home of the Nereids.

Black Fates: The Keres. Goddesses of Death. Tenebra, Kes, and Orena.

Bloodsand: A black tree with red veins that grows in the Nine Hells. Created by warlocks who made pacts with the Underworld after the Fall. Can be used to summon war demons from the Nine Hells.

Blossom Silver: A silver derivative that can heal injuries caused by demonic weapons or black magic. Made by the Naiads.

Cabalista: Demonic organization. Agents include demons only. Headquarters in London.

Dark Blight: A powder black-magic users use in their rituals and which is poisonous to angels and other magic users. Made by Shadow Empire alchemists from the heart of a Dryad.

Demi: The offspring of a God of Heaven/God of the Underworld and a human or a being possessing divine powers. Can take on any appearance.

Electrum: Naturally occurring alloy of gold and silver, as well as copper and other trace elements. Used extensively by Argonaut in their weapons. Combined with steel, titanium, and Rain Silver to make their bullets.

Empyreal: The highest order of angels or demons, with powers equal to those of a Demigod.

Enchanter/Enchantress: A human who uses illusion

magic. Emits a scent of cedar.

Fiery: An angel or a demon who can wield Heaven or Hell's Fire.

Fractured Soul: A human's damaged soul core, extracted from the body – a powerful source of magic.

Furies: The Erinyes. Goddesses of Vengeance. Tisiphone, Megaera, and Alecto.

Ghoul: An evil spirit who consumes the flesh of humans. Emits a scent of rotting meat.

Glitterfang: A pale powder white-magic users employ in their rituals and which is poisonous to demons and black-magic users. Made by Nereids.

Hesperides: Nymphs of the West. Goddesses of the Evening. Guardians of the Sacred Tree. Erytheis, Hesperia, and Arethusa.

Hexa: Guild of magic users. Agents include magic users only. Headquarters in Seattle.

Incubus: A male demon who gains power from sleeping with humans and divine entities.

Ivory Peaks: Home of the Dryads.

Khimer: A creature born of the fusion of a Reaper and a living being.

Lucifugous: A heliophobic demon who abhors light and who can control darkness.

Mage: A human who uses an arcane staff to focus their magic powers. Emits a scent of Juniper.

Magic Levels: Classification of magic users based on their abilities, with Level Six being the weakest and Level One the strongest.

Messengers: Those belonging to the Third Sphere of Heaven and Third Hierarchy of Demons.

Moirai: The Fates. Goddesses of Destiny. Clotho, Lachesis, and Atropos.

Order of Rosen: Religious order affiliated with the Catholic Church. Agents include angels only. Headquarters in Rome.

Potamos: A male Nymph.

Rain Silver: A liquid-silver derivative that can injure and kill demons. Made by the Nymphs.

Rain Vale: Home of the Nymphs.

Reaper: A soul collector and guide of the dead. Emits a

scent of camphor.

Reaper Seed: A drug that can intoxicate most beings and which is fatal in high doses. Mined by Lucifugous demons in the Shadow Empire. Potent hallucinogen for Lucifugous demons.

Shadow Empire: Home of Ghouls, Lucifugous demons, and Dark Alchemists.

Sorcerer/Sorceress: A human born with powerful soul core magic. Uses the energies around them to manipulate magic. Emits the scent of Valerian.

Soul Core: A living being's life force. Red for demons, white for angels, and dirty gray for humans.

Spirit Realm: Home of Pan, the Gods of the Underworld, and lesser spirits.

Stark Steel: Strongest and most magic-resistant metal on Earth. Found exclusively in the weapons and armor of the Fallen.

Succubus: A female demon who gains power from sleeping with humans and divine entities.

Terrene: An angel or demon who can control earth and its derivative metals.

The Fall: An unexplained event five hundred years ago

that resulted in an army of angels and demons falling to Earth.

The Fallen: Angels or demons who fell to Earth.

The Nether: The space between Heaven, Earth, and the Nine Hells.

The Abyss: A forgotten realm beyond the Nether from where there is no escape. Also know as the Eater of Souls.

War Demon: Demon soldiers created for battle. Remnants of an ancient war between Heaven and Hell. Banished to the deepest parts of the Hells.

Warlock: A human who draws power from demons and the Hells and converts it to magic. Emits a scent of sulfur.

Wizard/Witch: A human who learns to use magic through spell books, and who utilizes potions and rituals to access their soul-core magic. Emits a scent of Frankincense.

PRELUDE

FIVE HUNDRED YEARS AGO, THE SEVENTH PURGATORY

THE DISTANT SCREAMS OF THE DAMNED ECHOED DIMLY in Atropos's ears as the chains holding her prisoner bit into her ankles and wrists. The dark shackles tightened, slicing into her flesh, the hateful susurration the links made as they writhed against one another grating rawly on her nerve endings.

Even though three hundred years had passed since she and her sisters had been locked up in Purgatory by the God of Darkness, Atropos still hadn't gotten used to the damn sound.

Sweat dripped from her chin and splashed onto the rock beneath her bare feet, dark blotches hissing and evaporating almost as soon as they formed. She shook her head lightly to clear the eternal grogginess clouding her mind. The effort cost her what little strength she had managed to garner in the past hour, her skull so heavy upon her neck it felt like it would fall off at any moment.

Hotness stained her skin, distracting her from the bleak thoughts spinning endlessly through her subconscious. Her breaths shuddered in and out of her as she twisted her head a fraction to look at her left arm. She clenched her teeth.

Elios's corrupt fetters seemed almost gleeful as they absorbed the red ichor and divine energy draining from her immortal body. It was one of the ways their treacherous brother had grown his powers since he'd imprisoned them down here. And it was helping him control her and her eight sisters, amongst other things.

Inky lines shivered under her flesh next to where the chains bound her, the eerie apparitions pulsing in tandem with the seed of darkness Elios had wedged deep inside her body to suppress her soul core.

Atropos swallowed down bile and dragged her gaze from the ghastly evidence of the abomination her brother had visited upon her, her head hanging heavy once more. Sulfurous fumes stung her eyes and burned her nostrils as she blinked sweat out of her lashes. Had she been in full possession of her godly powers, they would not have irritated her so.

Determination brought a fresh surge of life through her veins. *Soon. It will be over soon. We shall escape this accursed place and deliver the Fate that bastard truly deserves!*

A chorus of voices danced through her skull at that thought. *Yes, sister!*

Atropos's heart pounded at the fury they contained,

her sisters' emotions mirroring her own rage. She lifted her chin with some difficulty and gazed across the vast crater surrounding the rocky outcrop she was chained upon.

Even with her divine vision, she could barely make out the boulders they were bound to through the thick, yellow clouds pouring out of the giant gulfs of spitting lava that defined the hellish landscape of the Seventh Purgatory.

Still, though she could not see them, her sisters' voices lent her the strength she needed to continue pouring what little divine energy she could access across the tenuous bond that linked her to Lachesis, the second of the Moirai, and to Tenebra, the eldest of the Black Fates, also known in Heaven and the Hells as the Keres.

Atropos focused and cast her mind out to the Goddesses trapped in the Underworld with her. *Are you nearly ready, sisters?!*

Clotho replied first. *Yes. The thread is almost spun.*

Relief laced with urgency resonated through Atropos. Of the two conditions they needed to achieve their escape, the youngest Moira's task was the most important.

Tenebra?

The eldest Black Fate finally answered. *I am almost done too, sister.*

Despite Tenebra's steady tone, Atropos could hear a trace of pain in her voice. Frustration gnawed at her insides. The Black Fate's duty was the more arduous one for sure.

I'm sorry, Ten.

It was a moment before Tenebra spoke. *You have nothing to be sorry about, Attie. None of this was your fault.*

Guilt tightened Atropos's chest. Though she knew her sisters did not blame her for their wretched fate, there was no denying she might have been able to stop Elios had she acted in time. Her nails bit into her palms.

I should have cut that snake's throat the second I sensed his intentions!

I'm not sure about that, Attie, Lachesis said in a strained voice. *I am pretty certain Hypnos would have stopped you.*

Atropos swallowed. The second Moira was right.

Bitterness welled up inside her at the thought of Elios's twin. *And look where our foolish brother ended up.*

Her sisters stayed silent at her sour words. Hypnos's fortune was even worse than their own. Elios had shown his twin no mercy despite the latter's steadfast loyalty and blind affection over the millennia of their existence.

A flash in the sky caught Atropos's eye. She tilted her head, the muscles in her neck quivering with the effort of that simple act. Her pulse quickened as she observed the fading brilliance rippling across the crimson firmament.

It could only mean one thing.

It has begun!

Tension oozed through her as her sisters' feelings resonated with her soul.

Tisiphone's voice quavered a little. *Is there a chance he might actually win?*

The third Fury could not stop the hope lacing her words.

Though her sisters could not see her, Atropos shook her head, her heart leaden with remorse. *No. The Awakener* will *lose this war. For it is his Fate. He must fall to Earth with the others. And so it has to be, for all that is yet to come.*

A grim hush fell across her bond with her sisters.

Pity, muttered Alecto, the first Fury. *I always wanted to have a taste of that demigod. He is ripe for the taking.*

A chorus of groans echoed inside Atropos's head. She bit back a sigh.

Orena, the youngest Black Fate, sounded appropriately disgusted. *I can't believe you're letting your loins do the thinking right now, you shameful Goddess!*

Oh, come now, Rena, Alecto retorted, undaunted. *Don't tell me you haven't wondered what it would be like to bed the North Star?*

I have to admit to having been curious about this too, mused Kes, the second Black Fate. *Of course, there is no way in the Nine Hells Ivmir would ever let us find out how sweet a morsel Icarus is. That foulmouthed brother of ours is like a dog with a bone when it comes to his lover.*

Megaera, the second Fury, sniffed. *Ivmir is a dimwit.*

Hear, hear, said Tisiphone.

Atropos sagged against her chains. *Now is hardly the time to be talking about this, sisters. We have to—!*

Heat flared through her chest, drawing a gasp from

her lips. The sound was echoed by the rest of her sisters.

I am done! Tenebra exclaimed triumphantly.

A golden light flared north of Atropos's location. Her eyes widened, the hope pouring through her so strong it choked her lungs.

She could feel her connection with the eldest Black Fate growing stronger.

Tenebra's tone hardened. *Bear with me, sisters. This will hurt for but a moment.*

Pain engulfed the very heart of Atropos as Tenebra's Rot gripped the dark seed within her. She doubled over, blood pearling on her lip where she'd bitten it.

This is but a fraction of what Tenebra has endured all these years. I must weather it!

A grunt escaped her throat as the Black Fate started destroying Elios's hold upon her from the inside out. She ground her teeth, the agony of the assault threatening to tear apart her very being.

She could feel her sisters' hurt across their bonded minds and souls.

Tears sprang to her eyes, not so much from the torment ripping through her and her beloved kin as from regret. A regret she would have to live with forever more.

It has taken too long! I should have put this plan in action three centuries ago! Maybe—maybe we could have stopped what's coming!

Don't do this to yourself, Attie, mumbled Tisiphone, her voice thin with pain. *You may be a Goddess of Destiny but you are not infallible. None of us is!*

Her tortured words were a brief balm upon Atropos's wretched heart.

Just a little more, sisters! Tenebra growled.

Atropos shuddered as the Black Fate's divine energy seared her soul. Elios's black core finally shattered, the sound so loud it resonated through every cell and fiber of her body and drew a scream from her lips. Power flooded her with her next heartbeat, robbing her of breath, the taste so sweet and wonderful after going so long without it she could only sob.

The dark chains that had held her captive for three hundred years hissed and dissipated as they fell, the God of Darkness's corrupt shackles vanishing in the divine light throbbing from her flesh. Her gold, laurel crown bloomed into life upon her head at the same time dazzling white wings unfurled from her back.

Points of radiance dotted the distance as her sisters regained their godly powers.

It had taken one hundred years for Tenebra to rot the corrupt kernel within herself. One hundred years of slowly and agonizingly chipping away at the evil energy entrapping her soul, every nick and scratch likely filling her with immeasurable agony.

Atropos knew what it must have cost the Black Fate to achieve this almost unsurmountable feat. She fisted her hands.

I will not let her efforts go to waste!

A storm bloomed above her as she rose from her prison and converged on her sisters, the wind whistling in her ears and ruffling her long, silver hair. Dark clouds were rushing across the firmament, the formations twisting in eldritch shapes that heralded what was to come. Lightning cracked, the accompanying thunder so loud it rattled Atropos's teeth.

The Nether was about to tear, just as she had foreseen.

They met in the center of the crater and clasped and kissed each other for long minutes, their faces full of tears, the love that existed between them brightening their bond. Though they had been given different titles and tasks upon their creation, they would always be tied by their affection for one another.

"How goes the thread, Clo?" Atropos asked urgently.

Clotho smiled and showed them her hand. In it was the gold thread she had been spinning for the past hundred years. *"It is finished, sister."*

Relief rushed through Atropos. She shuddered and briefly closed her eyes.

She had known the task she had given the youngest Moira would be nigh impossible. To spin a different Fate for them was technically forbidden. But, considering the Gods of old continued to hide in the Heavens and had done nothing to stop Elios, Atropos had decided bending the laws that ruled them was justifiable in this instance.

They can punish me all they want afterward. Atropos squared her shoulders. *And I shall tell them what I think of them straight to their cowardly faces!*

Tenebra's Rot had freed them from Elios's hold. But it was the Fate Clotho had created for them that would ensure their escape from the prison where Elios had trapped them. They just needed the right distraction to keep the God of Darkness's eyes away from the Seventh Purgatory long enough for them to make their getaway.

The ground trembled as the havoc in the Nether reverberated across all the realms. Giant slabs of rock detached from the walls of the crater and crashed down with dull roars. Debris and dust filled the air, casting turbulent billows in the sulfurous clouds filling the depression and exposing the lava bubbling violently from the crevasses snaking across the hellish landscape.

"Here they come," warned Kes.

Figures loomed into view atop the distant cliff's edge. More crowded the sky. They encircled the Goddesses' prison, their number some five hundred strong. Atropos's knuckles whitened.

The regiment of war demons and the thirty Nephilim and Cyclops Elios had tasked with guarding them looked daunting even at a distance. Fury ignited her blood as her brother's face swam before her eyes.

She reached out a hand to her right. *"Come!"*

A pair of giant, golden shears shimmered into existence in her palm, the weapon manifesting from where it had lain hidden within her soul. She gripped the handles and separated the blades to form two deadly sabers.

Her sisters' weapons appeared in their grasp, their faces full of the same rage burning through her.

"Wait for it," Atropos warned.

The disruption in the sky accelerated. An uncanny

light pulsed through the inky formations roiling above them.

Any second now!

Atropos's ears popped when a deafening silence befell them. Her heart slammed a rapid tempo upon her breastbone. She could sense the same hush spreading across every realm connected to the Nether.

The space where the four Guardians lived and carried out their duties to protect them all from the Abyss fractured with a noise that heralded the ending of worlds. Violent quakes shook the Seventh Purgatory. The land beneath them started to split.

A dark crack tore across the sky.

"*NOW!*" Atropos barked.

They shot out of the crater and arrowed toward the fracture line high above them, nine points of golden light that caused sonic booms to rip the sulfur-laden atmosphere. Nine Goddesses full of the wrath gathered over half a millennium and the iron-clad determination to best the foul God who had intended to trap them in that hellhole for eternity.

The war demons and the Nephilim moved. Crimson radiance bloomed in the Cyclops' eyes as they directed their deadly gazes at them, their mouths opening to release their paralyzing screams.

Blood and ash clouded the space around Atropos as she and her sisters transformed and engaged the monsters who would stop them, their dresses morphing into gold armor that shielded them from the neck down while their crowns extended into winged helmets that framed their faces. The divine power they emanated canceled out the soundwaves the Cyclops directed at them, just as their speed evaded the monsters' beams.

The Furies' brass-studded scourges found their targets with unerring accuracy, their black wings cracking the air like thunder as they flew straight and true. Clotho's spinning staff and Lachesis's rod cracked skulls and limbs where they danced between their enemy. Atropos whizzed around the war demons and the Nephilim, her golden blades carving their flesh to the bone.

"We cannot be tardy!" she shouted as she sliced off the heads of two fiends and smashed another one in the face with the handle of a saber. *"That opening will close soon!"*

She indicated the tear in the Nether. Her sisters nodded grimly.

A giant stone club whooshed past Atropos's left flank. Her scowling gaze found the Nephil beneath her. Though the creatures could not fly as fast nor as high as the war demons, they more than made up for it with their formidable strength.

Tenebra and Kes smashed into the giant and raked his face and eyes. The Black Fates had taken on their full forms, those of terrifying, bloodthirsty Goddesses of Death with wicked talons as long as their forearms. Shadows boiled around their inky wings as they slipped through the silent Nephil's attacks, their movements so fast only someone with divine powers could detect them.

Atropos silently thanked her sisters and focused on

the war demons who stood between them and their escape route.

"*To me! We do this together!*" she barked. "*No one gets left behind!*"

Divine strength flooded every cell of her body and thrummed across her bond with the other Goddesses as they converged on her location. They ascended as one through their opponents' ranks, their weapons tearing through flesh and bones and wings until their faces and armor were drenched in blood. But though they fought valiantly, their progress remained agonizingly slow in Atropos's eyes.

Frustration churned her stomach. *Damn it! At this rate, the Nether will—!*

The sky rippled above her. Terror squeezed Atropos's heart. Her worst fears were being realized. The crack was starting to close.

"*Go!*" Tenebra yelled.

She dropped toward the war demons and Nephilim closing in on them, her face full of grim purpose. Clotho, Lachesis, and two of the Furies, Alecto and Megaera, followed her.

"*Noooo!*" Atropos screamed. "*Come back!*"

Orena and Tisiphone grabbed her arms as she made to go after them.

"*It is better that some of us make it out of here than none of us does,*" Kes said in a strained voice where she floated beside her.

"*She's right, Attie.*" Tisiphone's knuckles blanched on her scourge. She met Atropos's tearful gaze before glaring at the war demons in their path. "*Take heart, sister. Elios will not kill them. Upon my honor as a Goddess, we shall come back and free our kin!"*

The firmament shuddered as the tear in the Nether continued to seal itself. Atropos faltered for a timeless moment before nodding jerkily. Her gaze shifted forlornly to the five Goddesses fighting to secure their escape.

Her sisters were right. It was better that some of them escaped this place and made plans to defeat Elios, rather than all of them becoming his eternal prisoners.

The four of them ascended toward the shrinking rift in the sky. Their chests heaved and their breaths shuddered out of their bodies in labored gasps and grunts as they worked their way through the troop of war demons trying to stop them, their weapons growing slippery with black blood.

By the time they reached the tear that would lead them out of the Seventh Purgatory, Atropos's limbs were trembling from exhaustion. She cast a final look at the Goddesses far beneath them before she entered the rift, her heart heavy and her soul bruised.

"We shall return, sisters!" Her voice broke. *"We shall be together once more!"*

"Take care, Rena!" Tenebra shouted at her youngest sister before ripping a war demon to shreds. *"Watch over her, Kes!"*

Tears streamed down Orena's face as she beheld her eldest sibling. Kes took her hand, her chin quivering.

"Stay strong, Tis!" Alecto and Megaera yelled at Tisiphone.

Tisiphone nodded and sniffed.

"*Be well, Attie!*" Lachesis called out.

Clotho met Atropos's gaze, her eyes bright with affection. "*I love you, sister.*"

Their figures disappeared amidst the crowd of teeming war demons and Nephilim surrounding them as the rift closed.

Darkness and silence engulfed the four Goddesses who had escaped Purgatory.

Tisiphone's expression was haggard with fatigue and the pain of losing their kin. "*What now?*"

"*We find somewhere safe for us to rest and restore our divine energy.*" Atropos swallowed, grief giving way to a resolve that would not be broken. "*Then we search for our allies.*"

They stared sorrowfully at the space where the tear in the Nether had sealed in on itself before twisting around and heading into the gloom.

"*We shall return, sisters,*" Orena whispered. "*Wait for us.*"

CHAPTER ONE

Cassius Black stepped out of the elevator on the top floor of his and Morgan King's building and headed for his apartment. His phone buzzed with an incoming message when he reached his front door. He juggled the grocery bags in his arms, slipped the cell out of the back pocket of his jeans, and checked the display.

It was a text from Lilaia.

He smiled, tapped out a reply, and opened his apartment, only to be greeted by the sounds of an argument.

"*Now look what you've done!*" Loki's singsong voice declared out of sight.

"Look what I've done?!" Morgan snapped. "I'm not the one who damaged the apartment with his giant head, you damn imp!"

Cassius's shoulders slumped. *What now?*

He trudged inside, rounded the corner of the living

room, and rocked to a halt. "What happened to my ceiling?!"

Loki and Morgan jumped guiltily where they stood beneath a two-foot hole in the plaster, hair and fur covered in dust and chunks of debris littering the ground at their feet.

Cassius dropped the bags on the kitchen counter and scowled at the exposed metalwork and wires. He directed an accusing look at the imp and the demigod. He could hazard a guess as to what had transpired in the brief time he'd left to do some last-minute grocery shopping for Lilaia's belated baby shower.

The animosity between Loki and Morgan had gotten ten times worse since their return from Europe. It seemed the imp had not appreciated the detour Morgan had encouraged Cassius to take on their way back from London. A detour which had involved Paris, a decadent five-star hotel suite, and room service for the entire time they'd spent in the city.

"Sightseeing my demonic ass!" Loki had growled at Morgan when they'd come back. "I bet the only thing that saw any action during those five days is that snake between your legs, you depraved demigod!"

To his chagrin, Morgan could not exactly deny this. They hadn't left their hotel suite once. Cassius had actually been grateful to catch up on some sleep on their flight back home.

Still, their side trip didn't fully explain why Loki seemed so tense these days. Cassius was certain something was worrying the imp. What that was he still hadn't figured out.

Maybe I should just ask him outright. But first things first.

Cassius crossed his arms.

"Well?" he said coldly.

Loki's tail and ears drooped. Morgan opened his mouth before closing it again.

Cassius surmised from this that they were both equally at fault for the damage to his ceiling. The doorbell rang. His eyes shrank to slits.

"Don't think the arrival of our guests is a get-out-of-jail card for you two. You're both in the doghouse."

Loki shrank down to his demon cat form and slinked off in the direction of the bedroom, a forlorn meow rumbling out of his chest. He paused on the threshold and cast a wretched look at Cassius over his shoulder.

The demigod resisted the imp's limpid eyes.

"In. The. Doghouse," he repeated in a steely voice.

Loki made an annoyed sound and disappeared, tail swishing with irritated flicks.

Cassius met Morgan's contrite gaze. "*You* can explain later."

He twisted on his heels and headed down the hall to open the front door.

"What's wrong?" Julia Chen asked right away.

Cassius accepted the drinks the Terrene angel handed him. "What makes you think something's wrong?"

"There's a muscle twitching in your jawline," Adrianne Hogan said in a helpful tone.

"Considering you have the patience of a saint, something must have happened," Suzie Myers drawled.

The owner of *Occulta* had her elbow hooked around Zach Mooney's arm.

The Aqueous demon made a face. "Morgan screwed up again?"

"My bet is on the imp," Bailey Green murmured, piqued.

The wizard had still not forgiven Loki for the hell he'd put Morgan's team through when he'd been recuperating from the injuries he had incurred fighting a Nephil in London.

"Reuben and Jasper had to go to New York at short notice. They send their regards." Charlie Lloyd marched briskly past Cassius, a white carton in hand. "Is there space in your fridge?"

"Yeah." Cassius stared at the carton while Suzie and the rest of Morgan's team traipsed in. "What's in the box?"

"A cake," Charlie replied guardedly.

Adrianne blinked. "You made it?"

Charlie lifted his chin defensively. "Jasper made it, as a matter of fact."

Cassius almost walked into Zach and Suzie, the demon and the witch having stopped abruptly in their tracks. Adrianne sucked in air. Even Julia looked shocked.

"Jasper bakes?" Bailey said leadenly.

Charlie furrowed his brow.

"He's pretty good at it," the enchanter almost growled.

Now in a firmly established relationship with Jasper Cobb, the demon director of the San Francisco branch of Cabalista, and Reuben Fletcher, the angel who commanded the local Order of Rosen, Charlie had grown more assertive, and acerbic, of late. Cassius suspected he was finally letting his true personality shine through his normally reserved demeanor, something Morgan often half-heartedly complained about these days.

The angel greeted Suzie and his team with a subdued air when they entered the living room. He was crouched down with a dustpan and brush and was clearing the mess he and Loki had made.

Julia indicated the hole in the ceiling. "Did Loki's head do that?"

"Yeah," Morgan muttered. "That imp is a menace."

Cassius's chest twinged a little at his lover's morose expression.

He steeled himself the next instant. *No, both he and Loki need to learn some boundaries. They can't keep going on the way they have been. They'll wreck the damn building one day during one of their arguments.*

"Shouldn't the guests of honor be here by now?" Suzie asked curiously.

"They're on their way."

The doorbell rang on cue.

A stuffed unicorn hit Cassius in the face when he opened the door. He grabbed the overly purple toy before it fell to the ground and was greeted by an enthusiastic "Agaboo!" by his attacker.

Phebei, Lilaia and Bostrof Orzkal's daughter,

beamed at him toothily from where she was strapped in a baby carrier to the Lucifugous demon's chest. She had inherited her mother's build and refined features, and her father's eyes and dusky complexion.

"Sorry," the former king of the Shadow Empire said in a harried tone. He took the toy off Cassius and gave it back to his daughter. "No hitting people with Lola."

Phebei giggled and threw the unicorn at her father's head. "Booya!"

"I swear I don't know where she gets her aggressive personality from," Lilaia muttered, wearing the tired look of a first-time mother.

She took Phebei out of the baby carrier and wiped her nose with a hanky that looked like it'd been sewn by the Gods. Cassius recognized the handiwork of the Nymphs of Rain Vale.

He decided not to point out that Phebei had probably inherited that trait from both her parents and kissed Lilaia's cheeks. "It's good to see you."

Phebei blew raspberries at Cassius from her mother's arms. Though she was less than a month old, she already resembled an infant five times that age. She owed her fast growth to her Lucifugous father.

"I think my daughter's lost her heart to you," Bostrof grumbled.

"Your kid fell in love with a chocolate pie last week," Cassius observed wryly. "It was a clown a few days before that. This too shall pass, I'm sure."

Lilaia brightened. "She could do worse. Cassius is Queen Nephele's grandson after all."

Cassius and Bostrof observed the Nymph's zealous

expression with a trace of shared unease. Lilaia's esteem for Cassius had only grown stronger since she'd discovered his identity as a prince of Rain Vale before he'd inherited the title of Awakener and North Star.

"Phebei's too young for him," Bostrof protested with the look of a demon engaging in a battle with a foregone conclusion.

"That hardly matters when it comes to our kind, husband." Lilaia arched an eyebrow. "Besides, may I remind you of our age gap?"

Bostrof flinched. Lilaia flashed him a saccharine smile and went inside the apartment.

Phebei waved her unicorn forlornly at Cassius over her mother's shoulder. "Aboo."

Cassius stared from the departing Nymph to a pink-faced Bostrof. "Wait. She's younger than you?"

"It's the other way around, actually," Bostrof admitted grudgingly. "And it's only a difference of a few hundred years."

Cassius masked a smile at the Lucifugous's defensive tone.

The elevator doors whooshed open to his right. Francis Strickland stepped out. Cassius's gaze dropped to the Argonaut director's hands.

The mage was holding a bouquet of flowers and a black bag bearing the gold logo of the most expensive chocolate boutique in San Francisco.

"I didn't know what to get for a Nymph's baby shower," Strickland said awkwardly.

Cassius swallowed a grin.

"Is there any alcohol in there?" Bostrof asked in a hopeful voice as they headed inside the apartment.

He indicated Strickland's gifts.

"Or course not. It's a baby shower." The Argonaut director grimaced at Bostrof's crestfallen face. "I see the joys of fatherhood are sinking in." He froze when he entered the living room. "What happened to your ceiling?"

CHAPTER TWO

MORGAN STIFFENED WHERE HE WAS PUTTING OUT PARTY food and drinks.

Cassius sighed. "Loki and Morgan had a fight, the imp transformed into his Gargantua form, and, well, you can guess the rest."

"Want me and Suzie to fix it?" Julia asked drily.

Cassius brightened. "If you wouldn't mind."

Loki emerged from the bedroom just as the Terrene angel and the witch finished repairing the damaged plaster. Seeing how attached he was to Lilaia and her baby, the imp couldn't resist coming out to greet them. Happy purrs rumbled from his chest as he allowed Phebei to pick him up.

"Watch she doesn't squeeze you too hard," Bostrof warned the demon cat.

Loki gave the Lucifugous a puzzled look. His eyes bulged when Phebei's chubby arms suddenly tightened around him.

"Not so strong, sweetie," Lilaia rebuked.

Phebei pursed her lips and loosened her hold on the wheezing imp. She brightened, grabbed a fish cake from her mother's plate, and fed it to Loki with a determined "Ba."

Bostrof observed his daughter with a thoughtful expression. "I wonder if she could lift a ten-pound dumbbell."

Lilaia accepted a drink from Adrianne and cut her eyes to her husband. "We're not putting our one-month-old daughter in your gym to test out that idiotic theory."

Morgan sniggered as Phebei smeared a cream doughnut all over Loki's face in an attempt to fill his belly. Everyone looked at him.

"What?" he said defensively at their faintly accusing stares.

Cassius sighed. "You're such a child."

"Well, I'm yours for better or worse, so get used to it," Morgan muttered.

The demigod's eyes flashed with a hint of heat that warmed Cassius's cheeks and reminded him of all the wicked things Morgan had done to him last night, in the very next room.

Cassius hardened his resolve. "Don't think you can just charm your way out of the doghouse you're in."

Morgan's mouth tilted in a smile that went straight to Cassius's heart and stirred his groin. "Sure."

Loki's eyes shrank to slits at the simmering sexual tension between them, his tail moving with irritated flicks. Lilaia noted his dissatisfaction with a sigh.

"Wow. I bet that kid crushes the balls of any boy who messes with her when she starts kindergarten," Suzie remarked in a tone full of admiration.

Everyone followed her gaze. Zach grimaced. Lilaia and Bostrof blanched.

Phebei had squeezed a handful of hard candy to smithereens and was trying to stuff the pieces in Loki's mouth.

"I think you might be right about that ten-pound dumbbell," Strickland told a worried Bostrof.

Cassius grinned.

The next few hours passed in a blur of easy conversation and laughter. Cassius's heart lightened when he went in the kitchen to get more drinks and turned to see the people he cared for gathered happily in one place.

This has been a long time coming.

He was glad he'd decided to hold a party for Lilaia and Phebei, however belatedly. It was a much-needed distraction from what was dominating the news headlines these days and the unease building inside all of them.

The events that had resulted in Inner London temporarily relocating to the Seventh Hell before it was forcibly transported back to the earthly realm by Cassius and the reborn South Star, Theophile Serrano, were still sending ripples across the world. Ripples that were making themselves felt in ways none of them could have anticipated.

Though most of the official gateways between Earth and the other realms remained broken, now that the governments of the world had become aware of Theo's ability to open stable interdimensional portals, there was talk of whether the Fallen and the rest of the otherworldly who had come to this realm should take their fight with Elios elsewhere.

It was a conversation that was happening at every level of society, from grannies at bridge parties to the highest councils that oversaw the human world. And it was one that was threatening to compromise the peace established after the Hundred Year War by Victor Sloan, among many others.

Because, truth was, the Fallen had found a home on Earth they wished to protect, while the humans who had formed attachments to them did not want to see them leave. After all, those alive today could not recall a world without the supernatural beings who walked among them.

Cassius frowned slightly as he opened a bottle of juice. He wondered if Elios had foreseen this. According to Victor, the God of Darkness had admitted to controlling the Fates during their clash in London.

Well, all except Atropos.

The eldest Moira had been spotted by one of Bostrof's spies in the Nine Hells a while back. It was she who had given them the clue they needed to locate Boreas, the Winter God Elios had captured and imprisoned in the Underworld.

Cassius had glimpsed the growing disquiet in Adrianne, Bailey, and Charlie's eyes since their return from London as the debate about whether to force the

Fallen and all otherworldly to leave Earth raged in the news and on social media. The same unrest now thickened the corridors of Argonaut and darkened Suzie's gaze when they visited *Occulta*.

Morgan and their team were aware of the vision Regina Bvarvik, the Dryad kingdom's royal seer, had had concerning the final battle with Elios. It would take place on Earth and determine the fate of all realms.

They had shared Regina's warning with the heads of Argonaut, Hexa, Cabalista, and the Order of Rosen, who, in turn, had related it to the leaders of the human world. It seemed the latter had ultimately decided they could avoid the Dryad seer's prophecy altogether by forcing the principal players of that battle out of their realm.

But leaving Earth was not an option for the Fallen, nor was it one for Cassius, Morgan, and their allies. What Regina had foreseen would become reality. They just had to find a way to convince the human leaders of this.

"You okay?"

Cassius startled. Morgan had come up behind him and slipped his arms around his waist. He hesitated before relaxing against his lover's chest, Morgan's heat easing his mind.

"Yeah. Just thinking."

"Let me guess." Morgan's breath tickled his ear as he lowered his head. "You're wondering about all the naughty things we're gonna do after they leave?"

Cassius's belly clenched on a wave of desire at the demigod's seductive words.

Loki shifted into his imp form in the middle of the living room and glared at them, hands on his waist. "Hey! What happened to the doghouse?!"

"He's still in it," Cassius protested.

He pulled away from Morgan.

Morgan tsk-tsked. Loki gloated. Lilaia and Julia rolled their eyes.

It wasn't until everyone had left later that night and he and Morgan had finished tidying the apartment that Cassius finally got to the bottom of what was worrying Loki.

"Want a coffee?" Morgan said.

Cassius nodded. His gaze found Loki.

The imp was sitting on a lounger on the terrace, his arms wrapped around his legs and his knees tucked under his chin. His ears and tail drooped limply, as if he carried the weight of the world upon his shoulders.

"Why don't you go talk to him?" Morgan dropped a kiss on Cassius's forehead. "Maybe he's finally ready to tell us why he's been such a grumpy little asshole lately."

Cassius smiled faintly. It was clear Morgan was equally worried about Loki's mood despite their clashes.

The imp didn't stir when Cassius came outside and took the seat next to him. They gazed at the starlit sky above San Francisco, a companionable silence settling between them.

Morgan emerged from the apartment and handed him a steaming cup of coffee.

Loki frowned when the demigod passed him a glass of hot chocolate. "I'm not a child."

"Just shut up and drink it," Morgan ordered gruffly.

Loki hesitated before clasping the glass and doing as he was told. The hot chocolate painted a mustache on his upper lip that would have been funny were it not for his downcast expression. He put the empty glass on a side table a moment later.

"What's wrong, Loki?" Cassius said.

The imp flinched. It was some time before he spoke. "I'm scared."

Cassius startled. His pulse quickened in the next instant. A faint, golden light had started to throb in Loki's belly, the Eternity Key resonating with his turbulent emotions. Morgan pressed a hand on his shoulder as he made to rise and go to the imp.

"I had a dream before you returned from London." Loki's eyes gleamed when he turned his head and finally met their gazes. "A premonition."

Cassius's heart slammed against his ribs, the fear reflected on the imp's face tightening his chest with a growing dread. "What kind of premonition?"

"Darkness." Loki's head swiveled. He stared at the sky once more, his face haggard. "I saw a darkness that will soon swallow this city and this world." His chin wobbled. His voice broke. "And I—I fear it's one neither of you will be able to defeat!"

Cassius finally moved. He picked up the trembling

imp and cradled him in his arms. Loki clung to him, his tears soaking silently into his shirt. Cassius looked over anxiously at Morgan.

The dark foreboding filling him was reflected in his lover's eyes.

CHAPTER THREE

MORGAN STEPPED OUT OF THE BATHROOM. "IS HE asleep?"

Cassius nodded as he closed the bedroom door, his face still reflecting unease. Loki had insisted on sleeping in the living room tonight. The imp seemingly needed some alone time.

Cassius glanced at Morgan's wet hair. "You showered already?"

"Yeah." Remorse bit Morgan at Cassius's mildly disappointed tone. "I wasn't sure how long it was gonna take to calm him down."

Cassius dipped his chin briskly. "I'll be ten minutes."

He walked past Morgan and disappeared into the bathroom.

Morgan crossed the floor to the glass wall overlooking the terrace. The imp's warning echoed in his mind as he stared out into the night.

He knew not to ignore Loki's instincts.

Whatever the Keeper of the Eternity Key had

foreseen would likely become reality. And it didn't take a genius to figure out who was the most likely culprit behind the threat that would soon be upon them.

The peaceful lull they'd experienced since defeating Elios in the Seventh Hell was a boon that was bound to end.

I wonder what that bastard is up to now. Morgan frowned. *Let's hope Loki is wrong about the part where we lose.*

The sound of running water distracted him. Morgan hesitated before twisting around and retracing his steps to the bathroom. He stopped silently on the threshold and watched as Cassius showered, his back to him.

Heat warmed Morgan's blood as his gaze danced down Cassius's naked form. The demigod's physique was perfection incarnate, his flawless skin a superb match for the toned muscles and hard angles it hid. Cassius demonstrated the most brutal strength in battle. Yet he was always soft and pliant under Morgan, as captive to the pleasure they found in each other's arms as Morgan was.

Morgan's cock stirred as he recalled all the times those strong legs had clung to his waist while he plundered that powerful body and that tight ass.

His heated gaze locked on Cassius's cleft and the treasure it hid.

A treasure his dick could happily spend the rest of its life inside.

"I can literally feel you drilling a hole into my ass with your eyes."

Cassius looked over his shoulder, his expression half amusement, half exasperation under the pouring water.

"There's another part of me that wants to drill into your ass more," Morgan said bluntly.

Cassius's lips parted hungrily at this shameless confession. He slicked his hair back with a hand, his gaze dropping to the magnificent erection Morgan now sported. He turned around, revealing his own swelling dick where it jutted from his groin.

"I can see that," he said in a breathy voice that pushed all of Morgan's buttons and made the bond that linked their soul cores come to life with a hot sizzle of sexual tension. The demigod licked his lips and cocked his head to the side. "How about you come here and show me what you want to do to me?"

He wrapped a hand around his hardening shaft and gave himself a few strokes.

It was all the invitation Morgan needed. He stormed across the bathroom, his hands discarding his clothes with an urgency that matched his desire for the demigod enticing him with a seductive smile.

He stepped under the hot spray, grasped Cassius's waist, and backed him up against the wall. "I thought I was in the doghouse."

"You get a reprieve for being nice to the imp." Cassius closed his eyes and hissed as Morgan bent his knees slightly and rubbed the head of his cock along the underside of his trembling shaft as he rose. "Shit! That feels good."

He clung to Morgan's shoulders and rolled his hips.

Morgan grinned and nipped at Cassius's lower lip with his teeth as they worked their groins together in an exquisite bump and grind that soon had them both panting.

"Want me to do something that will make you feel even better?"

"Do you even have to ask?" Cassius groaned.

His breath hitched when Morgan slipped a hand around his back and traced his cleft with a light touch. A low hum rumbled out of his chest as Morgan found his hole and ran the pad of a finger over his twitching pucker.

Color stained Cassius's cheekbones and his breathing grew ragged. Morgan captured his wrists above his head and plastered their bodies together, chest to chest, groin to aching groin.

Morgan could tell from the way Cassius's pupils constricted and dilated and the flare of seraphic light in the dark depths that he loved the submissive position he now found himself in. He smiled and lowered his head.

"Where do you want to come first, in my mouth or in my hand?" he whispered in Cassius's ear before gently biting the delicate shell.

A strangled sound left Cassius. He twitched and shivered. Morgan swallowed a groan when he felt the demigod's precum anoint his cock.

The intoxicating scent was nearly too much for him to bear.

Cassius pulled back a little. His feverish gaze dropped to Morgan's lips. "Your mouth."

Lust and a heady feeling of possessiveness almost had Morgan turning Cassius around and bending him over so he could fuck him there and then.

He absolutely loved when Cassius got this way. When he became brazen and showed Morgan exactly how much he wanted him. When he stated his needs and ordered Morgan to fulfill them.

He took Cassius's mouth in a blistering kiss before dropping to his knees, and fixing his hips with his hands.

A guttural sound left Cassius when Morgan swallowed him whole. He grasped Morgan's hair in a punishing grip and dropped his head back against the tiles as Morgan started sucking him, lips dragging sensuously along the hot, silky skin of his throbbing cock.

"Fuck! That feels—*Ah!* Yes! *Shit!* Your tongue is—!"

Cassius's throaty moans and cries echoed around the bathroom as Morgan worked his shuddering shaft with powerful contractions of his jaw. It didn't take long for him to explode, his orgasm so powerful he rose on the tips of his toes and shouted out his release.

Morgan swallowed most of the hot cum filling his mouth and throat. He let go of a trembling Cassius, turned him around, and used the rest to lubricate and stretch open his hole.

Cassius whimpered and hung on to the wall as Morgan worked his ass. Morgan scissored his fingers a final time before pulling out and rising to his feet. He aligned their bodies, his heart pounding a violent tempo against his ribs.

Cassius groaned when Morgan entered him. Morgan panted heavily, gaze on where his cock was disappearing inside Cassius's hot, tight passage.

They both cursed lustfully when he bottomed out.

Cassius's body fitted him like a glove.

He was made for me. For this!

Morgan grasped Cassius's hands where he clung to the tiles, bowed his back, and pulled out before sliding back in with a powerful thrust. Cassius cried out, his voice raw with pleasure.

Morgan repeated the motion.

"Yes! More! Harder!" Cassius begged, his ass clenching tightly around the thick rod impaling him.

Morgan sank his teeth into Cassius's shoulder and fucked him with savage strength, just the way he liked it. The erotic sounds Cassius made echoed the carnal ones their flesh gave rise to as Morgan pounded his hole with wild abandon, knuckles white where he'd laced their fingers together.

"*Coming!* I'm coming!" Cassius gasped moments later. His neck corded as he threw his head back, his mouth opening on a guttural rasp that made Morgan's orgasm race deliciously down his spine. "*Morgan!*"

A feral sound left Morgan when Cassius convulsed beneath him, his passage contracting with violent spasms that soon sent him over the edge. Morgan's cock throbbed as he crested the dizzying wave their mating dance had led him to. He grasped Cassius's hip and pumped his pulsing dick in and out of the demigod's twitching hole as he ejaculated.

It was a while before his erratic motions seized and

he shuddered to a stop. Morgan sagged, crowding Cassius against the wall, still buried deep inside him. He pressed his face against the side of Cassius's neck and let out a shaky sigh as hot water poured over them.

The fire that had blazed between their soul cores still smoldered in his belly, a connection he would never tire of.

Cassius moaned and twitched when Morgan nudged his swelling cock inside him.

Morgan rained soft kisses along his nape. "Want to go again?" he said huskily. He rolled his hips and drew a gasp from Cassius.

The demigod bit his lip, his expression feverish as he turned his head and locked eyes with Morgan. "You're already going."

Cassius reached behind and grasped Morgan's cock where he was sinking it in and out of his pleasantly used hole.

"*Fuck.*" The dual stimulation almost had Morgan's eyes rolling into the back of his head. "I'm not going to last long if you keep doing that!"

Cassius nipped at his jaw. "That's the whole point, isn't it?"

Morgan groaned at his teasing expression. Then he kissed him, pinned his hands to the wall, and took him for another wild ride.

CHAPTER FOUR

"Anyone know what this is about?" Julia asked curiously as they headed inside the elevator.

Morgan shook his head.

It was the morning after Lilaia's baby shower. Strickland had called them an hour ago and requested his team's presence at Argonaut. He'd refused to tell them why, except to state that they should get there ASAP.

Morgan could not stop the twinge that tightened his chest when he glanced at Cassius. The demigod had hardly slept last night, Loki's words weighing heavily on his mind once more after they'd finished making love. Instead, he'd lain quietly in Morgan's arms, his fingers hot where he'd tucked Morgan's hands against his heart, his steady breaths warming Morgan's throat. He'd woken Morgan at dawn, his touch and his kisses carrying a hint of desperation that had tugged at Morgan's soul, his hips undulating sensuously as he'd ridden Morgan and claimed the pleasure only he could give him.

They both knew not to take Loki's foreboding lightly.

Unfortunately, the imp hadn't been able to elaborate further on the vision he'd had when they'd questioned him that morning before they'd left the apartment. All he could say for certain was that he had sensed Cassius's despair and Morgan's pain deep within it.

There hadn't been any sign of Elios since London.

Could the darkness Loki saw be Elios himself? He clenched his jaw. *Is he finally preparing to attack Earth, like Regina foresaw?*

He was distracted from his grim thoughts by Cassius stroking his knuckles lightly across the back of his hand. Morgan turned his palm over, clasped his lover's fingers, and flashed him a comforting smile. Cassius's worried expression smoothed out.

The elevator door opened on the tenth floor of the building that housed the San Francisco branch of Argonaut, bringing with it a drone of voices. The bullpen was starting to fill up with agents on the day shift.

"Hey," Zakir Singh said morosely when he spotted them.

The Argonaut wizard looked like he had something weighing on his mind.

"What's wrong?" Zach asked.

"You tell me." Singh cocked a thumb in the direction

of Strickland's office. "I haven't seen that many VIPs in his office since, well—never."

Morgan traded a troubled glance with Cassius and the others. They headed briskly for the director's room. Cassius slowed as they approached the door.

His face brightened. "Oh."

Morgan's pulse accelerated when he sensed what his demigod lover had felt a heartbeat before him.

Cassius entered Strickland's office ahead of them. His gaze found the man his soul core had recognized. "Theo!"

Theophile Serrano turned where he sat on a couch next to Victor Sloan. A smile as bright as the sun lit his handsome features. Gold sparked in his pupils. He jumped to his feet and met Cassius halfway across the room.

"Cassius!"

They hugged each other fiercely, their faces full of affection.

Theo wasn't just the new South Star. He also carried a fragment of the soul of Rohengar, Cassius's older brother and the demigod who had been destined to rule Rain Vale. Though he had been born in the human realm and was not of divine descent, Theo had been chosen by a mysterious Fate yet to be revealed to become the fourth Guardian of the Nether.

Victor cocked an eyebrow at Morgan. "You look like shit. Is the imp giving you a hard time?"

"You don't know the half of it," Morgan grumbled.

Now that Loki had unburdened himself of his troubles, the imp was back to his sardonic self. A feeling of fellowship danced through Morgan as he beheld the demon who headed Cabalista. It was a sharp contrast to how he'd felt about him a few months ago, when he'd realized Victor had been the first to gain Cassius's affections after the Fall.

Morgan had truly despised the demon at the time.

Cassius had been Morgan's fated soulmate in their past life, just as he was in this one. The knowledge that Victor had claimed the demigod in intimate ways had ripped Morgan's heart apart when he'd finally recalled their true identities as Ivmir and Icarus and the soul bond that linked them. Add to this the truth Victor had recently revealed, about being the one who had inflicted the scar on Morgan's chest during the War in the Nether, when he'd fought by Elios's side as the dark demigod Coraos, and it was a miracle Morgan could talk to the guy without wanting to stab a sword through his heart.

Whether it was because they now knew themselves to be brothers birthed from the same Goddess mother, or because of their shared experiences and the battles they had fought alongside one another since Cassius had come to San Francisco, the antagonism that had existed between them had faded. Morgan knew Victor had done everything he could to subconsciously atone for his sins ever since he fell to Earth. Sins that had almost rendered the demon mad with grief when he'd recalled them.

It had taken time and Theo's arrival into their lives for Victor to start to forgive himself. Even then, a sad light occasionally darkened his gaze when he looked at

Cassius, as if he were wishing he could undo all his past deeds and the many ways he had wronged the demigod who wielded Heaven's Light.

Someone rapped the floor imperiously. "Not that this isn't nice and all, but maybe we should get down to business?"

Morgan's head swiveled. Amal Kazmi, the head of Argonaut, was frowning at them from her perch on the edge of a chair to his left, her walking stick clasped firmly before her. The tension in the air was palpable.

Jasper Cobb and Reuben Fletcher stood framing her. Charlie brightened when he saw his lovers.

Cassius met Strickland's troubled gaze as he slowly released Theo. "What's wrong, Francis?"

CHAPTER FIVE

The Argonaut director hesitated before indicating his guests. "It would be better if this came from them."

Cassius observed Reuben and Jasper sharing a curt glance.

"Jasper and I went to New York to attend a special U.N. Security Council meeting yesterday," Reuben said grimly. "Amal and Victor were there too."

"There's no easy way to say this." Faint lines wrinkled Victor's brow. "There's a plague ravaging parts of the Southern Hemisphere. One this world has not seen before."

"A plague?" Morgan repeated skeptically.

"Yes," Jasper said bitterly. "At the rate it's progressing, both the medical and magical experts who work for the Security Council estimate that it will affect ninety-nine-point-nine percent of the Earth's population within the next two weeks. And we're not just talking people. It's killing all animal and plant life too."

Adrianne paled. "Magical?"

"You mean, this disease is caused by magic?!" Bailey asked, aghast.

"No, it's not caused by magic, as far as we've been able to ascertain," Kazmi said. "But it is an illness that has so far eluded all known human, magical, and otherworldly cures."

Julia and Zach traded a cautious glance.

"Ninety-nine-point-nine percent?" Zach frowned. "Does that mean the otherworldly in this realm are not affected by it?"

Kazmi dipped her chin. "You are correct. So far, the otherworldly in the areas being devastated by this disease have yet to fall victim to it. We do not know why."

"What about magic users?" the Aqueous demon asked in clipped tones.

Cassius knew he was thinking of Suzie and all their human friends in Argonaut and Hexa.

Kazmi sighed. "We know of a couple of Hexa members who have survived it, but barely. They were Level One magic users."

Cassius's mind raced in the fraught silence that ensued. *Is this what Loki foresaw in his dream? Is this disease the darkness he spoke of?!*

Theo cast a worried look his way. "What is it?"

Cassius looked at Morgan. Morgan dipped his chin, his expression equally troubled.

"Loki told us something last night," Cassius

confessed. "He said he'd had a dream. A premonition of a darkness that would soon engulf this realm."

The others startled.

"You believe this plague is what the Keeper of the Key was referring to?" Kazmi said sharply.

Cassius nodded reluctantly. "It's too much of a coincidence."

Theo's eyes had darkened. "Darkness? Is this Elios's doing?"

Cassius hesitated. "I suspect so."

"How exactly have you guys managed to keep this out of the news?" Julia asked in a hard voice, her gaze sweeping over Victor, Kazmi, and Strickland.

"With a lot of foresight and some targeted bribery." Kazmi sighed at their slightly shocked looks. "There's enough going on in the world right now what with everything that happened in London."

Theo flinched.

Kazmi did not miss his reaction.

"The people of this realm do not need yet another troublesome thing to worry about," the Argonaut mage added tactfully.

Morgan's brow knitted. "If the Security Council's calculations are correct, you won't be able to keep this under the lid for much longer."

Kazmi's face grew discomfited. "That's why I'm here."

Strickland's expression darkened slightly, as did Jasper's. Only Victor and Reuben managed to maintain a neutral air.

Morgan narrowed his eyes. "Why do I get the

feeling I'm not going to like what you have to say next?"

Kazmi avoided his suspicious stare and cleared her throat delicately. "The U.N. Security Council will be putting a statement out in full shortly. But the essence of it is this. The Fallen and the otherworldly who came to Earth will be allowed to stay in this realm if you get rid of this problem."

Adrianne drew a sharp breath. The air became heavy with tension.

Morgan scowled and took a threatening step forward. "What?!"

Cassius laid a hand on his arm. Though his pulse raced, his voice was calm when he addressed Kazmi.

"This is the excuse they're going to use to backtrack on their original intentions?"

Kazmi's shoulders sagged a little. A wry smile curved the elderly mage's mouth as she met his unblinking gaze. "I suspected you would be the first here to grasp the true significance behind their words, just as Victor did."

Morgan and the rest of their team exchanged puzzled looks.

"What do you mean?" Bailey asked, confused.

Cassius's nails bit into his palms. "What happened in London created a situation Earth's leaders had not faced before. They needed to appease the humans who felt betrayed by the Fallen who had put their lives at risk *and* allay the fears of this realm as a whole." He paused. "They never dismissed Regina's prophecy.

They just needed to find a reason to allow us to stay here."

A wretched expression darted across Theo's face then.

Cassius touched his shoulder. "Stop blaming yourself. Remember, Elios is the real culprit behind what took place."

Victor rose and came over to hug Theo. "Cassius is right." He pulled back and pressed a soft kiss to Theo's forehead. "And I might never have met you were it not for Elios hastening your awakening."

"Like Cassius said, human leaders have had to find a way to save face," Kazmi confirmed. Her gaze swept the room. "They're confident you will find a solution to this problem. And they will fully support your wish to remain on Earth once this is all over."

Morgan's face darkened. "By 'you,' do you mean Cassius?"

Cassius's heart twisted at the anger simmering in his eyes. Morgan hated the fact that he'd been used repeatedly by the very people who'd professed to loathe him over the centuries since the Fall. Which was why he'd threatened to take Cassius and leave Earth so as to reclaim his rightful place as the heir to the Dryad kingdom's throne, if the world's leaders and the organizations that governed the otherworldly and magic users did not admit to Cassius's achievements.

The resulting official statements had turned Cassius into a hero almost overnight when they'd been released a few months ago, something the demigod still hadn't gotten used to.

Kazmi shook her head, her face somber. "No. This one's on all of you Fallen."

Theo paled, as did Charlie.

Jasper made a frustrated sound. "Humans may be confident we can resolve this situation, but I'm not." The demon met Cassius's uneasy stare. "I know you're strong, but this? *This* is on a whole other level."

"This plague takes the form of a black mist that leaves death and suffering in its wake," Reuben explained. "Those who survive the initial contact with the disease all perish a few days later, and agonizingly at that. This thing is like," he waved a hand vaguely, "an entity scouring the land it passes through clean of all life."

"I'm pretty sure there's an otherworldly at its root." Crimson glimmered briefly in Jasper's pupils. "One we have yet to face and who is insanely strong."

Cassius stilled.

"Jasper is right," Victor said quietly at his shocked look. "We both sensed it when we saw the pictures from the devastated areas. The bodies of the sick and the dead are marked with putrid wounds and blemishes reminiscent of something you might see in the Nine Hells."

Blood pounded heavily in Cassius's skull at their warning. He scowled, his nails biting into his palms.

This has to be Elios's doing! Only he would think of something so terrible!

A commotion outside the door distracted him. He stiffened when he recognized the soul cores drawing closer. Morgan's eyes similarly widened.

Galliad Fenhorn and Cedric Esteban stormed inside Strickland's office, Eden and Brianna Monroe in their wake.

CHAPTER SIX

"Eden?" Cassius mumbled, stunned.

The young woman looked like a completely different person compared to the last time he'd met her. Gone was the reserved and nervous girl who had thought herself an outcast of the magic community she lived in and had long wished to escape. In her stead was a bright-eyed, confident mage who'd finally come into her powers.

Born with a bloodcursed soul core that should have killed her while she was still a young child, Eden's magic had been secretly bound by her mother Brianna and a group of powerful Hexa mages upon her birth. It was Elios's machinations that had caused the young girl's latent abilities to awaken and ended in her claiming the Bloodcursed Devilwood Summoning Staff, one of a number of divine artifacts that had sealed Chaos in the Abyss, as her weapon.

Eden had once remarked that it was the other way around. That it was the staff that had deemed her powerful enough to wield it and granted her permission to bind their magic cores together.

The weapon lay snugly against the base of the young woman's throat in its tree-shaped pendant form and was doing its best to look innocuous. Cassius was not fooled. He could tell the thing was sentient and watching them all closely.

Eden's frown cleared when she saw Cassius. Pleasure brought a surge of color to her cheeks. "Cassius!"

She strode past Cedric and hugged Cassius tightly.

Cassius closed his arms around her, his surprise fading to affection. "It's great to see you, Eden. You look well."

She pulled back and smiled at him. "It's good to see you too."

Cedric failed to disguise his chagrin at the sight of his fiancée clasping another man in her arms.

"You should do something about your girlfriend," Morgan grumbled at the second prince of the Dryad kingdom.

"That's rich coming from a guy whose boyfriend keeps innocently seducing every man, woman, and otherworldly under the sun," Cedric retorted.

"He's not wrong," Brianna drawled.

Julia and Zach bit back a smile.

Morgan's eyes shrank to slits. "May I remind you that I'm your superior?"

"Yeah, yeah," Cedric muttered.

The fact that Morgan was the de facto king of Ivory

Peaks seemed to have no influence on the prince's attitude toward the demigod.

Morgan muttered something under his breath before casting a shrewd look at Galliad and Brianna. "I doubt the two of you are here for a social visit."

Brianna's expression sobered.

A muscle jumped in Galliad's jawline. "You would be right."

A fresh wave of dread wound through Cassius at the older man's expression. He'd never seen the former Head Mage of the Dryad royal court this agitated before.

Officially, Galliad ran a rundown pawn and gift shop in Chinatown. Unofficially, he was the diplomatic liaison between Earth and Ivory Peaks, and Cedric's guard when the prince visited the human realm. Which was often these days, what with Cedric having technically already married the only bloodcursed mage in existence.

"What's wrong, Galliad?" Morgan said guardedly.

Galliad took a shallow breath. "I bring a warning from Regina." He paused, his tone hardening. "And a direct plea from the Dryad royal family to our kingdom's true sovereign."

Cassius's belly clenched at his words. Victor frowned.

"A warning?" Morgan repeated.

Galliad bobbed his head. "Regina received a vision. A Harbinger."

Cassius's pulse stuttered. Morgan's pupils flared.

"What the hell is a Harbinger?" Jasper snapped.

"Let him speak, Jasper," Brianna rebuked gently.

Galliad did not answer Jasper's question straightaway. "Regina foresaw two things." His words fell leadenly in the strained hush hanging over the room. "A darkness that will sweep through all the realms. And the war that will follow it."

Kazmi and Strickland stilled, their expressions darkening. Cassius and Morgan shared a nervous look.

"A darkness?" Deep lines now furrowed Victor's brow. "What kind of darkness?"

"One that carries the wrath of a deity."

There was a sharp intake of breath all around.

"Do you mean Elios?" Theo asked harshly.

Galliad shook his head. "No. Regina did not divine the God of Darkness's corruption in this contagion."

Reuben flinched. "Contagion?"

"So, this darkness is a disease?!" Jasper asked sharply.

Cassius clenched his jaw. "What makes a Harbinger different from Regina's other visions?"

"Regina's premonitions normally come to her in dreams. She rarely sees them during the day. If she does, she enters a trance-like state, like she did when the war demons attacked our capital." Galliad paused. "A Harbinger is delivered to her by a divine messenger or a divine being, while she is fully conscious. Her mind is transported to a neutral void between worlds for the span of a moment that can last a heartbeat in our time, but which may stretch over several minutes in the other." Dread clouded his expression. "Regina has only ever received one

Harbinger before. And that concerned the War in the Nether."

Cassius's heart thumped heavily. "By divine being, do you mean a God?"

Galliad dipped his head. "Yes. In this instance, it was a Goddess. One of the Fates, to be precise."

Cassius's chest tightened. He shared a stupefied look with Morgan. "Atropos!"

Galliad's eyes rounded. He looked wildly between them. "How did you know?!"

"She's the one who helped us find Boreas," Morgan said dazedly.

A thousand thoughts swirled through Cassius's mind as he stared at the floor. *Has Atropos been assisting us from the shadows all along? If so, why has she not made her presence known to us?!*

Reuben went over to Strickland's computer, logged into a secure database, and brought up a series of images on the digital display on the wall. "This contagion. Does it look something like this?"

Eden paled. Brianna cursed. Cassius's stomach roiled.

The faces of those who had died from the mysterious disease they'd just learned of were almost unrecognizable under the black stains and pustulant sores distorting their flesh. The hairs rose on Cassius's nape when he saw the clouds captured in some of the images. He'd thought it was smoke at first. But the satellite shots did not lie.

The plague's true form was a dark fog that was moving rapidly across the Earth.

Blood drained from Galliad's face.

"By the Gods!" he mumbled hoarsely. "It's already here?!"

Kazmi rose, a heavy frown marring her brow. "*This is what your seer saw?!*"

Galliad swallowed heavily and nodded. His gaze swiveled to Morgan. "Which brings me to the plea. This plague appeared in Ivory Peaks twelve hours ago. It's already killed a hundred Dryads and decimated a large section of forested land to the east. By our count, it will ravage the entirety of our kingdom within five days."

Cassius's mouth went dry. Shocked gasps echoed around the room.

Jasper's brows met. "But—this thing hasn't affected the otherworldly on Earth. How come it's killing Dryads?"

"Jas is right," Reuben said with a puzzled frown.

"Is that true?!" Galliad croaked.

"Yes," Cassius mumbled.

The Dryad shuddered and closed his eyes, his features distorted by a pained grimace. "At least that's a small mercy, considering what Regina was warned about." Resolved brightened his pupils when he opened them once more. He turned to Morgan. "I do not know why this plague is making our people sick, but not the otherworldly here. But I am certain of one thing. We need *you* to save Ivory Peaks. Only a direct descendant of Queen Atlanteia can wield the divine magic buried within its bones and protect the realm."

Morgan's heart slammed a rapid tempo against his ribs as Galliad's words faded into heavy silence.

He was conscious the mage, and by default the Dryad royal family, would not be asking this of him unless they were truly desperate. He met Cassius's anxious gaze and saw the answer he wished to deny in his beautiful eyes. The answer that had come unbidden to his own throat and that he was choking back, knowing instinctively that it would mean their separation.

"You have to go," Cassius said quietly. His knuckles whitened at his sides, betraying his true feelings. "You are the demigod who inherited the Dryad realm. It is your duty to—"

The rest of his sentence was swallowed by Morgan's lips.

Cassius froze before melting against him, his eyelids fluttering closed and his hands rising to clasp Morgan's face with equal heat.

Someone cleared their throat after a moment.

Morgan slowly lifted his mouth from Cassius's. Color stained his lover's cheekbones as their soul cores resonated with the love and passion that burned eternally bright between them.

He pressed his forehead against Cassius's.

"Come with me," he whispered.

Cassius touched his cheek and shook his head, his eyes darkening. "You know I can't do that. It looks like Loki's dream and Regina's Harbinger are one and the same. Which means there's a good chance this plague will soon be upon this city."

Galliad drew a sharp breath. "The Keeper of the Key had a similar premonition?"

"Yes," Morgan replied reluctantly.

"Cassius is right, Morgan," Eden said. "That's why I'm here. My staff told me our city is in imminent danger. And he thinks we can help fight whatever is coming."

Reuben and Jasper stiffened. Victor's brow furrowed. Kazmi and Strickland stared at Eden's pendant, their unease evident.

"Your staff *told* you?" Strickland said dubiously.

Brianna sighed.

Eden dipped her head. "Woody can talk." She grimaced. "Well, kinda. I can hear his voice in my head."

Bailey blinked. He leaned toward Zach. "Did she just call the Bloodcursed Devilwood Summoning Staff *Woody*?!"

"That's what it sounded like," the demon muttered in a voice laced with pity.

The weapon sagged a little against Eden's throat. It was clear it did not approve of its mundane name.

"I'll go with Morgan."

Morgan and Cassius turned, surprised. Theo's face fell.

Victor shrugged. "I can't exactly let my idiot younger brother die in another realm now, can I?"

Morgan bristled. "Hey, who're you calling an idiot?!"

"I know for a fact that you're one," Victor muttered.

Theo chewed his lip.

Victor raised a thumb to his lover's mouth and stayed his nervous gesture. "Besides, I'm a demigod of darkness too." Crimson glinted in the demon's pupils. "My powers may very well help Morgan against whatever is attacking the Dryad kingdom."

Galliad and Cedric shared a determined look.

"We shall accompany you, of course," the prince told Morgan and Victor.

A heaviness settled in Morgan's chest. He knew this course of action was the right one to take. Still, he could not stop the foreboding twisting his insides.

If Loki's right, this battle will not be an easy win.

The look in Cassius's eyes reflected his thought.

Cassius turned to Theo. "Can you open a portal to Ivory Peaks on the rooftop of this building?"

Theo hesitated.

"Yes," he replied reluctantly.

CHAPTER SEVEN

Morgan sensed the wrongness of the realm beyond the dimensional doorway even before he exited it with Victor and the two Dryads accompanying them. They emerged onto the terrace of the palace overlooking the royal gardens to a sky scored by turbulent clouds and an atmosphere rife with the smell of despair.

He didn't have to be a genius to divine that the Dryad kingdom was under attack. Heat pulsed through his belly as his soul core throbbed in tandem with the magic that lived deep within Ivory Peaks. A magic that was currently in turmoil judging from what he could sense.

Embedded in the very crux of the realm by Queen Atlanteia herself as a last line of defense against any who would harm her kingdom, Morgan had only become aware of the immense pool of power beneath his feet when Cassius had used his abilities as the

Awakener to re-establish his connection to the divine force only he could wield.

"Morgan!"

Morgan turned.

Hildur Esteban, the queen of the Dryads, had rushed out of the throne room. Her husband, Roald, and Cedric's three brothers followed in her steps as she crossed the terrace.

Hildur clasped Morgan's hands and kissed his cheek, the relief in her voice reflected on her face. *"May Atlanteia's blessing be with thee."*

"I receive her blessing and grant thee the same," Morgan murmured.

Hildur exchanged the official Dryad greeting with Victor. "Thank you for coming. Both of you."

Roald welcomed Morgan and Victor somberly while Cedric hugged Leiv, Arfinn, and Tor. Regina appeared with Elwyn Fremaine, the Head Mage who had taken over Galliad's role.

Dread quickened Morgan's pulse as he looked from their strained faces to the glittering city that hugged the highest ice-capped elevation in the mountainous range forming the backbone of Ivory Peaks. He could sense the fear shrouding the capital and its inhabitants even from a distance.

"How bad is it?"

Hildur's mouth thinned. "Bad."

"A new wave of the contagion was spotted some hundred leagues south of here," Elwyn explained stiffly.

Galliad cursed. "When?!"

"Two hours ago." A muscle jumped in Leiv's cheek. "Thalia went to investigate whether the rumor was correct. She should be back any moment now."

"I vastly underestimated how long it would take this abomination to reach us here." Regina's knuckles tightened on her ash-wood staff. She whirled around, her robes swishing around her legs. "I beseech you, my liege." Her pleading gaze swept the royal family. "You *must* leave the kingdom! Your bloodline is too precious to be—"

Roald stayed the distressed seer's words by laying a gentle hand on her shoulder. "We belong here, Regina."

Hildur smiled tremulously as tears pooled in Regina's eyes. "We shall not abandon our people, my friend." She turned to look over the city beneath them and the vale beyond, her expression growing steely. "If we are to die here, then it is our Fate." Her knuckles whitened at her sides. "But mark my words; we will fight to the bitter end."

The queen froze mere seconds later, her gasp echoed by Regina's. Morgan's head snapped around. Victor lowered his brows as he followed their gazes.

"Looks like we're about to find out whether death awaits us all today," Galliad said grimly.

A dark line now edged the horizon to the south, where none had been before.

The black mist that heralded the plague was pouring over the far-flung peaks that rimmed the valley the capital overlooked. Birds darkened the sky ahead of it as they fled the ominous phenomenon.

Power detonated across the terrace, startling

Morgan. The dense wave pressed against his body and shoved him back a couple of steps. Victor grunted beside him, feet similarly skidding across the flagstones.

The air shimmered emerald as the Dryad royal family and their retinue unleashed their magic. Emerald symbols manifested on the staffs that appeared in their hands. Twigs and shoots sprouted on their flesh and in their hair, the blossoming leaves and buds shimmering with potent force as they unfurled. The scent of the forest swelled around Roald, Hildur, and their sons when they manifested the blackthorn and alderwood crowns that denoted their lineage.

"That's a sight you don't see every day," Victor murmured.

Galliad's eyes flashed. Relief brightened his face. "Thalia!"

Morgan and Victor looked in the direction he stared. Pale shapes glimmered into view against the dark haze growing in the distance. They multiplied, forming a solid line of gleaming armor that thickened and grew in size.

An army of Dryad soldiers upon giant golden eagles were racing ahead of the darkness about to engulf the land. They passed over the city and crossed the palace walls minutes later.

Thalia Fenhorn, Galliad's wife and the chief commander of the Dryad army, landed heavily a short distance from where they stood, her eagle kicking up clods of dirt and grass with his claws. The Dryad warrior dismounted and turned swiftly, her cape billowing in the breeze raised by her alighting troops. She stumbled to an abrupt halt when she registered Morgan, Victor, and Galliad's presence. Her eyes rounded.

Thalia sagged. "Thank the Gods!"

Galliad closed the distance to his trembling wife and took her in his arms. Roald and Hildur approached the couple.

"Our people?!" the queen asked in a brittle voice.

Thalia stepped out of Galliad's hold, her fear fading as her fingers found his hand. "They hide inside the mountains and flee along the rivers like we planned, my liege. So far, the plague has spared those regions, even in the east." She dipped her head at Regina. "Your counsel was wise. We have curtailed the loss of life for certain."

Regina's mouth thinned. "We can thank the Goddess who brought me the Harbinger for that tip."

Winged shadows danced across them before Morgan could ask the seer about Atropos. A large flock of eagles had appeared from the direction of the military aviary. The birds landed noisily in the garden, the soldiers atop them holding staffs and weapons blazing with green magic as they readied for battle.

Asteria, Leiv's eagle, came over and lowered her colossal head. She studied Morgan with a beady, ochre eye before peering forlornly around him.

"Cassius isn't here, you dumb bird," Morgan muttered.

He patted her flank nonetheless. Something that sounded like a sigh huffed out of the eagle. Her wings drooped.

Leiv grimaced as he grabbed her harness and climbed onto her back. "I swear she'll dump me in a flash if Cassius so much as suggests she come to Earth."

Unease darkened Thalia's gaze.

"This second wave is behaving differently from the first," she told the king and queen.

"It's accelerating." Regina frowned, her glowing gaze focused unblinkingly on the looming threat. "I don't know how nor why."

Galliad fisted his hands. "Accelerating?"

Morgan stiffened, a singular truth resonating through him then. He saw the same realization dawn in Victor's flaring, crimson pupils.

Hildur's face tightened. "What is it?"

"Acceleration means intent," Morgan said grimly.

Heat blossomed in his belly.

"And intent means someone is actively controlling this plague," Victor concurred in a hard voice.

The fresh scent of an ancient forest enveloped Morgan as he drew upon the divine energy that dwelled within his soul core, the force that flooded his veins and soaked into his bones now as familiar as breathing. Black wind and emerald light exploded around his winged form, his Stark Steel armor shimmering into view at the same time an oak crown sank into his hair. The Sword of Wind whooshed into life in his right hand, the blade of inky currents swarming with Dryad magic and green shoots.

Fire bloomed around Victor as he unleashed his broadsword and manifested his battle suit. He spread his wings, flames, feathers, and armor turning the color of night as the power bequeathed him by their Goddess mother Nyx and his demigod father Nimexis pulsed violently from his body.

Awe filled the faces of the Dryad soldiers in the palace gardens.

Victor raised his head and sniffed the air. "Can you smell that?"

Morgan lowered his brows. "Ozone."

A muscle twitched in Victor's jawline. "There is a God present in this realm."

Hildur and Roald exchanged a shocked look.

Dread underscored Leiv's words. "Do you mean Elios?"

"No," Morgan said in a deadly voice. "This isn't Elios."

He extended his wings and rose above the palace grounds, Victor at his side.

"It looks like this fight will be upon us sooner than we expected." Victor's mouth tilted in a wry half-smile as he looked over at Morgan. "Try not to die, will you? Cassius will have my hide if you do."

Morgan met his gaze steadily. "I'm counting on you to watch my back."

Surprise widened Victor's eyes. They darkened with emotion in the next instant. He dipped his head solemnly.

The knowledge that the demigod beside him would do his utmost to protect him in the battle to come was all the encouragement Morgan needed. He took a deep breath and focused on the land beneath him, seeking Atlanteia's magic.

CHAPTER EIGHT

ELATION FILLED MORGAN WHEN HIS SOUL CONNECTED
with the power he had been born to wield. His pulse
spiked, his senses registering the life force of every
living creature and plant in Ivory Peaks as his heartbeat
synchronized effortlessly with that of the kingdom he
ruled by virtue of his birth. He blinked, a little stunned.

This is...easier than the first time around!

Brightness flared around them. Victor sucked in air.
It was the demon's first time seeing the phenomenon
that was unfolding.

A sparkling viridescence was spreading through the
air, the living manifestation of the magic of the land
responding to Morgan's presence. A thought came to
him, unbidden.

*Could this form a protective barrier, like Theo did in
London? Is that even possible?*

The kingdom sighed beneath him, the answer it
breathed reaching him on a whisper. He clenched his
fists.

"What's wrong?" Victor asked tensely.

"I'm…going to attempt something."

Morgan took a deep breath and closed his eyes. *Please work!*

He willed his racing pulse to slow and centered his soul. A deep sense of peace gradually filled his mind, superseding the dread that sought to overwhelm it. Words danced through his subconscious as Atlanteia's magic soaked into his flesh, a susurration that soon formed a command.

Morgan opened his eyes and barked out the decree, knowing in the very essence of his being that it carried a will that could not be defied. "*By the powers vested in me by my father, Isdar, and my ancestor, the Goddess Atlanteia, I command thee to shield this realm and every living thing upon it!*"

An ungodly blaze scorched his insides as the final word left his lips. His voice boomed across the palace grounds, the echoes defying physics as they multiplied and spread far beyond the city and the valley below.

Victor stiffened.

Morgan's scalp prickled. *It's—it's working!*

His heart thundered as he watched the green mist spread across the Ivory Peaks faster than the speed of light. The haze thickened before condensing down into a thin, shimmering barrier that hugged the highest mountains and treetops in the land and wrapped around all its life forms.

Even though he could not see beyond the vale, Morgan knew in his soul that the entire kingdom was now being shielded by Atlanteia's magic. How long that defense would last was anyone's guess.

Better get rid of what's threatening Ivory Peaks before it collapses then!

Leiv was staring at the semi-lucent layer hovering above his flesh and Asteria's body, his face pale. "What —what is this?!"

The eagle remained serene beneath him, as if she knew what the light sparking across her feathers meant.

"It's Atlanteia's protection."

"What?!" Hildur breathed.

Regina and Elwyn exchanged a shocked look.

"You never fail to surprise me," Galliad mumbled in admiration.

"It will keep you safe from this plague."

Morgan's gaze shifted from the dazed Dryads to the approaching threat hurtling toward the capital. The dark wave boiled agitatedly as it thinned and spread sideways, as if it sensed the new magic protecting the realm it wished to decimate. It stretched into a ring that soon encircled the city and the palace. Shadows raced across the gardens as the sky darkened. The stench of ozone saturated the air.

"Morgan," Victor warned.

Morgan scowled. "I see it."

Gold flashed amidst the black fog rolling rapidly toward them, a bright spot that winked in and out of sight as whoever controlled the plague shielded themselves within the living miasma.

Morgan's stomach lurched when the dazzling light suddenly split. "Dammit! There's two of them!"

Victor's knuckles whitened on the handle of his sword. "Here they come!"

Morgan caught a glimpse of bloodshot, gold-speckled eyes and a female face distorted by fury before something rammed him with enough force to rattle his teeth and choke his breath. Surprise jolted him when he heard the crunch of his Stark Steel armor. Fire raked his flank.

Victor's battle cry sounded close by as the landscape blurred around him.

Morgan plowed through the wall of the palace, smashed into the central concourse of the throne room, and carved a deep groove in the marble floor before fetching up hard against the steps of the dais holding the gilded chairs of the king and queen of the Dryads. He sat up and shook his head dazedly, trepidation tightening his chest.

It had been a long time since he had lost the upper hand in a battle so quickly.

Metal glinted at the corner of his vision.

Morgan cursed and rolled. Blood smeared the pale tiles from the wound his attacker had inflicted when she'd damaged his suit and cut his flesh.

A brass-studded scourge smashed into the ground where he'd been a heartbeat ago. Debris erupted, the shards missing him by a hairbreadth as he spread his wings and shot backward. Morgan's heart thumped violently when his foe finally emerged from the mass of seething shadows hovering in mid-air.

The barefoot, black-winged Goddess wore a tattered, golden dress that exposed her glittering flesh in places. Unkempt, dark hair covered her greasy scalp and writhed around her head, the ragged ends tipped with hissing snake heads. The metal and leather whip in her hand twitched sinuously, the lashes moving as if they were alive.

"Who are you?" Morgan raised the Sword of Wind in a defensive stance. "Why are you attacking this kingdom?!"

The Goddess glanced at his sword. Her lips stretched in a smile that did not reach her dark eyes. *"That's because we mean to steal your blade and kill you, brother."*

Morgan's pulse stuttered. *Brother?!*

The fist that smashed into his stomach crushed his armor and bruised his flesh. He gasped, eyes rounding as he sailed backward across the hall.

Shit! I didn't even see her move!

Air locked in his lungs when he collided violently with one of the oak pillars that lined the concourse. His skull thumped the trunk hard. Black spots swarmed his vision.

The Goddess charged, as swift as wind, her scourge whistling in her grip.

Both she and Morgan froze as wood creaked and foliage slithered ominously above them. The oak tree he'd crashed into folded its flower and fruit-laden boughs protectively around him.

The Goddess cursed as Morgan disappeared inside

a living cage of greenery, her momentum floundering. He blinked, equally startled.

Warmth was filling his veins. *Wait! Is this—?!*

Magic from the tree was suffusing him. It was Atlanteia's strength and it was pouring out of Ivory Peaks into his soul core.

Morgan swallowed convulsively, recognizing the life force the Dryads and all living things in the realm were lending him so he could fight this unholy battle. Resolve filled his heart. His wound and bruises started to heal.

Shock curdled his blood.

Not only had his enemy broken through his armor as if it were made of eggshells, the injuries she had inflicted had not repaired themselves as they should have, given his demigod status.

How—how is that possible?!

The Goddess's enraged scream filled the hall and scattered his alarmed thoughts. Morgan's breath caught when he spotted her through a gap between the branches shielding him.

Her scourge was on the ground.

The other trees in the throne room had bowed to twine their branches around her limbs and wings, holding her prisoner in mid-air.

That was when Morgan remembered the myth of the place he found himself in. Legend had it that the palace had sprouted from the body of the consort of Queen Atlanteia. It seemed the fallen deity was not pleased with the unwelcome visitor in his realm.

Glass exploded to his left.

Victor smashed through a giant window and landed hard on the floor some fifty feet away. He rolled to one knee and raised his blade in time to block the enraged, dark-winged Goddess trying to claw out his eyes.

She too wore a tattered, golden dress and wielded a brass-studded scourge.

Morgan's belly twisted on a fresh wave of dread when he saw Victor's wounds. Deep slashes scored the dark demigod's Stark Steel armor. Blood was trickling from the wounds and a deep gash in his temple.

He wasn't faring any better against their enemy.

Crimson filled Victor's pupils. The black flames around him roared, thickening and swarming the Goddess.

For a second, Morgan thought he would win.

Corruption blasted across the throne room. It dispersed the demigod's fire and shoved him back several feet. The Goddess who'd attacked him emerged from the fading inferno.

Her eyes had shifted to obsidian from edge to edge. Inky lines snaked under her skin, the thin threads pulsing with the sinister power that had repelled Victor's attack.

A dark premonition turned Morgan's blood to ice. *Wait! Is that—?!*

The Goddess bared her teeth and charged Victor.

He braced and swung his sword. She ducked beneath the blade, her figure blurring. Fresh lacerations appeared in Victor's armor, metal giving way as if it were gossamer. Blood bloomed along the wounds. The demigod clenched his teeth, steadied his stance, and barely managed to parry her next attack.

A mocking smile stretched the Goddess's mouth as she danced out of the way of his counter swing, shadows roiling on her feathers.

"You're too slow, brother!" she teased, her gleeful voice full of malice.

"Watch out!" Morgan yelled.

The oak tree unwound its cage and released him just as the Goddess somersaulted backward on one hand. She twisted in mid-air, kicked off a nearby pillar with enough force to dent the wood, and smashed Victor in the jaw with her left heel.

Bone cracked.

Morgan's pulse stuttered. He caught a glimpse of her chest as she took the demigod to the ground and started squeezing his neck with her thighs.

Fuck! I was right!

Power surged through him from his replenished core. He shot toward the clashing pair, black wind and Dryad magic erupting around him in a violent storm.

"Victor, I think they're being controlled by Elios! They seem to be after me and the Sword of Wind!"

Victor grunted where he was attempting to stop his attacker from choking him, his broken jaw visibly swelling. His eyes flared when he saw what Morgan had detected.

Something dark throbbed within the Goddess's body. Something that looked eerily similar to what

Elios had used to bind Boreas's powers when he'd imprisoned him in the Sixth Hell.

A violent tremor rattled the hall, halting Morgan's charge. His alarmed gaze found the first Goddess. His breath froze on his lips.

No!

CHAPTER NINE

THE OAK TREES MAKING UP THE PILLARS OF THE THRONE room were dying, their leaves and flowers turning black and their branches twisting into dry husks as the vile energy pulsing from the deity they had entrapped drained them of their life force.

Agony scored Morgan's heart, the loss of the millennia-old entities echoing through his very marrow. He felt sorrow spread through the Dryads in the kingdom as they sensed the ancient trees' demise.

The Goddess dropped down from her dead prison, her inky wings spread wide. The shadows swarming her parted for a heartbeat when her feet touched the ground, revealing the same black seed pulsing within her too. Her wrathful stare found him as her scourge levitated into her grip.

Morgan widened his stance and hoped he would see her blisteringly fast attack when it came this time. He concentrated his power into his blade, aware he would only get one chance to land a blow.

Dazzling arrows brimming with Dryad magic sailed through the jagged opening behind the Goddess as they launched toward one another with ungodly roars. Morgan recognized Hildur's bolts.

Most of them missed the Goddess.

One pierced her left Achilles tendon and another her right pinion, slowing her by a millisecond.

Now!

Morgan dove beneath her swinging, brass-studded whip and spun as he rose. The Sword of Wind sang in his hands as it carved a deep slash in her flesh from her left hip bone to her right shoulder.

The Goddess shrieked. Her expression cleared, incandescent fury giving way to pain and awareness. Gold bloomed in her pupils. Her gaze landed on him.

Recognition flared on her distraught face.

"*Iv—Ivmir?!*" she mumbled, confused.

Shock reverberated through Morgan. A volley of viridescent spell bombs carrying the magic of the Dryad royal family and their mages smashed into her back and choked her breath before he could ask her how she knew his true name.

The second Goddess's head snapped around. Gold pierced her dark eyes. She paled, wings drooping as her rage faded to alarm.

"*A—Alecto?*" She looked at her hands, disorientated. "*What—what's going on?!*"

Blood drained from the first Goddess's face, as if she were seeing her companion for the first time. "*Megaera!*"

Victor took advantage of the distraction, yanked his

attacker close, and headbutted her viciously in the nose. Bone crunched. Megaera howled and stumbled back.

The demigod shoved her off him and regrouped with Morgan.

Galliad, Elwyn, Regina, and the Dryad royal family appeared through the breach in the palace wall. Though the plague was trying to attack them, it could not penetrate Atlanteia's protection. They raised another barrage of magic attacks.

"Wait!" Morgan shouted. "They're being manipulated by Elios! I—I think we can still get through to them!"

Victor scowled. "Are you sure about that?!"

Morgan's stomach plummeted. The miasma bubbling around the two Goddesses had thickened where they'd met in the center of the throne room. Whatever consciousness they'd briefly regained was gone, fury and madness filling their faces once more. He clenched his fists.

Dammit!

The hairs rose on his nape. Victor cursed.

The dark mist was taking the form of an object in Alecto's hand. One that drenched Morgan in a cold sweat. A vicious smile curved the Goddess's lips when she noted his expression. Her next words confirmed his suspicions.

"Fear not, little brother. This will not make you his slave. It will eat your core and kill you instead." She glowered at Morgan. *"Be grateful for that small mercy, you ingrate!"*

Shadows exploded around the Goddesses. Their figures blurred.

"Morgan!" Victor shouted.

The demigod moved to shield him.

Alecto and Megaera were faster.

Icy fingers closed around Morgan's throat. Dark streams swarmed him, trapping his body and the Sword of Wind. Alecto and Megaera lifted him off his feet and drove him upward. They plowed through the roof of the throne room as if it were parchment.

Wind whistled in Morgan's ears as they rose fast above the palace. He glanced over his shoulder. They were taking him toward the mountain that stood guard over the capital.

Morgan's gaze darted to the Sword of Wind. It could normally negate Elios's corruption.

Why isn't it working?!

Alecto sneered, like she knew a truth he had not yet perceived.

A boom shook the air as the Goddesses folded their dark wings and accelerated. The temperature plummeted. Morgan's breath misted in front of his face, the sheer momentum of their motion bringing tears to his eyes. Horror filled him when he grasped their intent. His core pulsed as he struggled violently against his restraints.

"Please! Wait! You need to fight Elios's control over you! You don't know what he's compelling you to do!"

Megaera brought her face closer.

"What makes you think we want to fight it, brother?!" she hissed.

"Because you're both still in there!" Morgan choked out. "I glimpsed the real you, only a moment ago!"

Alecto startled for an instant, her grip loosening on his neck and her wings fluttering agitatedly. The black core within her throbbed, suppressing whatever resistance it had just encountered.

"*Wrong answer, brother!*" she growled.

Victor flashed into view behind the Goddesses, the Dryads racing a short distance beyond him on their eagles.

"*Morgan!*" the demigod screamed, voice full of dread.

Pain filled Morgan's world as Alecto and Megaera smashed him into a vertiginous cliff face. The mountain trembled. Ice and snow shuddered high above.

The rumble of an avalanche reached Morgan dimly as the two deities carved a hole in the flank of the elevation with his body, his Stark Steel armor and their rage blasting effortlessly through millennia-old rock. Numbness bloomed on his back. His limbs. His entire body grew cold as the light faded around him. His consciousness flickered.

His soul core throbbed, jolting him awake with a gasp.

Atlanteia's magic was soaring through his veins. But it wasn't just the ancient Goddess's energy that had roused his fading mind.

Ivmir!

Morgan's heart stuttered. *Icarus?!*

Whatever he thought he'd heard was gone. What was left in its stead was the power of the Goddess whose blood he bore and the love of the demigod who owned his heart and soul.

Fresh resolve surged through him. The Sword of Wind raged in his grip, inky currents twisting agitatedly as it fought the darkness confining it. The shackles started to dissipate as divine energy and Dryad power rattled his bones and poured out of his very flesh.

The Goddesses faltered.

"*Im—impossible!*" Megaera gasped.

Morgan broke free of his prison with a roar, bound the Goddesses with magic and black wind, and slowed their descent. The two deities screamed and raged as they began to rise. The gloom rapidly receded as he gained momentum.

Brightness filled his vision as they shot out of the mountain scant seconds after smashing into it. They emerged under a tempestuous sky, fragments of rock falling from their hair and bodies while snow and ice crystals formed sparkling trails behind them.

Victor slammed into Megaera with a sound of pure rage. She choked on a curse as he dragged her away from Morgan, his flames swarming her flesh.

The Dryads' magic struck Alecto, drawing a pained grunt from her throat.

Morgan grasped the Sword of Wind in both hands and scowled as he aimed it at the corrupt mass within the Goddess. "I'm sorry! This is gonna hurt!"

Alecto's eyes widened. A smirk twisted her mouth. *"You're right."*

Morgan jerked and froze. It took a heartbeat to realize what had just happened.

His stunned gaze dropped dazedly to where the Goddess had punctured his belly with her hand.

When—how?!

Megaera escaped Victor's hold, closed the distance to Morgan in a flash, and snatched the Sword of Wind from his grip. His fingers clawed empty air, his hand blindly seeking the blade that was bonded to him. Coldness engulfed him, the evil energy contained within the inky seed Alecto had lodged inside him swarming his soul core.

Morgan threw his head back and screamed, the agony of the assault so fierce he felt he was being torn apart from the inside out. He glimpsed Victor and the Dryads beyond the two Goddesses smiling contemptuously at him as his consciousness started to falter. Their mouths were open on shouts he failed to hear, their expressions pure anguish and horror.

Morgan blinked, a stark truth dawning upon him. *Oh. I'm dying. That's why they look so upset.*

Darkness encroached the edges of his vision. Cassius's face blurred into view as his soul core started to creak under the immense strain it found itself under.

Once it shattered, he would be gone.

Bone-deep sadness filled him at that wretched thought.

"I'm sorry," Morgan mumbled, barely aware of the

tears falling silently down his cheeks. "May we meet again in our…next lives…my…beloved…"

A crack tore the sky open. Golden light filled the valley.

"*LET HIM GO!*"

CHAPTER TEN

Victor's head snapped up, his throat raw from screaming Morgan's name and his jaw throbbing from a wound that was too slow to heal. His eyes widened, the torment squeezing his heart at the reality of losing his brother giving way to shock once more.

The two Goddesses arrowing down from the closing rift wore golden armor and expressions of grim resolve. The one in the lead had dazzling white wings that matched the long, silver hair fluttering from under her winged helmet. She wielded twin, shining, gold blades. The second one bore black wings and dark hair and held a brass-studded scourge similar to Alecto and Megaera's weapons.

"*Release him, sister!*" the silver-haired Goddess roared.

Shadows shrouded Alecto as she extracted her hand from Morgan's body. She barely managed to block the blades arcing toward her. Her curse was lost in the boom that shook the valley as she was driven toward the ground by her attacker.

Morgan fell, body limp and face ashen.

Victor dove and caught him. Fear choked his lungs when he felt the coldness of his brother's flesh. His harrowed gaze found the bubbling darkness within the demigod. He clenched his teeth and raised a hand to touch it, dark flames engulfing his fingers.

"Don't. It will only hurt you."

Victor stiffened, head swinging jerkily toward the figure who had appeared beside him. It was the dark-haired Goddess who had come to their rescue. He hadn't heard her approach.

The Dryads hovered close by, faces full of apprehension as they looked from her to the warring deities below. Sonic explosions marked their passage, their movements so swift the only way Victor could detect their presence was by the thin trails of gold and darkness etched in the air. The Goddess beside Victor ignored the clashing pair, her unblinking eyes locked on something in front of them. He followed her gaze.

Megaera floated silently some hundred feet away, her face twisted with loathing. The Sword of Wind shuddered in her grasp as it tried valiantly to resist the power overwhelming it.

But it wasn't just hate Victor read in Megaera's features. Gold sparked faintly in her pupils and her fingers twitched, as if she were fighting whatever was controlling her.

"I'm sorry, Megaera," the dark-haired Goddess said quietly. *"I cannot let you leave with Ivmir's sword."*

Megaera blinked. Her expression cleared for a moment. "*Ti...Tisiphone?!*"

The plague engulfing her thickened. She cried out, a sound of pain.

"*Megaera!*" Tisiphone barked, alarmed.

She darted toward the shadow-wreathed Goddess. Megaera assumed an icy mask of fury once more.

Tisiphone fended off her scourge inches from her face and shot back to a safe distance. "*Snap out of it, sister!*"

A rift reeking of corruption formed next to Megaera. The Goddess smiled savagely and stepped inside it. Tisiphone bolted toward her once more.

"*Tis! No!*" the silver-haired Goddess yelled from below.

Tisiphone rocked to a halt, her expression one of pure grief.

Victor's pulse thrummed with trepidation. The distraction had cost the silver-haired Goddess the battle. Alecto was rising, her cursing attacker on her tail. Divine power drenched the air with a golden haze when she reached the portal where Megaera had vanished with the Sword of Wind, slowing her movement.

The silver-haired Goddess stopped a short distance from the dark doorway, her pupils bright and her body radiating holy energy. Tears brimmed in her eyes and coursed down her cheeks, leaving stark, silver trails in their wake.

"*Alecto,*" she whispered in a voice full of misery. "*My sister. My kin.*"

Tisiphone stretched out a hand toward the Goddess being controlled by Elios. *"Alecto! It's me, Tisiphone!"* Anger and regret distorted her features. *"What has that bastard done to you?!"*

Alecto froze, one foot inside the rift. The air shivered around her.

Victor's scalp prickled. *She's trying to fight it!*

The Goddess gritted her teeth and looked over her shoulder. Blood soaked her palms as she scored her flesh with her nails, the grimace on her face laced with awareness.

"Find us, sisters!" Alecto choked out. *"Find us before Elios kills Clotho and Lache, and devours Tenebra's sanity!"*

Tisiphone froze, horror rounding her pupils. The silver-haired Goddess made a tortured sound.

Alecto shuddered, her body and mind falling under Elios's spell once more. She glared at them before vanishing inside the rift. It closed silently after her fading figure.

The Goddesses who had saved Morgan and Ivory Peaks sagged, wings drooping and their strength visibly draining out of them. They exchanged a distraught look.

Hildur appeared beside Victor, fear rendering her ashen. "Morgan!"

"How is he?" Roald mumbled.

Victor looked down at the unconscious demigod in his arms. Morgan's chest rose and fell shallowly, his skin so pale it looked like his veins had been drained of all blood. Guilt twisted his gut.

I failed to keep my promise.

"Is he—is he dying?!" Cedric asked shrilly.

His brothers touched his back, their faces reflecting the second prince's sorrow. Galliad joined them, an equally worried Thalia at his side.

"Not yet."

Victor straightened. His guarded gaze met that of the silver-haired Goddess as she approached. Her expression softened behind the metal framing her jaw and cheeks when she registered their suspicious stares.

"Look beneath you."

They did as she told them.

Regina's pupils flared. "Oh!"

"That's right, Seer." The Goddess's face hardened as she studied the viridescent magic still protecting the realm. *"Atlanteia's power would have faded back into Ivory Peaks if Ivmir neared Death's door."*

Victor's heart raced, hope surging inside him. Her next words dashed it cold.

"He's not out of the woods yet. Not by a league. And he will die if we do not act soon." The Goddess removed her helmet and shook her silver hair before dragging her fingers through the tousled locks. A frustrated sigh fell from her lips. *"Damn the Gods! I did not foresee this complication."*

Regina's eyes bulged. *"Atropos?!"*

Shocked murmurs left the Dryads.

Victor stared. *This is the eldest Moira?!*

"You have done well, Seer," Atropos told Regina curtly. *"You can leave the rest in our hands."*

Tisiphone was staring at the sky, her expression troubled. *"We must make haste, sister."*

Victor blinked, a vague memory resurfacing from what remained of Hypnos's spell. *She's...a Fury. So are Alecto and Megaera.*

He followed her gaze, stunned by what he'd just recalled, only to draw another shocked breath. Clouds were racing across the firmament, the formations spiraling in ominous shapes.

"What's happening?" Hildur asked anxiously.

A muscle jumped in Atropos's jawline. *"The Awakener is angry."*

A sudden intuition blasted through Victor. His stomach clenched. Atropos met his stiff stare.

"Remember what he did when he thought he'd lost Ivmir and Rohengar?" the Moira said grimly.

Victor's knuckles whitened. *Shit! I was right!*

Galliad's wary gaze swung between them. "What is it?"

Victor swallowed heavily and gazed at the sky. "Cassius's rage may very well be about to tear open the realms once more!"

CHAPTER ELEVEN

"How soon will it get here?" Kazmi said grimly into her cell phone.

Cassius's stomach churned as he glanced from the head of Argonaut to the live satellite feed on the digital display in Strickland's office.

It had been fifteen minutes since Morgan and Victor had left for Ivory Peaks with Cedric and Galliad. Kazmi had just received a call from the Argonaut headquarters in New York warning her that a new source of the plague had been spotted three hundred miles from the Western seaboard.

The phenomenon was a tiny, dark spot on the screen. Cassius was not fooled by its size. The second wave was approaching San Francisco fast, its unnatural progress and the way it was expanding suggesting it was moving with intent.

Or someone controlling it is.

Cassius shared a guarded look with Theo and Eden. He could tell they could sense it too. Someone powerful was drawing close. Someone whose aura was drenched in death.

Kazmi closed her eyes briefly, the answer she'd been given evidently not the one she'd been looking for.

"Okay," she said in a leaden tone. "You know what needs to happen if I don't survive. Just follow protocol." The Argonaut mage ended the call and met their apprehensive stares steadily, as if she hadn't just given her subordinates instructions on what to do upon her death. "We have fifteen minutes before that thing reaches us."

Brianna paled and clasped Eden's hand, her fingers trembling.

Jasper and Reuben huddled closer to Charlie. Julia and Zach framed Adrianne and Bailey protectively.

"Goddammit!" Strickland smashed his fist on his desk, face twisted in a bitter scowl. "Even if we give orders to evacuate the city right now, there will still be thousands of casualties!"

Something scratched the glass outside his office, making everyone jump.

Cassius's eyes rounded at the sight of the small, black shape on the narrow ledge beyond one of the windows. "*Loki?!*"

The demon cat's faint meow reached him as he stormed across the room.

"How the hell did he get up here?!" Bailey muttered.

Loki looked nervously at the drop behind him while Cassius carefully opened the casement. The demon cat purred affectionately when Cassius scooped him up into his arms. He rose to lick Cassius's face and leapt out of his hold, body shifting into his imp form before his paws hit the ground.

Theo came over and hugged him as he shook out his fur. "That was dangerous!"

Delight brightened Loki's expression. "Theo!"

He rubbed his face against the demigod's chest, his ears and tail flicking contentedly for a moment. The imp sobered when he pulled back and spied the barrage of tense stares directed at him.

Kazmi studied him with a heavy frown. "Cassius tells us you foresaw this plague?"

She indicated the screen on the wall with her cane.

Loki's eyes darkened as he studied the shadowy band racing for the coastline. "Yes. That's why I'm here." Crimson flared in his pupils. "I think…I know what's causing it."

Cassius startled, his surprise reflected on everyone's faces. "You do?!"

Loki bobbed his head. "This energy smells familiar. I am pretty certain we're dealing with one of the Black Fates."

A memory flared into life in Cassius's subconscious.

"You mean the Keres?" he said sharply. "The Goddesses of Death?!"

"The what now?" Bailey said numbly.

Loki ignored the wizard. "Not just death. They are bringers of plagues and disease too."

Julia clenched her fists. "Why the hell is one of the Black Fates attacking Earth?!"

A muscle jumped in Zach's jawline where he stood beside her.

"It's Elios," Theo said flatly. "It has to be! He must be behind this!"

"Finding out who's at fault is not going to help us right now!" Brianna snapped. She jerked her chin at the satellite display. "By my count, we have less than thirteen minutes before that thing reaches the city."

Eden dipped her head. "Mom is right. We have to stop this plague." She met Cassius and Theo's gazes, her expression resolute. "The three of us are the only ones who stand a chance against her."

"The four of us," Loki said in a hard voice.

The Eternity Key appeared in his hand, the golden dagger blazing with power.

Cassius knew not to dissuade the imp. Loki had proven himself in battle more than once before.

"Eden," Brianna murmured.

The witch was staring at her daughter, face ashen.

The young mage smiled faintly. "Don't worry. Woody and I will not fall prey to this disease."

The devilwood pendant quivered against her throat. Eden's confident tone seemed to allay some of Brianna's fears.

"Be careful."

Cassius's heart pounded as he crossed the floor to the screen showing the satellite feed. He pointed at a spot over the ocean some thirty miles from the shoreline.

"We should make our stand here," he told Theo and Eden. He turned to face the rest of the room, his gaze sweeping the humans and otherworldly who would stay behind to defend the city. "Try to get people as far below ground as you can. Subways, the basements of buildings. Anywhere deep that can slow down the spread of this plague if it does make landfall!"

❦

DARKNESS SWARMED THE GODDESS'S MIND. AN ETERNITY of darkness. Just as coldness swallowed her body whole, the chill of it so deep it would have frozen her bones were it not for her divine powers.

She could not recall a time when she had been warm.

Has there ever been such a time?

Her thoughts scattered to the winds, like they always did. Whoever she had been had long succumbed to the will of the one who controlled her. She would have felt anger had she retained a fragment of her consciousness. But she had none.

She did not even recall her own name.

And so she moved, relentless in the task she had been assigned by a merciless God, raining death and destruction in her path across the realms he'd chosen to attack. The screams of the dying did not reach her ears. The stench of rotting carcasses never filled her nostrils.

Instead, she fed on the despair of all those she killed and funneled it into the dark seed her master had carved inside her body, so he could feast upon it and grow stronger still where he bided his time in the Nine Hells.

Strong enough to destroy all worlds.

Strong enough to kill the Gods themselves.

Something shimmered in the distance. Points of light. The coastline grew defined.

A city of man appeared, towers of glass and metal gleaming under the sun as they soared toward a pale blue sky.

Not for long. Soon, they will be but ashes and ruins blemishing the Earth, just like all the others.

Nothing survived her passage. No man. No creature. No tree. No building.

Well, almost nothing.

A trace of unease flitted through her, only to be consumed by the corruption dampening her mind. She had been vaguely aware of the otherworldly souls and the few humans who had not breathed their last when she had scourged the lands to the south of mankind's realm. Since they were inconsequential to her mission, she had not paused to investigate the reason for their survival.

After all, their world would soon be dead and their hopes crushed.

Something drew her divine gaze. Another source of light.

The Goddess frowned.

It was arrowing toward her at supersonic speed, the ocean parting beneath it in a V-shaped trail of foam-tipped waves.

Whatever it is, it too shall fall.

The dark mist she travelled in thickened as it started to drop through the atmosphere, the plague eager in its intent to destroy everything upon the land ahead of her.

The point of light grew. Expanded. Became blinding.

The Goddess squinted, her seraphic vision rendered sightless for an instant. *What is that?*

A figure appeared. A man. One with fair hair, blazing white wings, and a dazzling sword swarming with crackling light.

The Goddess blinked. Something fluttered through her skull, a memory slipping through the shadows suffocating her consciousness. It slowed her charge a fraction.

Awake...ner?!

The man frowned, his bright eyes full of resolve. His shape blurred when he got within three hundred feet of her.

The Goddess rocked to a halt and followed his breakneck ascent with her gaze, her mind bent under the will of the one who commanded her once more. A sound reached her ears. The growing roar of water. She looked down.

Her eyes rounded.

A giant tidal wave was headed straight for her and the band of darkness stretching out on either side of her.

That was when the Goddess realized how foolish she had been.

CHAPTER TWELVE

Cassius's heart slammed heavily against his ribs as he watched the storm surge he had raised swallow the dark mist and the shadowy figure at its center. The tidal wave crashed back down upon the ocean with a noise like thunder, currents churning with violent eddies that would stretch for miles.

He doubted it would end the plague or the Goddess who wielded it.

Still, so long as it buys Theo the time he needs!

"Here she comes," Loki warned.

He clung to Cassius's back. Cassius felt the power of the Eternity Key throb against his body as it extended into a golden sword in the imp's grasp. The sound of the turbulent sea beneath them was superseded by a rising whine. A dark shape bolted out of the choppy waters.

It reached them in a single heartbeat.

Cassius grunted as he blocked a set of long, curved claws with his blade. The Eternity Key quivered in

Loki's grip, the sword similarly curbing the inky talons that would have shredded the imp's face.

The Black Fate looked past them to the city, the plague mist bubbling into existence around her once more. A gruesome smile distorted the dark-winged Goddess's monstrous features. Corruption boiled in her pupils.

"*Clever.*"

She vanished in the blink of an eye. Cassius's stomach plummeted.

Shit!

Loki grabbed on grimly to his armor as he went after the escaping deity. She was aiming straight for Eden and Theo where they levitated before the city.

Scarlet flared in Eden's eyes, the power she wielded reflected in the shimmering, red light that exploded around her body and the staff in her hand. Her hair rose around her head, a golden halo sparking with crimson flashes. The runes on her weapon overspilled the wood and carved their magic into their mage's flesh.

Her bloodcursed spell bomb found the Black Fate as lightning-charged clouds detonated above her. Sulfur and ozone suffused the air, the devilwood staff blasting open a portal to the Hells. The phenomenon started to spin, creating a swirling updraft that swallowed the plague mist within its inky currents.

The Goddess smashed into Eden. The mage grunted as she was shoved back some fifty feet before she braced to a halt. Her weapon blurred in her grasp, the staff moving of its own volition to foil the counterstrike that would have blinded its mage.

"Bloodcursed Devilwood Summoning Staff," the Black Fate said coldly. *"I see you have found a new Magus."* She brought her face close to Eden's. *"Do you think the power of the Underworld is enough to stop me, little girl?"*

A dark smile curved Eden's mouth. "No. But he can."

The Black Fate flinched. She moved.

Cassius was faster.

Heaven's Light exploded along his sword as he raised it above his head and dropped toward the Goddess with a roar. He carved a deep slash across the deity's back at the same time Loki sprang from his shoulder and stabbed the Eternity Key into her left wing.

The Goddess screamed as the blades pierced flesh and skewered tendons and bone. Gold flashed in her pupils.

Pain drained her features of color as she regained some semblance of her normal appearance. The plague mist started to dissipate, revealing her tattered, golden dress.

Her tortured gaze clashed with Cassius. Awareness filled her face.

"Icarus?!"

Cassius's pulse stuttered. *I—I know her!*

A name came to him then. One he had not uttered in hundreds of years.

"Tenebra?!" he mumbled.

Recognition flared in the Black Fate's golden eyes at

the sound of her name. Sorrow swamped her ashen features when it faded on the wind.

Cassius knew instinctively she was not acting of her own free will. He started toward her.

"*Stop!*" Loki barked.

Cassius froze, sensing the overwhelming force the imp had detected an instant before him. It was swarming Tenebra's soul once more. Goosebumps broke out on his skin when he recognized its pungent aftertaste.

That's Elios's power! He's—he's stronger than before!

"Is her mind being controlled by Elios?!" Cassius asked Loki.

The imp scowled. "Yes. And I'm pretty sure he subdued her the same way he did Boreas and Demetrius!"

Cassius clenched his jaw. "We have to free her!" His heart thundered as he focused his divine powers and sought out the corrupt seed Elios had embedded within the Goddess. "*There!* It's in her—!"

He grunted as darkness exploded around Tenebra. The blast sent a cursing Loki crashing into the ocean with Eden. It would have cast Cassius there too, had he not braced his wings and used Heaven's Light to buffer the impact of the detonation.

Tenebra spun around and bolted toward the city, her eyes full of madness, the plague thickening and shrouding her once more.

She got to within one mile of the shoreline before smashing into an invisible wall.

Golden sparks erupted as she bounced off the

barrier with a cry, the force of the collision briefly dispersing the shadows around her. She recovered and glared at the translucent dome protecting San Francisco.

Her gaze found the demigod responsible for it. *"You! Is this your doing?!"*

Theo smiled savagely where he hovered some hundred feet above the divine shield. He raised a hand and barked out a command.

"Suspend!"

Tenebra cursed as the time spell froze her wings and limbs. The Spear of Light whooshed out of Theo's grasp and sailed toward her. His weapon glanced off the plague currents that had shot out to protect Tenebra.

Theo scowled.

A grimace distorted the Goddess's features as she fought the spell. It broke with an audible snap. She came at him, murder in her dark gaze.

"Dimensional Gate!" Theo snarled.

He vanished just as her claws carved the air where he'd been. Tenebra cursed and pulled up sharply. A grunt left her when Cassius smashed into her.

She twisted around, her talons scoring his Stark Steel armor and raking his skin as he drove her relentlessly toward Theo's barrier.

Cassius ignored the slashes and gritted his teeth. "Now, Theo!"

Tenebra's shriek of rage choked off into a soundless gasp.

Theo had reappeared out of a portal behind her and

stabbed the Spear of Light through her back and into the corrupt seed next to her heart.

Elation filled Cassius. *We did it!*

Tenebra blinked at him. Gold slowly filled her pupils as her awareness returned.

The pain that squeezed Cassius's belly with his next breath made his soul core throb with bloodcurdling violence and drew an abject cry from his throat. It took him but a heartbeat to grasp that it was not his own suffering he was experiencing.

It was that of his demigod soulmate. Ice filled his veins, the terror that seized him in its cold clutches so overwhelming he feared he would lose his mind.

Ivmir!

Morgan's voice sounded faintly inside his skull. *Icarus?!*

Cassius blinked through the silver tears obscuring his vision, unsure if he'd imagined his lover's distant shout.

Theo let go of Tenebra and bolted toward him, face pale with dread. "Cassius!"

"No!" Cassius swallowed convulsively and shook his head despite the horror leeching the heat from his body. "You must—you must destroy the core Elios put inside her first!"

Theo faltered, his wings fluttering agitatedly as he rocked to a halt.

Elios's vile power flooded the atmosphere.

Resolved tightened Theo's eyes. He turned and arrowed toward Tenebra. "Suspend!"

A vicious bellow left the Black Fate, the time spell

breaking as quickly as it formed. She yanked the Spear of Light from her body and cast it into the ocean.

Cassius's mouth went dry as the God of Darkness's corruption healed the crack in the inky seed within her body. The gold faded from Tenebra's pupils, Elios's unholy energy subjugating her all over again.

There was movement below them. Eden rose from the sea inside a crimson sphere, Loki at her side and the devilwood staff vibrating angrily in her grip. She'd caught the Spear of Light before it could sink into the ocean.

Theo snatched his weapon out of mid-air when she lobbed it at him. He joined her and Loki as they charged Tenebra. They smashed into the Black Fate with enough force to churn the ocean and disperse the clouds in the sky. Bloodcursed magic and divine light erupted around them as they combined their powers to subdue the Goddess and attempt to destroy the dark core inside her.

For a moment, Cassius thought they might win.

The plague engulfed Theo, the mist a living weapon that bound his wings and the Spear of Light. He cursed. Eden choked and Loki snarled as Tenebra evaded their attacks and grasped their throats, her claws slicing thick lines into their flesh.

Sweat beaded Cassius's forehead. He headed jerkily toward them, his movements rendered awkward by the vicious agony still gripping his body.

Theo gagged as the plague infiltrated his mouth and nose.

Eden's face started turning purple. Loki's eyes

bulged and rolled back in his head. The Black Fate smiled coldly and squeezed the mage and the imp's windpipes even more.

Panic turned Cassius numb. *No!*

The scream of denial bubbling up his throat finally ripped from his lips.

"*STOP IT!*"

The air split open next to the Black Fate. Cassius's pulse stuttered.

Two dark-winged Goddesses in golden armor bolted out of a portal and crashed into Tenebra, their eyes bright with seraphic power and their bodies swarming with shadows. The Black Fate cursed as she lost her hold on her would-be victims.

"*Stand down, sister!*" one of the Goddesses yelled.

She cursed and parried the talons curving toward her face with her own claws.

The second Goddess charged the Black Fate with a battle cry that made the air vibrate. "*Come to your senses, Tenebra!*"

She slammed into the Black Fate and drove her toward the sky, her companion following. Sonic booms punctuated the ozone-heavy atmosphere as the two strangers engaged the Goddess who had attacked San Francisco.

CHAPTER THIRTEEN

Blood pounded dully in Cassius's skull. He was struggling to keep track of their movements. He pressed a shaky hand to his belly and swallowed a whimper.

His armor felt hot to the touch, the heat his soul core was emitting strong enough to sear the skin of a normal human.

Ivmir! Mor—Morgan! Please be okay! I beg of you!

Bile flooded the back of his throat at the agony that threatened to rip his body apart with his next breath. He threw his head back and screamed, seraphic light bursting from his eyes in bright beams that pierced the dark clouds gathering above them.

He knew in the very marrow of his being what this pain meant.

His soulmate was dying.

Rage bloomed inside Cassius, superseding his despair and suffering. It blasted out of his subconscious and bubbled through his veins, robbing him of his wits.

Of his sanity. His soul core trembled as incandescent fury overwhelmed every cell in his body, the power of the Awakener surging from within him and rattling his bones.

He thought he heard Theo scream his name.

Strong arms closed around him. A familiar scent filled his nostrils.

Theo's tortured face swam before Cassius's blurry vision. The young demigod's pupils brimmed with divine light within his sage green and sapphire irises.

"*No, Icarus!*" the South Star shouted, his voice underscored by the sweet tone of the one whose soul fragment he carried within him. "*You must not lose control, brother!*"

The power of Summer drenched Cassius's entire being as Theo and Rohengar surrounded him with their warmth and their love. It brought with it a semblance of lucidity that pierced the fire inside him and dampened the ungodly force about to tear open the walls between worlds.

Cassius tasted blood on his tongue as he ground his teeth and desperately hung on to the sliver of awareness Theo had granted him. He scored his palms with his nails, attempting to subdue his wrath.

He knew only too well what would happen if he let his powers loose in such an unrestrained manner. The memory of what he had done during the War in the Nether made him shudder all over again.

I cannot! Even if I lose him! Sorrow squeezed his heart so tight he wished it would kill him there and then. *I cannot destroy so many—!*

"Calm yourself, Awakener."

Cassius's stomach flip-flopped.

The smell of camphor was imbuing the air around him.

The tendons in Cassius's neck twinged as he fought the madness controlling his body and slowly turned his head.

The Reaper God had stepped out of a portal beside him. He was in his human guise, his robe of shadows fluttering around his body and his somber face, his long, dark hair still under the hood. A circle of bones and black flames glowed starkly against the snow-white skin of his left ring finger.

"Your soulmate has yet to cross Death's door," the Reaper God told Cassius, his gaze locked on the unholy battle taking place in the sky. *"So, breathe, Awakener."*

Cassius did just as he said. He took shaky inhales and exhales, his labored breathing echoing in his ears. The blaze threatening to consume him started to abate.

It felt like a lifetime before he managed to bring his powers back under his control.

"Cassius," Theo mumbled in a pained voice, still holding on to him.

"I'm—I'm okay." Cassius sagged and leaned his forehead against Theo's shoulder, his body weak and his soul core bruised and aching. He closed his eyes and soaked in Theo's warmth for a moment before raising his head and seeking the flashes of gold and darkness in the sky above them with his gaze. "Who are they?"

"They are Kes and Orena, the second and third Black

Fates." The Reaper God met Cassius and Theo's shocked stares briefly. "*They are Tenebra's sisters.*"

"Are they here to destroy Earth too?!" Loki asked harshly.

He and Eden had joined them.

"*No.*" The Reaper God shook his head. "*They wish to stop the eldest Black Fate before she—*"

A sinister energy saturated the atmosphere. The Reaper God froze. Cassius's eyes widened.

The plague mist surrounding Tenebra had grown into a howling storm of darkness.

"I think she's pissed," Eden mumbled.

Coldness raised goosebumps on Cassius's flesh. The ring of bones and dark fire on the Reaper God's finger had morphed into an eight-foot-tall, black scythe that was sucking the warmth out of the atmosphere.

The Reaper God moved, flesh giving way to his skeletal form. "*Stop, Mother!*"

Cassius and the others startled.

The Reaper God's roar was swallowed by the sound the Ring of Death made as it connected with Tenebra's claws. He leaned close to the Black Fate's furious face.

"*REMEMBER WHO YOU ARE, GODDESS WHO BIRTHED ME!*"

His voice boomed across the ocean and dispersed the clouds above them.

Tenebra blinked. Gold glinted in her dark pupils as Kes and Orena joined the Reaper God.

"*Kes?!*" she mumbled. "*Rena?*" Her gaze shifted to the Reaper God. "*Temir?!*"

Her breath choked off, the corrupt core within her seeking to control her once more.

The Reaper God's orbits bloomed crimson and gold. He raised the Ring of Death and brought it pointed tip down toward her chest and Elios's dark seed.

The plague mist blocked his attack.

Madness filled Tenebra's face. She was about to charge the Reaper God and her sisters when something made her pause. Her scowling gaze locked on a spot a short distance to Cassius's left.

Cassius's breath froze. The way his soul core was pulsing could only mean one thing. Theo sucked in air, his face brightening as he too sensed what was drawing near.

A rift opened before them.

Two Goddesses in golden armor stepped out of it, the one who'd carved open the portal with her blade sporting long, silver hair and white wings, while the other had rippling, coal-black locks and dark wings.

"Shit," Loki muttered, the word underscored by unease even as recognition flared on his face. "When it rains, it pours."

Cassius's gaze flitted across the deities' strangely familiar faces before focusing on the shadows inside the portal, his heart racing with equal trepidation and hope. Victor emerged from the gloom.

He sported a bruised jaw and a nasty cut on his temple and was holding an ashen-faced Morgan around the waist.

Horror widened Cassius's eyes. Their Stark Steel

armor was dented and covered in slashes, blood congealing on the metal.

Morgan raised his head weakly where he clung to Victor. A weak smile stretched his mouth as he met Cassius's tearful gaze.

"Hey," he croaked. "I hope we're not late for the party."

Cassius was barely aware of the wetness staining his cheeks as he took his lover from Victor and gently hugged him.

Theo bolted into Victor's hold, his eyes glittering. He faltered before carefully pressing their lips together. Victor closed his arms around the demigod and kissed him back with wild abandon, unheeding of his wounded jaw.

Morgan's warmth slowly thawed Cassius's frozen heart as they embraced. Cassius swallowed a sob.

He could feel the dissonance within his lover. The wrongness in his soul core. Morgan was not out of danger yet.

"Cedric?" Eden looked anxiously past Victor to where the portal had closed. "Is he—is he okay?!"

Victor reluctantly lifted his mouth off Theo's and dipped his head at the young mage. "He's alright. He's helping his family deal with the aftermath of what happened in their kingdom."

Eden sagged, face pale with relief.

Cassius's insides churned at the guarded light in Victor's eyes and his careful tone. He could smell the demon's trepidation. Whatever had happened in Ivory Peaks had scared the demigod.

They jumped when a voice boomed across the sky.

"It seems I must put this fight on hold for now."

Cassius and the others turned to face the Black Fate who had attacked San Francisco. A portal had appeared next to Tenebra. She made to enter it.

"Don't go, Ten!" Kes yelled.

Orena and Kes rushed toward the Black Fate. The Reaper God and the dark-haired Goddess who'd accompanied Victor and Morgan blocked their path.

"Get out of our way, Tisiphone!" Kes snarled.

Orena scowled. *"Move, Temir!"*

The dark-haired Goddess shook her head, her expression full of sorrow. *"You cannot follow Tenebra where she is going, Kes."*

"She is right," the Reaper God said calmly.

He had assumed his human appearance once more.

A muscle twitched in Tenebra's cheek. She fisted her hands, fighting a force she could not hope to defeat.

The silver-haired Goddess hovered a short distance from the shadow-wreathed Black Fate. *"Is it true, Ten?"*

The air trembled around her, her divine strength drenching the atmosphere with a golden haze that warmed Cassius's cold flesh even though her voice was devoid of emotion.

"Does he torture our sisters, like Alecto told us?"

Tenebra closed her eyes briefly. Her head swiveled, slowly, painfully, as if she were a puppet fighting the strings controlling her. A silver tear bloomed in her left eye and tumbled down her cheek.

She vanished silently inside the rift, the brief

awareness that had flitted across her face gone as quickly as it had appeared.

The silver-haired Goddess was still for a timeless moment. Then she raised her face to the sky and howled her rage at the weak Gods of Heaven who had allowed all that had come to pass to unfold.

CHAPTER FOURTEEN

"It's called Rot," Atropos said quietly.

Tension churned Cassius's stomach.

The Goddess sat next to his and Morgan's bed. Her armor and helmet had returned to the golden dress and laurel-leaf crown that denoted her station. His gaze shifted from her flawless face to his lover.

Morgan slept fitfully, his jaw tight with pain and his flesh soaked in sweat. His fingers twitched from time to time in Cassius's grasp.

Cassius gently wiped the demigod's brow with a cool towel. It took all of his willpower to quell the fresh wave of panic threatening to swallow him. Morgan was never cold. Yet, his skin felt so icy it almost burned his hand.

"Is that what attacked Ivory Peaks and is trying to destroy Earth?" Victor asked.

The demigod was leaning against the wall opposite the bed, his expression somber.

"Yes." Atropos clenched her jaw. "We had hoped to find

Tenebra and the Furies in time to stop what Elios intended, but it seems we were late, once again."

Her frustration made the air vibrate and spark with flashes of gold. Loki's ears twitched where he'd curled up next to Morgan's pillow in his demon cat form, his ochre eyes focused unblinkingly on the Goddess. A mirror rattled on the wall.

Atropos's face fell. *"I'm sorry."*

She reeled in her divine energy and glanced at the sleeping demigod in the bed. Cassius could tell from the tortured light that danced in her pupils that she blamed herself for what had happened to Morgan. Yet he could not find it in himself to condemn her for her failure.

Somehow, he had a feeling that he owed Atropos a lot. That they all did.

Theo entered the bedroom.

"Was that an earthquake?" he asked suspiciously.

"No," Victor murmured, his face brightening a little.

He accepted the cup of coffee his lover handed him. Though the bruise on his jaw had faded a little, the wound on his temple had yet to fully heal.

Theo eyed the demigod's injuries worriedly before coming over and passing Cassius another steaming cup of coffee. "Drink it."

"I'm not—" Cassius started.

"Either drink it or you'll be wearing it in the next five seconds," Theo grumbled.

Cassius reluctantly accepted the cup. Atropos's lips twitched.

Theo caught her amused expression.

"What?" he said warily.

"I was right. You make a wonderful South Star."

Cassius stilled, his fingers frozen around his drink. Theo's eyes rounded.

Victor lowered his brows and took a threatening step toward Atropos. "What do you mean by that?!"

A faint sound from the living room distracted them. Judging by the smell of camphor infusing the apartment, the Reaper God had returned. The doorbell rang an instant afterward.

Someone started pounding on the door exactly one point five seconds later.

Cassius swallowed a sigh. He could sense Adrianne and the soul cores of the rest of Morgan's team outside the apartment. They weren't alone.

The Reaper God poked his head through the doorway.

"Would you like me to get that?" he asked politely.

Loki huffed and rolled his eyes. He leapt down from the bed and transformed into his imp form. "Stay here. The last thing those guys need right now is you scaring the crap out of them."

The Reaper God looked faintly abashed at that. He hovered awkwardly by the dresser.

Adrianne rushed inside the bedroom ahead of Loki.

"How is he?" She paled and rocked to a stop when she saw Morgan. "Is he—is he gonna be okay?!"

The rest of Morgan's team walked in, their expressions grim.

"Shit," Bailey mumbled. "He looks even worse than I thought he would."

"Lucy's on her way," Julia said in clipped tones.

Lucy Walters was an Argonaut medical mage and one of the best healers in the country.

Loki shifted back into his cat form and climbed onto the bed. He curled up next to Morgan, his flank hugging the demigod's side. The tightness in Cassius's chest loosened a little. For all their arguments, Loki truly cherished Morgan.

Strickland stood in the doorway of the bedroom. "Somehow, I have a feeling Lucy won't be able to help."

His brow furrowed as he looked from Morgan to Atropos.

The Goddess dipped her chin at his shrewd stare. *"You are correct, mage. Your magic cannot heal him. What ails Ivmir is not of this world."*

Silence fell in the wake of her somber statement. Strickland's knuckles whitened at his sides. The Argonaut director looked like he had a hundred things to say to the Goddess. Theo's voice stayed his words.

"Is Victor sick too?" Though his voice quavered, the demigod glared at Atropos. "I mean, his wounds should have healed by now and they—" Theo stopped and swallowed convulsively, "—they haven't!"

Victor took his trembling lover in his arms, unease darkening his eyes. "Hush, my love."

"The poison hasn't affected Coraos as badly," Atropos said. *"Still, it would be best if it were out of his system soon."*

Theo chewed his lip at her stiff words.

They all jumped when Strickland's phone rang.

The Argonaut director straightened when he saw the screen. He took the call.

"How are things looking?" Relief flooded his face as he listened, making him look ten years older. "Good. Keep me posted." He ended the call and met their tense stares. "That was Reuben." He frowned at Atropos. "It appears your plan to control the plague is working," he admitted grudgingly.

"*Tenebra may be the strongest Black Fate, but Kes and Orena are a force to be reckoned with.*"

Cassius glanced between Strickland and Atropos, his pulse racing. "They used their powers to stop Tenebra's contagion from spreading?"

"*Yes. They share the same abilities, after all.*"

Cassius's belly clenched on a wave of hope.

"Does that mean they could do the same for Morgan and Victor?" Theo asked before Cassius could voice the very same question. "Can they stop the Rot inside them?"

Atropos hesitated. "*No. Once a Black Fate's poison enters someone's blood, the only thing that can end it is the one who unleashed it.*" Her knuckles blanched on her lap. "*In Morgan's case, Tenebra's Rot is already eating at his soul core.*"

CHAPTER FIFTEEN

Fear choked Cassius's lungs. Loki let out a soulful meow.

Adrianne stifled a whimper and covered her mouth with her hands, her eyes round with horror. Julia touched the sorceress's trembling shoulder, her own expression dark with grief and anger.

"What about Ivory Peaks?" Victor asked roughly in the tense hush. "The plague there—"

"*Tenebra would have given Alecto and Megaera a seed of her powers to unleash the contagion. Now that they are no longer in that realm, it will die a natural death.*"

Cassius blinked. He turned and stared through the glass wall overlooking the terrace at the same time as Atropos. Loki's ears twitched. The demon cat raised his head, his posture wary. Three divine soul cores were fast approaching the building.

Relief colored Atropos's voice. "*They're here.*"

The glass rattled when Kes, Orena, and Tisiphone alighted outside the apartment. The shadows around the Black Fates receded as they retracted their powers. Tisiphone's scourge disappeared into thin air.

The Goddesses headed for the sliding door that separated the bedroom from the terrace, their armor and helmets melting into golden dresses and laurel-leaf crowns as they tucked their dark wings against their backs.

Kes opened the door and traipsed inside like she owned the place. Orena and Tisiphone entered more gracefully in her wake.

Loki shot under the bed with an angry hiss. Cassius sensed there was some kind of history between the Keeper of the Eternity Key and the Goddesses.

Kes frowned at the spot where the imp had disappeared before looking around critically. *"Hmm. This place is smaller than I thought it would be."*

Atropos smiled faintly. *"Well done, Kes, Rena."*

Kes flashed Atropos a fierce grin and gave her a thumbs up. *"All in a day's work, sis."*

Atropos's face glazed over a little at her vernacular.

"Are we sure they're Goddesses?" Adrianne asked Julia out of the corner of her mouth. "They don't talk like Goddesses."

"Oh." Surprise danced in Tisiphone's golden eyes. *"Breenelle and Orramgauth."* She was staring at Julia and Zach. *"It has been a long time."*

Bailey traded a startled glance with Charlie. "Bree what now?!"

Julia made a face. Zach sighed. Breenelle and Orramgauth were their true names from before the Fall. They had yet to make that public.

Tisiphone brightened when she spotted Cassius. She dug an elbow sharply in Orena's side.

"*Hey, don't you think Icarus looks even hotter now?*" the Fury said in a stage whisper loud enough to reach Downtown.

"*Hush, you floozy,*" Orena admonished.

She blushed and glanced between Cassius and Theo from under her lashes, as if she couldn't decide who to look at.

"*It seems Icarus has some competition, huh?*" Kes seemingly had no such problem with that decision and was shamelessly ogling Theo. "*I must say, sisters, Rohengar's replacement looks good enough to eat.*"

Victor shifted protectively in front of his befuddled lover.

A feeling of sympathy coursed through Cassius at Atropos's pained expression. He couldn't help but surmise that she was used to this kind of verbal exchange.

Kes misinterpreted her sister's look and came over to pat her heartily on the back. "*Chin up, Attie. Why, not only did we manage to foil Elios's plans, we even saved our unworthy brothers.*" She beamed at Cassius and Theo. "*And now, we get to claim our long-coveted prizes.*"

"Bro—brothers?!" Theo said in a strangled voice.

"*Yup.*" Kes cocked a thumb at Morgan and Victor. "*Tweedledee and Tweedledum over there are our younger half-brothers. Why, we used to regularly whoop their asses when they were kids.*"

Adrianne spluttered. Charlie opened and closed his mouth soundlessly. Even Strickland looked shocked.

Tisiphone was studying Morgan with an amused half-smile. *"That Ivmir sure was a crier."*

Orena arched an eyebrow at Victor. *"Whereas Coraos could charm his way out of most arguments."*

Kes sniggered. *"Hey, remember when Ivmir threw up on Tenebra at the centennial banquet of the Gods?"*

"Yeah." Tisiphone chuckled. *"She almost destroyed a star chasing the little rat."*

Bailey leaned toward Zach. "What the hell happened to, you know, time out and no dinner?!"

Atropos muttered something under her breath and pinched the bridge of her nose.

"Hey, what exactly did you mean by prizes?" Victor growled at Kes.

The demigod had evidently decided to overlook the Goddesses' offensive observations and focus on what was irking him the most.

Kes smirked. *"Did the fight with Alecto and Megaera affect your brain, little brother? It means we want some private time with Icarus and the new South Star."* Her grin widened. *"And by private time, they'll be naked and so will we."*

The handle of Victor's cup snapped, spilling coffee down his pants. Black flames bloomed around him.

"Hmm," Cassius murmured while Theo tried to calm his lover down. "How about we all—?"

"He returns."

The Reaper God's voice made Strickland and Morgan's team flinch. They whirled around and gawped at the dark-robed apparition clinging to the shadows of the bedroom.

"When did he get here?!" Adrianne croaked.

The Reaper God sniffed reproachfully. *"I have been here all along."*

"Oh, hey Temir," Tisiphone greeted him warmly.

"Ca—Cassius?"

Cassius's head swiveled around so fast he almost sprained a ligament. Morgan had opened his eyes and was blinking blearily at him.

Cassius grasped his hand, relief sending his pulse into the stratosphere. "How are you feeling?!"

Morgan grimaced. "Like someone used my body for a punching bag."

Loki crawled out from under the bed, jumped onto the top sheet, and bumped his head against Morgan's cheek.

"Hey there, flea ball." Morgan lifted a heavy hand and scratched the demon cat behind his ears. He froze when he clocked the crowded bedroom and the sea of stares locked upon him. "Did I die? This is Hell, right? I mean, why else would all of you be here?"

Adrianne and Julia narrowed their eyes. Tisiphone's mouth flattened into a thin line. Orena's expression turned sour. Atropos blew out a heavy sigh.

Kes shook a fist at Morgan. *"Why, this ungrateful little punk!"*

CHAPTER SIXTEEN

"Will Tenebra return to attack Earth?" Cassius asked Atropos.

Morgan could feel the tension vibrating though Cassius where they sat beside each other in the lounge. Cassius had helped him shower and get dressed in a fresh change of clothes. That simple act had drained Morgan of what little energy he'd been able to muster since he'd awoken. But that wasn't what was worrying him.

They'd barely spoken while Cassius had redressed his wounds, Cassius's face locked in rigid lines and his eyes barely meeting Morgan's. The injuries Alecto had inflicted were still bleeding and had soaked through the bandages the Dryads had hastily applied before he and Victor had left Ivory Peaks with Atropos and Tisiphone.

Morgan knew the fact that he had yet to heal scared Cassius like little else could. To be fair, it made his stomach churn too. And that wasn't even the half of it.

Tenebra's Rot felt like a block of ice where it sat lodged deep inside him, slowly eating away at his soul core. He knew that it would have killed him had Atropos and Tisiphone not intervened and stopped Alecto.

"*I am not sure,*" Atropos replied in the stark silence. Faint lines furrowed her brow. "*There are certain things I cannot...see anymore. But I believe Elios achieved his goals when he separated the two of you.*" She glanced from Cassius to Morgan. "*I doubt he will call upon Tenebra to unleash another plague in this realm.*"

Surprise shot through Morgan at that. He saw his reaction reflected on Cassius's face.

"You mean to say Elios timed the plagues on Earth and Ivory Peaks so as to deliberately split our forces?" Victor asked sharply.

Morgan's team exchanged shocked looks. A muscle twitched in Strickland's cheek.

Atropos dipped her head and met their tense stares steadily. "*Yes. Though I granted Regina a Harbinger, I did not foresee that the Dryad royal family would call upon Ivmir to protect their realm from Alecto and Megaera. With Tenebra threatening Earth, Icarus was bound to stay here and do his duty.*"

Cassius flinched. Morgan laid a hand on the back of his rigid knuckles, aware his lover had interpreted Atropos's words as an accusation she never intended. Cassius recoiled a little before accepting Morgan's touch. He swallowed heavily, a scowl marring his brow when he realized he'd almost pulled away.

Morgan's stomach clenched. They needed to talk.

To clear up this terrible misunderstanding between them. Morgan knew Cassius was blaming himself for the fact that he had nearly died. But now was not the time for a private conversation.

His heart thumped in his chest as he recalled his battle with the Furies. "Alecto and Megaera. Their target was the Sword of Wind, wasn't it?"

Cassius startled and stared at Morgan. Loki raised his head where he lay between them in his demon cat form.

"*Yes.*" Atropos's eyes darkened. "*But, from what unfolded, it appears Elios also ordered them to kill you.*"

Cassius blanched. This time, he didn't shrink away when Morgan clasped his hand.

"Why does Elios want me dead?" Morgan faltered. He let out a bitter chuckle. "I mean, I *know* he wants me dead. He wants all of us dead. But why now?"

"*I am not certain.*" Atropos rubbed the lines wrinkling her forehead. "*But it must have something to do with his original intentions.*"

Cassius curled his fingers into fists. "To release Chaos from the Abyss?"

"*Yes. As you know, the Sword of Wind was one of the divine weapons used to seal away the first Primordial God, just as the Eternity Key and the Bloodcursed Devilwood Summoning Staff were too.*"

Loki's ears twitched. Eden stiffened where she perched at the kitchen bar. She'd arrived a short while ago, having convinced a worried Brianna that this was where she needed to be.

"*I've been giving that some thought.*" Kes pursed her

lips. *"The Sword of Wind is bonded to Morgan's soul core. With Morgan still alive, Elios cannot wield it. Could this be why he wishes him dead?"*

"Oh." Tisiphone blinked. *"Of course. His weapon is like ours."* She snapped her fingers. Her brass-studded scourge appeared in her hand. *"They reside within us when the bond is active."*

"That...would make sense," Atropos said slowly.

Cassius jumped to his feet. "Wait. Does that mean Elios now possesses a piece of Morgan's soul?!"

Heaven's Light shivered around him, his powers surging with his emotions. The room trembled. Glass chimed and dishes rattled in the cupboards.

"Cassius," Theo mumbled, his voice raw with reflected pain.

Cassius shuddered and closed his eyes. The brilliance dancing across his flesh subsided. The tremors shaking the apartment stopped.

"No, Awakener," Tisiphone said. *"That is not how it works. In fact, were it not for Tenebra's Rot weakening Ivmir, he could likely summon the Sword of Wind, right here, right now."*

Shock jolted Morgan at the Fury's words.

Orena made a face at his stunned look. *"You'd forgotten?"*

"He was never the brightest of our siblings," Kes muttered.

Morgan narrowed his eyes.

"When I fought Elios in London, he said he had the Moirai under his control," Victor said guardedly. "Did he mean your—" he paused and grimaced, "I mean, *our* sisters?"

"Yes." Grief tightened Atropos's face. "*Elios still holds Clotho and Lachesis prisoner.*" A small, sad smile curved her mouth at his belated correction. "*I realize you and Ivmir lost most of your childhood memories to Hypnos's spell, but know that you were truly cherished by all your sisters.*"

"*Cherished is pushing it a bit, Attie,*" Kes murmured. "*I mean, I could tolerate the smarmy bastards in small doses.*"

Victor glowered at the Black Fate.

"What did you mean when you said you cannot see anymore?" Cassius said. "Is that why you turned up when you did?" His tone turned harsh. "You are a Goddess of Fate. Why did you not stop this before it all started?!"

Morgan's heart twisted. He could sense the fresh anger bubbling through Cassius's veins. An anger directed squarely at the Moira who sat opposite them.

Orena lifted her chin defiantly. "*We may be Goddesses but we are not infallible, Icarus. We did the best we could, under the circumstances.*"

"Is that the truth?!" Cassius spat out. Seraphic light brightened his pupils. "Did you really do the best you could?! If so, why—?!"

"*Calm yourself, Awakener,*" the Reaper God warned.

Shadows swarmed Kes as she stormed across the floor. She grabbed Cassius by the neckline of his shirt and yanked him to his feet.

"*What do you know of our efforts?!*" she hissed in his face. "*What do you know of all we suffered in the Hells while you and your lover cavorted together in the Nether? What do you know of the terrible deeds Elios visited upon us even as he charmed the ancient Gods of Heaven, tricked Coraos into joining his side, and plotted to overturn the very order of this universe and all of Creation?!"*

"*Sister,*" Atropos whispered in a voice full of sorrow.

"*I won't have it, Attie.*" Tears glimmered in Kes's golden eyes. She glared at Cassius, her knuckles white where she clutched his shirt. "*I won't have them look down on you and condemn you when they do not know the agony you went through. That we all went through.*" She closed her eyes and shuddered. "*When they do not know what we lost to get here!*"

Orena gently touched Kes's shoulder. "*It's okay, sister.*"

Kes slowly released Cassius.

Cassius swallowed and sagged, his expression miserable. "I'm—I'm sorry."

All the anger had drained out of him, leaving him ashen faced. Morgan rose despite the effort it cost him and gently took him in his arms.

Cassius trembled in his hold. He buried his face in Morgan's shoulder, his fingers clenching on Morgan's chest like he never wanted to let him go. The wetness soaking into Morgan's shirt made him want to weep too.

Despite the poison eating away at his soul core, he could feel all of Cassius's emotions. His love. His guilt. His rage. His despair.

Morgan ground his teeth. *I swear, I will kill you with my own bare hands, Elios!*

"I understand your frustration, Icarus." For the first time, bitterness underscored Atropos's voice. *"Trust me, I wish I could have stopped Elios when I divined his intentions. Alas, with Hypnos steadfastly at his side, there was little even us Moirai could do against him."*

Cassius finally lifted his head from Morgan's shoulder.

He took a shaky breath, wiped his eyes, and turned to face the Goddesses. "I'm sorry. I didn't mean to lash out at you."

"It is quite alright, Awakener," Atropos murmured graciously.

Tisiphone and Orena smiled gently.

"I'm only forgiving 'cause you're a hottie," Kes grumbled. *"Also, when we have private time, I get first dibs on you."*

CHAPTER SEVENTEEN

THEO swallowed a sigh. CASSIUS refrained from looking at the man beside him.

"What's this about private time?" Morgan asked suspiciously.

Adrianne grimaced. "Oh, yeah. You were out cold when they talked about that."

"I'll tell you later," Victor muttered to Morgan.

Cassius drew Morgan back down on the couch. They all watched Atropos, knowing she had more to tell them.

"The first I grew suspicious of Elios was some five hundred years before the Nether tore," the Moira said quietly, her gaze lost in the past. *"At the time, he still curried favor with the ancient Gods of Heaven and regularly trod the celestial halls of power. I had heard some disturbing rumors about him. That he had been spotted in parts of the Hells he had no business visiting. That he was talking to the war demons and the Nephilim, an act which would have brought him before*

the Council of the Gods had it been confirmed. I attempted to look at his fate then, but Hypnos blinded me, just as Clotho and Lachesis now obscure my vision. It was by chance that I found out he'd been whispering poison in Coraos's ear to try and turn him against Ivmir. Everyone knew of Coraos's interest in Icarus. Well, except for Icarus himself."

Cassius's chest tightened as the enormity of Elios's deception sank in.

Atropos spied Victor's wretched expression. She sighed. *"I do not blame you for what happened, Coraos. Love can make even Gods do foolish things. Besides, it was Elios who used Hypnos to brainwash you into becoming obsessed with Icarus and hating Ivmir after he claimed the Awakener's heart."*

Bile roiled at the back of Cassius's throat.

The blood had drained from Victor's face. "What? He—they *brainwashed* me?!"

Atropos nodded, frowning. *"You've seen how he was able to control Alecto and Megaera. Hypnos's powers were as effective as Elios's seeds of corruption."*

Victor sagged. His hands trembled as he covered his face.

"All this time. All this time, I thought I deliberately hurt Icarus and tried to kill Ivmir out of my own despicable greed!" the demon choked out.

Theo closed the distance to Victor and took him in his arms. Victor hugged his lover tightly and burrowed his face in the crook of his neck, eyes gleaming with unshed tears.

Cassius's heart ached at the torment radiating from

his oldest friend. Morgan's fingers clenched tightly around his hand.

"By the time I spoke to my sisters about my misgivings, Elios had already laid a trap for us," Atropos continued in a lifeless voice. *"He suppressed our divine cores with his corruption, captured us, and imprisoned us in the Seventh Purgatory."*

Movement startled Cassius.

Loki jumped down from the couch and shifted into his imp form. "That's where you were?! The Seventh Purgatory?! But I looked for you there and did not find you!"

Atropos's eyes widened.

"You—you looked for us?" Tisiphone stammered.

Orena and Kes traded an equally shocked glance.

Loki nodded, tail quivering agitatedly. "Yes! Pan, Boreas, and several other Gods joined the search too. We thought it strange that all of you had vanished at the same time. We scoured the realms, but in vain. Since the Eternity Key allows me to travel to the Hells, I was tasked with the search there." The imp fisted his hands. "Pan and Boreas warned Heaven that something was amiss, but none there took them seriously. It seemed Elios had done a really good job of convincing them that he was harmless."

Atropos looked blindly at the floor, still taken aback by this revelation. *"I'm—I'm sorry, Keeper. I did not know you had come looking for us. Our presence must have been shielded by Hypnos when you came to the Seventh Purgatory."* She exchanged a distraught look with her sisters. *"All this time, we thought we were alone. We should have trusted that other Gods would have become suspicious too."* Her gaze found Loki once more. *"I'm afraid you will struggle to make your way into the Hells as easily as before, Keeper. Elios's strength is now such that he can hide entire realms from our sight."*

Horror filled Loki's eyes. A strained hush befell them.

"What happened to Hypnos?" Cassius said. "Pan told us he disappeared after the Fall."

Atropos's face hardened. *"Elios cast him into the Abyss."*

Cassius's pulse spiked. Shook reverberated around the room.

"What?!" Victor said hoarsely.

"He killed his own twin?!" Morgan ground out.

"We knew he was an unfeeling asshole, but even we were stunned at the degree of his cruelty," Kes bit out. *"Hypnos was utterly blind to his brother's personality defects. In his eyes, Elios could do no wrong. He'd always followed Elios around like a puppy, even though he was the older of the two of them."*

"Wait." Gold flared in Theo's eyes. One iris turned sapphire blue as Rohengar made his presence felt. *"You said Elios cast Hypnos into the Abyss. How did he do that? I thought the whole point of him coming after Icarus was because he needed the Awakener's powers to access the forbidden realm where Chaos is trapped!"*

Atropos clenched her jaw, like she was steeling herself for a truth that would be hard to bear. Kes laid a hand on her shoulder.

Atropos grasped her sister's fingers gratefully. *"The*

Abyss did *open that day. When Icarus ripped the Nether and every other realm apart, he also tore a doorway into that dimension.*"

Cassius's mouth went dry at Atropos's admission.

"What?!" he said numbly.

Horror leached the color from Theo's face.

"*She is right, Awakener,*" the Reaper God said somberly. "*I felt it in my bones.*"

"*It was an infinitesimal opening. One so small, it closed almost as soon as it opened, partly because Icarus did not unleash all of his Awakener potential. Elios did not know this would happen, so he proceeded with what he'd intended. To throw Hypnos into the Abyss and draw out Chaos.*"

"Draw out Chaos?" Morgan said, confused.

Atropos nodded. "*A divine soul in exchange for another divine soul. The Abyss is the Eater of Souls, after all.*"

CHAPTER EIGHTEEN

THE GODDESS'S SHOCKING WORDS ECHOED THROUGH Cassius's skull.

I tore open the Abyss?!

"Let me get this straight. Cassius fractured the Nether and all the realms even though he held *back?!*" Julia said, aghast.

Zach looked similarly dazed beside her.

Atropos met Cassius's stunned gaze solemnly. *"We may call you a demigod, but whoever wears the mantle of Awakener is, by definition, the most powerful entity in all of Heaven and the Hells. In your fully roused state, you are likely a match for the first Primordial God himself."* She paused. *"Did you know that the role of Awakener was created after Chaos was imprisoned in the Abyss?"*

Cassius shook his head numbly.

"The Gods of old realized they needed a safety key in the future, in case another calamity like the one that shook all of Creation when they battled Chaos were to happen again. A safety key that could unlock all their latent powers at once.

But one they were confident would never grow arrogant and want to rule over them." Atropos spread her hands open. *"As you likely know, the default state of divine soul cores is that of dormancy, especially for the strongest among us. If we were to go about with our abilities on full display all the time, we would damage the realms."* A gentle smile curved her lips. *"You may have lost yourself in that moment of rage in the Nether, Icarus, but, deep down inside, you recognized the danger your powers posed to everyone and you curbed your own soul core. That is the true nature of an Awakener. Someone who is not only powerful, but kindness and mercy itself."*

Cassius blinked. "Oh."

He hadn't thought he could be more dumbfounded by the startling facts they had just heard, but Atropos had just proven him wrong once again.

"I wish we could have seen Elios's face when he realized his plan had failed," Kes grouched.

"One thing still doesn't make sense," Morgan muttered, bewildered. "If the Abyss tore even a fraction, Chaos could have escaped. Why didn't he?"

"Morgan is right," Victor said in a hard voice.

"I...do not know." Atropos lowered her brows. *"We were trapped in the Seventh Purgatory and blinded by Hypnos's spell, so I cannot surmise what exactly took place in that moment."*

"Besides, we were totally focused on making our escape at the time," Tisiphone muttered.

"Despite my powers being suppressed, I foresaw that the Nether would tear and that the Fall would happen," Atropos said, clocking their puzzled looks. *"I charged*

Tenebra with destroying the rotten seed Elios had implanted within her so she could free us from his corrupt shackles and I asked Clotho to spin another Fate for us just for that day. One that would guarantee our getaway from the Seventh Purgatory."

"What happened?" Cassius asked, his heart pounding. "How did Tenebra and the others end up getting left behind?"

Pain distorted Atropos's features. *"It was my fault."*

"No, it wasn't, Attie," Kes denied bitterly. *"None of it was."*

"Our sisters sacrificed themselves so we could escape." Orena's face tightened. *"We decided it was better that some of us made it out of that hellhole, than all of us be held captive there forever more."*

"But we didn't know Elios would do that to them." Tisiphone's voice trembled. *"We didn't know he would go to such lengths to punish us for running away. That he would—he would turn our sisters against us!"*

The four Goddesses huddled close, as if to comfort one another.

"Where have you been all this time?" Victor asked after a short silence.

Atropos shared a worn-out glance with her sisters. *"Hiding in the realms we could find and gathering our strength. We had planned to look for allies who could help us free our sisters and mount a counterstrike against Elios, but we soon discovered that the tear in the Nether made it nigh impossible to uncover their whereabouts."*

"What about the Nymphs of the West?" Loki frowned. "By the sounds of it, Elios only captured the

Moirai, the Black Fates, and the Furies. But there's still the Hesperides."

Surprise jolted Cassius. *I'd forgotten about the Hesperides!*

The awareness dawning on Victor and Morgan's faces told him they were experiencing the same recollection. His breath caught at the agony filling Atropos's golden eyes. The Goddess had turned gray.

"*I ordered the Nymphs of the West to go into hiding,*" the Moira whispered. "*This was before Elios ambushed us.*"

"*Attie.*" Kes squeezed Atropos's shoulder. "*You could not have known what would happen.*"

Dread tightened Cassius's chest at the other Goddesses' grim faces.

"*We tried to find our sisters after we escaped, but our efforts were in vain,*" Orena murmured. "*We finally discovered their last known whereabouts some two hundred years ago. Alas, their current location remains a mystery even our divine eyes cannot pierce.*"

Tisiphone's fisted her hands. "*They were in Argent Lake when the Nether tore.*"

Cassius startled. "The kingdom of the Naiads?"

Tisiphone nodded, her eyes glittering. A bolt of intuition shot through him at her abject expression. His stomach knotted.

Atropos's next words confirmed his sick feeling.

"*Erytheis, the eldest Hesperis, sacrificed her life to save Argent Lake.*"

Loki froze, his crimson eyes rounding. "Erytheis is dead?!"

Atropos bobbed her head, her chin quivering. Loki's

tail drooped. Cassius gathered the imp had known the Goddess well.

He touched Loki's hand. Loki flinched before looking at him, his expression tortured. Cassius wordlessly pulled him down next to him and wrapped a comforting arm around his shoulders. Loki trembled and leaned into him.

"Though we did not achieve what we had intended to do upon escaping the Seventh Purgatory, I still managed to foil Elios's machinations over the centuries that followed." Atropos's voice had hardened. She looked at Theo, her eyes bright with conviction. *"I found the perfect vessel for Rohengar's soul."* The Goddess's gaze shifted to Eden. *"I guided the Bloodcursed Devilwood Summoning Staff to the next Magus who would wield it."* Atropos's face softened a little as she gazed at a stunned Loki. *"And I made sure the Keeper of the Eternity Key found his way to Icarus."*

CHAPTER NINETEEN

MORGAN CAME OUT OF THE BATHROOM AND FOUND Cassius sitting in the gloom with his back against the headboard and his knees pressed against his chest. The demigod was looking out over the terrace and a moonlit-bathed San Francisco Bay, his gaze unfocused.

Cassius flinched when Morgan flicked the bedside lamp on. He turned to look at him, expression clearing.

He shifted down the bed. "Hey."

Morgan slid under the covers, tucked him against his flank, and kissed his hair. Cassius relaxed against him.

His hand found Morgan's belly, his touch hesitant. "Does it hurt?"

Morgan swallowed a sigh at the way his voice quivered. "I won't lie to you. It hurts. But the way you're acting hurts me even more."

Cassius flinched. He tilted his head and frowned at Morgan. "What do you mean?"

Morgan met his irate gaze squarely. "I don't like this

distance between us. And I hate that you think this was all your fault."

Cassius's expression grew mutinous. He pulled away and jerked upright. "It *is* my fault!"

Morgan bit back a curse and sat up. He winced a little at the hot shard that stabbed through his core before glaring at Cassius. "Every which way I look at this, I still don't understand how you came to such a stupid conclusion."

Cassius glared at him over his shoulder. "I should have seen what Elios intended!"

"How?" Morgan snapped. "By looking in your magic crystal ball?!"

Cassius's face fell. His lower lip trembled. This time, Morgan swore out loud. He pulled Cassius into his arms.

"You're such a stubborn brat," he muttered into his hair.

Cassius sniffed against his chest. "I'm older than you. Attie said so."

Morgan grimaced. "Since when did you start calling her Attie?"

"Since just now," Cassius mumbled.

They stayed silent for a while, their hearts thumping steadily against one another.

Morgan finally drew back and tilted Cassius's chin with a knuckle. "Stop blaming yourself for something you had no control over, Cassius. Even Atropos couldn't divine Elios's plans."

Cassius shuddered and closed his eyes. Tears

glimmered in the beautiful gray depths when he opened them once more.

"If I hadn't responded to his provocation during the War in the Nether," he whispered. "If I hadn't unleashed my powers and torn apart the realms. If I—!"

Morgan swallowed the rest of his wretched words with his lips.

Cassius went rigid before relenting and kissing him back.

Morgan savored Cassius's sweetness for a long minute before reluctantly lifting his mouth off the demigod's. "You heard what Atropos said." He pressed his forehead against Cassius's. "That we were destined to lose the War in the Nether. That the Fall was preordained."

Cassius clenched his jaw.

Atropos's words from a few hours ago flitted through Morgan's mind once more.

"*It is Cassius and Theo's presence on Earth that has stopped the Fallen and otherworldly in this realm from succumbing to Tenebra's Rot,*" the Moira had explained once they'd gotten over the blow of her latest revelations concerning Theo, Eden, and Loki. "*The holy power of two Guardians is a potent force that can negate even the most powerful of poisons and prevent it from infecting a soul core that contains divine energy.*"

"Why did you not come forward before now?" Cassius had asked the Goddess after a stunned silence. "Why act from the shadows for so long?"

"*Because it was the only way we would have a chance to win the war to come.*"

Tension had knotted Morgan's shoulders at her grim look.

"You mean the one Regina saw?" Cassius had said stiffly. "The vision you bestowed upon her?"

Atropos had dipped her head. *"Yes. We could not allow Clotho and Lache to tell Elios our plans. Just like they blind me, I can blind them, so long as I do nothing to reveal my hand."* The Goddess's face had softened at Cassius's harried expression. *"The conflict in the Nether was one we were all ultimately bound to lose. You. Me. Elios. Though my brother may think he won that battle, he set aside an incredibly useful pawn in the form of Hypnos and he failed to kill Ivmir and truly destroy Rohengar."* Her gaze had swept the room. *"The final battle will take place on Earth, like I revealed to the Dryad royal seer. And it will determine not just our Fate but that of every realm, including Heaven and the Hells."*

"Can you see how it ends?" Victor had asked harshly in the grave hush that followed her declaration. "Will we defeat Elios?"

Atropos's expression had grown shuttered then. *"I... do not know."*

Morgan couldn't help but feel that she'd lied to them in that moment. She never spoke more on the topic, even after everyone had left. But she had said one last thing that had curdled Morgan's blood before she and the other Goddesses had retired to his apartment for the night.

"Elios hates Icarus. Yes, he wanted to use his powers as the Awakener to tear the Nether, open up the Abyss, and release Chaos from his prison, but, ultimately, what Elios

wants more than anything is for Icarus to die. We can use that against him."

"What are you thinking about?" Cassius murmured presently.

"I'm thinking I really want to smack that bastard Elios." Morgan sighed ruefully. "Also, I want to make love to you badly right now, but I don't think I can summon the energy."

Cassius chuckled. "That's a first."

"Yeah, yeah," Morgan grumbled. "Just thank your lucky stars for the reprieve. Once I get rid of this stupid Rot, I'm not gonna let you sleep for a week."

Cassius pulled back and grinned. "Promises, promises."

Morgan's chest loosened. The fear and regret stamped on Cassius's face had faded to amusement.

Cassius arched an eyebrow. "You know, it takes two to tango."

Morgan blinked. "You want to dance?"

Cassius pursed his lips. "I kind of agree with Kes."

"What?"

"Nothing." Cassius pushed Morgan onto his back and climbed on top of him, his expression teasing. "How about I take care of you today?"

"Oh."

Morgan's pulse accelerated at Cassius's sultry look and the telltale bulge in his pajamas. Despite the dull throbbing of Tenebra's Rot deep inside him, he could still feel an echo of Cassius's desire in his core.

Cassius peeled his T-shirt off and leaned down to kiss Morgan. Morgan groaned when he pushed inside his mouth, his tongue moving languorously against Morgan's hungry flesh.

Morgan's cock swelled. Cassius moaned when he felt the solid evidence of his passion. Morgan rubbed their erections together and drew another groan from him.

Cassius's movements grew jerky as he got rid of the rest of his clothes and stripped Morgan naked. His touch seared Morgan's skin where he danced his hands over his body, his lips and tongue following the path his wicked fingers took.

Morgan's breathing grew ragged as Cassius made love to him, the sight of the demigod's flushed face and his leaking erection so hot he felt he could come there and then. And come he finally did, inside Cassius's mouth.

Cassius lavished Morgan's stiff rod with his tongue and fingers before swallowing him with his lips. Sweat beaded Morgan's face and his heart raced like a freight train at the pleasure Cassius was giving him. His fingers soon found Cassius's hair, his hips tilting and rocking his cock against the back of Cassius's throat. Cassius panted and maintained eye contact while he blew Morgan hard and deep, face taut with lust and fingers busy on his own erection.

By the time Cassius let go of Morgan's trembling shaft, he'd brought him to two shuddering orgasms and had painted the sheets with his own cum.

Morgan shivered.

Cassius had wiped his lips and was rubbing his sensitive flesh to a fresh erection, his heated stare full of desire. Air hissed through his teeth when he finally mounted Morgan and impaled himself on his rock-hard cock.

The sight of Cassius's body swallowing him whole had Morgan gnashing his teeth. He sank his fingers into Cassius's thighs as Cassius started moving, his hungry hole squeezing Morgan's flesh rhythmically as he danced up and down his shaft. Cassius's sultry moans soon turned to gasps and cries, the pleasure storming him brightening his pupils with seraphic light.

Morgan ran his hands up Cassius's legs to his belly and his chest. He pinched and tugged Cassius's nipples and was rewarded by Cassius's insides sucking him with a powerful contraction that drew a wanton groan from both of them.

It wasn't long before Cassius drove them both over the edge. Fire flooded Morgan's veins and sparked across his mind when the hard, hot knot inside his lower belly loosened with an explosive force that filled Cassius with his seed. Cassius's head dropped back, his face and chest flushed and his lips open on incoherent sounds as he accepted everything Morgan gave him, the hot stickiness of his own ejaculation drenching Morgan's stomach.

The scent of their lovemaking filled the bedroom when they finally collapsed in each other's hold. Morgan's heart raced wildly, the thumps echoed by Cassius's own frantic beats where he lay atop him.

Morgan squeezed his arms tightly around the demigod.

"I promise, I won't die on you," he mumbled into his hair.

Cassius stiffened. He lifted his head and stared into Morgan's eyes, determination darkening his gaze. "You better not. I will chase you to the end of the Hells if you do."

Morgan chuckled at that. Cassius sucked in air as the motion shifted Morgan's stirring cock inside his ass.

Morgan nibbled at Cassius's chin. "Wanna go again?"

"You're just a horny beast, aren't you?" Cassius grumbled, color staining his cheekbones afresh.

Morgan grinned. "And you love me for it."

CHAPTER TWENTY

"Wow. Look at that smug face," Kes muttered.

She studied Morgan with faint accusation from where she perched on a stool at the breakfast bar in Cassius's apartment.

Tisiphone sniffed. *"Like the cat that got the cream."*

Loki looked up and meowed before inhaling some gourmet salmon on the counter. He'd spent the night with the Goddesses and seemed to be in a more cheerful mood this morning. Orena scratched the demon cat behind the ears and leaned a hip against the worktop.

"This building could do with better soundproofing," the Black Fate observed mildly.

Heat flooded Cassius's face when he became the focus of the three Goddesses' shrewd stares. He squinted at Morgan.

Morgan arched an eyebrow. "Hey, you're the one who climbed on top of me."

Cassius blushed harder.

Kes propped her chin on her hand. *"How about you guys let us watch next time?"*

Morgan's amused expression vanished. He scowled. "Hell no!"

He slammed a cup of steaming coffee in front of her and spilled half its contents.

"Hey, be careful, dumbass!" Kes snapped.

They glowered at one another.

Atropos bit delicately into her smoked salmon bagel where she sat beside them, her expression that of someone pointedly ignoring the current inane exchange.

Cassius studied the faint shadows under Morgan's eyes as he put more bagels in the toaster. Though the demigod was acting like nothing was wrong, he could see past his mask to the pain he was trying hard to hide. He could also feel the deepening coldness of Tenebra's Rot within his soul core.

The way Atropos kept glancing surreptitiously at Morgan did little to reassure him. It was clear she was similarly worried.

Cassius picked up the remote to distract himself and switched on the TV, only to freeze when he saw the news headline. His pulse accelerated as he flicked rapidly through the other channels.

They were all broadcasting the same story.

That was when he discerned the sound of helicopters drawing close.

"Isn't that your place?" Tisiphone asked warily.

Morgan swore. One of the local channels was transmitting live from outside the apartment block. He snatched the remote from Cassius's slack grip and turned the volume up.

"The world is waking up to the incredible news that a group of Goddesses arrived on Earth in the last twenty-four hours to curb a devastating plague that has been ravaging the Southern Hemisphere of our planet, and to save our city from the nameless threat that caused our officials to raise the alarm of a possible terrorist attack yesterday morning," the female news anchor was saying where she stood amidst a huge crowd outside the glass facade of the foyer.

Her cheeks flushed with excitement as she continued. "We now know why we lost communication with several countries south of the Equator this past week and what the governments of the world have desperately been trying to hide from us so as not to incur global panic. It is only this morning that we began to learn of the deadly contagion that has ripped through large sections of populated territories in South America, Africa, and Asia, sparing no man or creature or even building it has touched. Coming up next are witness accounts from San Francisco citizens who saw the tidal wave that sprang up in the middle of the ocean some twenty hours ago and spied several fast-moving figures in the sky. This was shortly after city officials warned us to get underground. Chief among those spotted was Cassius Black, the fallen angel turned hero who we now know has secretly saved the world innumerable times before. We are bringing you this report directly outside the address where the Goddesses and Cassius Black are suspected to be—"

Morgan's phone rang. He muted the TV and answered the call.

His face tightened. "How did you get this number?!"

He disconnected, a muscle jumping in his jawline.

Orena grimaced. *"Humans sure are nosy, huh?"*

Morgan's cell rang again. The demigod scowled and stabbed the screen with a finger.

"Look, dipshit!" he snarled into the speaker, "I don't know who you—" He froze and swallowed the rest of his tirade, his expression turning chagrined. "Oh. Sorry, Francis." He met Cassius's worried stare before narrowing his eyes at the TV. "Yeah, we're watching it right now."

"So, this is what it feels like to be in a zoo," Kes remarked.

The Goddess looked more curious than anything. Loki stared unblinkingly at the TV screen where he sat next to her elbow, his tail straight.

Cassius's cell vibrated in his back pocket. He took it out and looked at the screen warily. Relief darted through him.

It was Adrianne.

"We can't get into your building," the sorceress said in a frustrated voice when Cassius answered.

He stared at the TV. "Wait. You're outside right now?!"

"Yeah. What the hell is going on, Cassius?!"

Cassius's fingers clenched on the phone. "It looks

like someone leaked information to the media about Atropos and the others despite every agency banning its operatives from talking to the press. Morgan's on the phone to Francis right now."

Zach's voice came from somewhere close to Adrianne. "Man, social media is on fire with this stuff. Someone even recorded yesterday's fight."

"That looks pretty epic," Bailey said brightly within earshot.

Morgan ended his call with Strickland. "Francis wants us to lie low for a while."

Atropos drummed her fingers on the breakfast bar. *"That might be a problem."*

Cassius's stomach clenched when he clocked her faint frown. Movement outside distracted him. He almost dropped his phone.

An annoyed-looking Theo was alighting on the terrace with Victor, wings and all. Eden rose from beyond the parapet inside a crimson sphere and landed beside them like she was out for a casual morning stroll.

The mage narrowed her eyes at the helicopters closing in on the building before exchanging words with Theo. Theo nodded.

"Was that Eden we just saw up there?" Adrianne said suspiciously in Cassius's ear.

"Wait. Don't tell me they're gonna—" he half mumbled to himself.

Theo and Eden raised a translucent, gold and crimson barrier around the apartment block without batting an eyelid. Victor looked on with the resigned expression of a man who knew when he was fighting a losing battle.

Kes chuckled. Cassius followed the amused Goddess's gaze to the TV.

The shield had levitated the entire crowd and dumped them some two hundred feet from the building. The whine of the news helicopters attempting to draw close enough to film the apartment reached his ears faintly as the otherworldly energy Theo and Eden had projected pushed them away.

"What the—?!" Adrianne gasped in Cassius's ear. "Was that Eden? Did that brat just kick us out?!"

"I can feel Theo's power in this too," Julia observed mildly close to the sorceress.

Cassius pinched the bridge of his nose and closed his eyes briefly. "We should meet up somewhere else."

Adrianne conferred with the rest of Morgan's team.

"How about Bostrof's place?" the sorceress suggested.

Guilt tightened Cassius's belly. He'd had several missed calls from Lilaia and Bostrof yesterday. He'd messaged briefly to say he'd talk to them later but had never gotten around to it, what with waiting for Morgan to wake up and everything that had followed.

"I'll text him. Make sure you're not tailed on the way there."

The terrace doors opened.

Theo entered the apartment and met Cassius's cool stare with an innocent expression. "What?"

Victor maintained a diplomatic silence.

"No, you can't blast them to smithereens," Eden was

grumbling at the devilwood staff behind them. "Because it's wrong, Woody! Just because they're getting on our nerves isn't a good enough reason to kill them." The mage scowled as she listened to her weapon's response. "That's it. No more video games for you."

CHAPTER TWENTY-ONE

Lilaia uttered reverently, bowing on one knee.

"*Rise, child of Nephele,*" Atropos ordered.

Lilaia stood up, her demeanor still humble before the four Goddesses. She flashed Cassius a narrow-eyed, sidelong glance that clearly broadcasted he should have told her the deities the whole world was currently talking about would be part of the party he was bringing to Bostrof's fight club.

Bostrof slowly straightened beside his wife, his beefy body towering over all of them.

Atropos smiled at the Lucifugous demon. "*It is good to see you again, King of the Shadow Empire.*"

"Former king," Bostrof murmured demurely.

Brightness flashed in Atropos's eyes.

"*We shall see about that,*" the Moira said mysteriously.

Lilaia and Bostrof exchanged a startled look.

Tisiphone pursed her lips. "*You should stop teasing people, Attie.*"

Lilaia's eyes rounded at the affectionate nickname. Atropos's expression turned mischievous.

Cassius's chest loosened a little. The tight lines in the Moira's face had faded, as had the permanent tension knotting Kes, Orena, and Tisiphone's shoulders. They looked relaxed for the first time since they'd come to Earth.

He could only imagine how they'd survived these past five hundred years. Always on the run from Elios, and Clotho and Lachesis's piercing gazes. Constantly living with the fear that he would capture them again and make them his slaves before they could free their sisters.

It must have been a horrible existence.

The look Atropos gave him told him she'd divined his thoughts.

"It was no worse than your fate, Awakener," the Goddess murmured with a sad smile.

Victor arched an eyebrow. "This place sure looks different."

Eden's gaze darted curiously around the room. It was her first time visiting *Ohomgath*.

"I gotta say, I like this decor better than the old one," Charlie muttered.

Bostrof followed their stares and grimaced slightly. His once sumptuous office was no more. The opulent furniture occupying what had once been a lavish space designed to intimidate his rivals and business partners had been replaced by soft couches with vivid cushions and washable floor mats. The dark walls were now a pale blue and the mini bar had transformed into a play area dominated by a giant dollhouse castle that looked suspiciously like Kalliste's palace in Rain Vale.

Seated in tiny wooden chairs in front of it were Crusher, Bostrof's champion, Akamon, the Lucifugous demon Cassius had saved in the sewers under the city, and Bostrof's bodyguards Vorzof and Goran. They were currently in the midst of a tea party with Phebei, the delicate, porcelain cups they held swallowed by their thick fingers.

"Aboo," Phebei said imperiously where she sat on the mat, her chubby legs stretched out before her.

The demons drank their invisible tea and made noises of approval, their nervous gazes darting to the visitors who'd just entered the room. Loki jumped down from Cassius's arms and shifted into his imp form as he headed over to them.

Phebei beamed when she saw him. "Kiki!"

Loki smiled at the little girl.

Kes studied Phebei thoughtfully. *"You two have a kid?"*

Lilaia bobbed her head and guided them to the couches.

"It is rare for interspecies relationships to bear fruit," Orena remarked as she sat down. *"You must have tried real hard."* She looked up and stiffened a little at their stares. *"What?"* It took another second and Kes's dirty smirk for the Black Fate to realize the sexual connotation in her last statement. She flushed. *"I mean, you must have* wished *for a child with all of your hearts."*

"His heart was an animal in the bedroom," Lilaia confessed, poker-faced.

Vorzof and Goran swallowed snorts. Spots of color bloomed on Bostrof's cheeks. He scowled at the bodyguards. Eden looked like she wanted to sink into the ground.

"Are you sure those reporters won't find us here?" Theo asked nervously.

"I doubt it," Morgan murmured. "*Ohomgath's* location is one of the best kept secrets in this city. Besides, they wouldn't want to mess with Bostrof."

Unease prickled Cassius's skin. Morgan looked a shade paler than before. He was sweating slightly, as if in the grip of a fever once more.

Lilaia did not miss Cassius's anxious expression. "Is something wrong?"

Bostrof frowned at Morgan. "You look a bit peaky."

Cassius swallowed. It took all his will power to stop his voice from trembling when he spoke. "Morgan's soul core is infected with Tenebra's Rot."

Bostrof's eyes bulged. "What?!"

"Tenebra?" Lilaia gasped. "You mean, the eldest Black Fate?!"

Cassius briefed the Nymph and the Lucifugous demon on the events of the last twenty-four hours.

Lilaia pressed a trembling hand to her mouth. "Alecto and Megaera attacked Ivory Peaks?!"

Victor nodded.

"If it weren't for Atropos and Tisiphone, things would have ended differently," he said grimly.

Dread tightened Bostrof's face. "The plague they're talking about on the news is of Tenebra's making? The same plague the Furies unleashed in the Dryad kingdom?"

"Yes," Cassius replied in a low voice. "We decided to keep this a secret for now. It would only induce further panic if the world was to find out that this contagion was not of earthly origins."

Guilt stabbed through him. He hadn't told Lilaia and Bostrof that he'd nearly torn apart the realms again in his rage yesterday. He glanced at Phebei.

I dread to think what would have happened to everyone I cherish if Theo hadn't stopped me.

"Elios is controlling the Goddesses still trapped in the Seventh Purgatory, like he did Boreas and Demetrius," Victor explained bitterly. "He's using them to do his dirty work."

Lilaia and Bostrof exchanged a troubled look.

"To what purpose did he attack Earth and Ivory Peaks?" the Lucifugous demon asked in a hard voice.

"He was after the Sword of Wind," Morgan muttered. "The plague on Earth was just a distraction to keep Cassius here, while I was lured to the Dryad kingdom."

Bostrof sucked in air.

Lilaia's knuckles whitened. "He has your weapon?!"

Morgan bobbed his head, his eyes darkening with regret all over again. Cassius reached over and clasped his hand.

"How are the Dryads doing?" Heavy lines furrowed

Bostrof's brow. "Did their realm incur significant losses?"

"There were fatalities. And some of their forests were destroyed by Rot." Victor glanced at Atropos and Tisiphone. "Like I said, things would have been much worse if our sisters had not come to our aid."

CHAPTER TWENTY-TWO

Bostrof's expression froze.

Lilaia's eyes rounded.

"Oh. I'd forgotten you and Morgan are the younger siblings of Nyx's daughters," she mumbled, her startled gaze darting from Victor and Morgan to the four Goddesses.

Kes frowned faintly. *"It seems Hypnos's spell still has a hold on some of your memories."*

Concern tightened Lilaia's eyes as she studied Morgan's wan features.

She gazed at Atropos. "Does Elios intend to use the Sword of Wind to free Chaos?"

Atropos dipped her head. *"We believe so, yes."*

Bostrof ground his teeth. Shadows trembled around the Lucifugous, his fury manifesting his unearthly powers.

"But he will need more than the Sword of Wind to do that." Lines furrowed the Moira's brow. *"The true goal of his current machinations remains a mystery to me."*

"What will happen to Morgan?" Lilaia asked in a low voice. The grim hush that followed her question gave her the answer she sought. Blood drained from her face. She pressed a trembling hand to her mouth. "No! That cannot be!"

Bostrof cursed out loud before glancing guiltily at Phebei where she played with Loki and the Lucifugous demons. The little girl hadn't heard him. Loki's ears twitched. A wretched look darted across the imp's face before he smiled at Phebei.

"How do we save him?" the Lucifugous said between gritted teeth. "There *is* a way to save Morgan, right?!"

Agony twisted Cassius's heart all over again. "Only Tenebra can do it. She has to remove her poison from Morgan's soul core. Same for the plague affecting Earth. Kes and Orena may have put a stop to its spread, but the only way to get rid of it for good is to free Tenebra from Elios's mind control."

Morgan turned his hand over and interlaced his fingers with Cassius's where he'd pressed his fists on his knees. Cassius shuddered.

Morgan's skin felt like ice again.

"Victor was infected with Rot too. It hasn't affected him as badly." Theo's worried gaze darted to the dressing on Victor's temple. "But his wounds aren't healing as they should."

"Is there no other way that Morgan can survive this contagion?" Bostrof asked Atropos harshly after a stilted pause, the deference he'd shown the Goddess up till now superseded by anger.

The Moira shared a strained look with the other Goddesses. She hesitated.

"There...might be another way."

❦

Morgan's pulse stuttered.

"What?" Cassius breathed. The same hope blooming inside Morgan brought a flush of color to his gray face. "Why didn't you say so yesterday?!"

Atropos's shoulders drooped. *"Because I don't know whether it could work."* She sighed and met their tense stares. *"I did my utmost to make sure Elios wouldn't get his hands on the Hesperides not just out of love for my sisters. It was also because of what they guard."*

Victor's expression slowly cleared, like he was recalling something.

"The Sacred Tree," he mumbled.

Puzzled lines wrinkled Theo's brow. "What?"

Julia blinked. "Oh."

"The Golden Apples," Zach muttered, dazed. "How could we have forgotten about them?!"

Memories floated up from the depths of Morgan's consciousness, sending his heart thundering against his ribs. He masked a wince at the pain that skewered his insides in response to his quickening pulse.

Tenebra's Rot was gaining ground, her poison eating insidiously at his soul core with every passing hour.

Cassius leaned forward, seraphic power flashing in his pupils. "The Golden Apples can cure Morgan?!"

"*Probably*," Atropos replied with a reluctant dip of her chin. "*Though it's never been done before, they are about the only things I can think of that could counteract Rot.*"

"What are the Golden Apples?" Eden said hesitantly.

"The Hesperides are the Guardians of the Sacred Tree, which grows in the Garden of the West." Excitement raised the pitch of Cassius's voice. "It's been known by many names in mythology. Yggdrasil. The Tree of Life."

Victor frowned. "Isn't the giant oak in the sacred forest in the Spirit Realm rumored to have grown from a branch of the Sacred Tree?"

Orena nodded. "*You are correct, little brother.*"

"*Every two hundred years, the Sacred Tree bears the Golden Apples of Resurrection,*" Kes declared somberly.

"*Their powers are such that they can even restore a divine soul that has returned to the cycle of life and death,*" Tisiphone elaborated at Eden and Theo's thunderstruck expressions.

"That's like the ultimate cheat," Adrianne mumbled.

Bailey and Charlie looked similarly overawed.

"*We were following a lead when Attie got wind of Elios's latest plans,*" Orena said. "*Someone had come across a Nereid who told them the dragon fell through a crack between the realms when the Nether tore. He apparently ended up in the Astrea Sea.*"

"The...dragon?" Adrianne repeated dully.

Tisiphone bobbed her head. "*The dragon Guardian, Ladon.*"

"Ah." Zach made a face like he'd remembered

something he would rather not have. "I'd forgotten about him."

"*He's a giant, three-headed beast who guards the Golden Apples along with the Hesperides.*" Orena wrinkled her nose. "*He's nothing but their glorified pet, really.*"

Bailey and Charlie paled.

"*That lizard almost burned the Sacred Tree down when he came out of his egg,*" Kes muttered darkly.

"*He was always so rude to us.*" Tisiphone sniffed. "*Our sisters spoiled him rotten, they did.*"

Orena's mouth flattened into a thin line. "*Remember how he did it secretly though, when his mistresses weren't watching?*"

Kes scowled. "*Yeah, about the only one he treated with respect was Attie, the sneaky little snake.*"

Atropos rolled her eyes. "*That's because you guys teased him mercilessly from the moment he hatched.*"

Orena, Kes, and Tisiphone failed to look abashed.

"You were on your way to the Astrea Sea before you came to help us?" Cassius asked tensely.

Atropos nodded. "*We'd heard that the Nereid who'd seen Ladon had returned to her realm after a long absence.*"

Cassius frowned.

"What's wrong?" Morgan asked.

"I've been to the Astrea Sea a couple of times since the Fall," he said hesitantly. "I would have heard something if a three-headed dragon was roaming the place."

"*We visited the place secretly once too, and found no trace of Ladon,*" Atropos confirmed. "*Still, this is the only lead we've had in the last hundred years.*"

Morgan studied the Moira, understanding dawning belatedly. "You believe Ladon can help you find the Garden of the West?"

"Just as Temir is Tenebra's child, Ladon is the offspring of the Hesperides. He was born from their combined powers." Atropos paused. *"He is connected to them in a way we are not. If anyone can find our sisters, he can."*

A noise broke the tense silence that ensued.

Phebei had pushed herself to her feet and was tottering over to the couches. Loki and Akamon hovered close behind, ready to catch her in case she stumbled.

Lilaia and Bostrof watched with trepidation as their daughter grasped Tisiphone's dress and attempted to climb onto her lap with little huffs and puffs.

The Goddess picked her up and plonked her gently on her knees. *"You're a brave little girl, aren't you?"*

"Aya," Phebei concurred with a grin.

Tisiphone eyed her critically. Shadows bloomed around her.

She leaned her face close to Phebei. *"BOO!"*

Lilaia made an incoherent sound. Bostrof paled. Atropos winced.

Phebei's smile faded when she saw the snake heads now tipping Tisiphone's hair amidst the halo of darkness surrounding her. She stared before breaking out into giggles.

"I knew there was more to this child than met the eye." Tisiphone looked up into their accusing stares. *"What?"* she said defensively. *"It didn't scare her."*

"No, but it made *me* crap my pants a little," Bailey mumbled.

Akamon was trembling and had stepped behind Loki.

"How about you try making funny faces or something at the child next time?" Atropos suggested with a frown.

Tisiphone grimaced. *"I tried that when Temir was small, remember? He bawled his eyes out for an entire day. Besides, this kid is gutsy. Why, I wouldn't be surprised if she* —Ouch!"

Phebei had gotten a hold of a handful of the Fury's hair and was yanking the snakes closer to try and eat them. "Yum!"

The serpents hissed in alarm as they struggled in her grip, tiny eyes bulging when her mouth loomed into view.

"Your daughter is insanely strong," Adrianne told Lilaia and Bostrof dully while Tisiphone carefully peeled the little girl's fingers off her hair.

CHAPTER TWENTY-THREE

Wind rushed in Cassius's ears as he and Tisiphone streaked toward the rugged coastline growing on the horizon.

The sea-locked continent jutting out of the ocean was ringed by dark, towering cliffs upon which waves crashed thunderously, the foam they churned rising hundreds of feet and misting the air around the landmass.

Their winged figures cast minuscule shadows across the archipelago rising from the western waters of the Astrea Sea, their passage too swift for the people in its towns and villages, or the fishermen in the vessels moored in its harbors and dotting its ocean, to discern against the pale sky and the dazzling light of the realm's two suns.

The scent of the sea and the taste of salt enveloped Cassius as they passed atolls enclosing sparkling, crystal-clear lagoons. The tangy freshness went some way toward clearing his mind and easing the tightness in his chest.

He'd been loath to leave Morgan when Theo had opened a doorway to the home of the Nereids on the terrace of their apartment building shortly after they'd returned from *Ohomgath*. Even in the hours since they'd been at Bostrof and Lilaia's place, his condition had deteriorated.

But Atropos's strategy made sense.

As long as Tenebra's plague remained a threat to Earth, it was best she and the Black Fates stayed put in San Francisco. With Victor, Theo, and Eden at their side, they at least had a fighting chance if Elios decided to attack again. Which left Cassius and Tisiphone free for the mission to find the Nereid who had last seen Ladon.

Loki had wanted to accompany them. Atropos had stopped him.

"*We cannot afford to lose another artifact to Elios, Keeper,*" the Moira had said quietly. "*If he intercepts you during your passage between realms, we may not be able to save you.*"

The imp had clenched his fists at her words, torn between the divine duty he had inherited and his affection for Cassius.

Morgan had ruffled his head gently. "You know she's right, flea ball."

The imp had squinted at him.

"I guess someone has to say here and look after your sorry ass," he'd mumbled with a sniff.

Morgan had rolled his eyes at that.

"Be safe," he'd murmured to Cassius when they'd hugged each other goodbye.

Cassius had swallowed and nodded, Morgan's fever almost searing his flesh. What he'd sensed in the demigod's soul core had made him want to weep.

Tenebra's Rot was winning.

"Make sure he rests," he'd told Victor and Theo before gazing at a distraught Loki. "Be good."

The imp had wiped his cheeks before nodding.

"Elios may already be aware of our intentions," Atropos had told Tisiphone grimly. *"Now that we're having to work in the open, I see no need to hide our presence from our friends. Go meet the queen of the Astrea Sea and seek her help."*

The Fury's voice broke through Cassius's thoughts. *"We have company."*

Cassius's gaze found what her divine sight had spotted first.

They were fast approaching the wall of mist shrouding the looming landmass from view. Something glimmered against the haze rising above the wind-tossed waters at the base of the cliffs. It grew into a troop of armored figures atop winged seahorses.

Tisiphone and Cassius slowed to a hover some hundred feet from the line of soldiers. The leader of the Nereids cut an impressive figure on her mount as she came toward them, her hold firm on her reins and the trident in her hand.

"Identify yourselves!" the sea Nymph barked.

Tisiphone's eyes brightened with divine power. *"I am*

the Fury Tisiphone, daughter of Nyx." Her voice boomed against the invisible cliffside and sent the seabirds nesting beyond the mist flying into the sky. She indicated Cassius. "*My companion is Icarus, the North Star and Awakener.*"

The Nereid commander sneered. "The Awakener? Do not jest, woman who dares mimic a Goddess!"

Tisiphone's face fell. She looked pointedly at Cassius. "*You're gonna have to do your thing.*"

Cassius sighed. They'd agreed in advance how they would go about convincing the Nereids of the authenticity of their claims.

Well, at least this is better than fighting with our future allies.

Heat bloomed inside him. He unleashed Heaven's Light.

The Nereid commander squinted as brightness flared across the ocean and lit up the pale backdrop behind her. She raised a hand to shield her eyes, only to freeze when her vision cleared. Shocked gasps rose from her soldiers. Their seahorses reared in alarm at the sight of Cassius's full demigod form.

The creatures could also feel his divine force.

Cassius retracted his powers. The stark radiance surrounding him faded.

The Nereid commander bowed stiffly at the waist, her face ashen. Armor clattered as her troop followed suit.

"Forgive my transgression, Goddess, Awakener," she begged. "I was not forewarned of your visit. I am Nais, captain of the Royal Guard. We came here because we detected the presence of two powerful entities in our realm."

"*You are forgiven, Nais,*" Tisiphone said graciously. "*Our mission must be kept secret, hence why we did not send a messenger in advance.*"

Puzzlement flashed in Nais's eyes as she raised her head.

"I understand," she said with a firm nod. "I shall take you to our queen."

"*Please do.*"

Cassius smiled. "Thank you."

Nais blinked. Several of the sea Nymphs blushed.

Tisiphone smirked and jabbed an elbow in Cassius's side. "*Way to go on the charm offensive.*"

Cassius masked a wince and rubbed the rib she'd almost broken.

Nais cleared her throat and turned her mount around. Her soldiers made way for her as she approached the vertical wall of mist. She raised her trident.

"*Reveal!*"

Cassius's skin prickled as the divine power of the Goddesses who had established the Astrea Sea brightened the tips of the weapon. The air shimmered, molecules vibrating under the unearthly force drenching them.

The pale wall parted with a low rumble. It revealed an enormous waterfall crashing into the sea at the base of the cliffs and a glittering city high above.

Cassius stared. The few times he'd sneaked into the Astrea Sea after the Fall, he'd used one of the short-lived portals that occasionally cropped up between Earth and the realm of the sea Nymphs. His covert missions had never brought him as far as its capital. Now that Hypnos's spell was almost completely broken, his recollections of the trips he'd made to the kingdom when he'd still been the second prince of Rain Vale were slowing returning.

The sea Nymphs framed Cassius and Tisiphone as they ascended past the roaring waters of the cascade, Nais in the lead. They shot out over the bluff a moment later and finally came in sight of the capital of the Astrea Sea.

A white palace sparkled to their left, its towers and spires rising gracefully toward the cerulean sky. It towered above the metropolis hugging the shores of the lake that narrowed to a channel and a promontory that gave rise to the chute kissing the ocean beneath them.

The river that birthed the body of water split the city in half, its meandering course crisscrossed by an array of glittering bridges that ended at a giant watergate set in a defensive wall protecting the capital where it faced an undulating landscape of hills and forests. An enormous mountain range was visible in the far distance, its peaks lost in pale clouds.

Nais dove toward the palace. "Follow me, honored guests."

Cassius and Tisiphone went after her, their escort keeping a respectful distance.

They passed the parapets and guard towers of the palace walls and crossed a bevy of courtyards and exquisitely maintained gardens. An immense quadrangle of pale flagstones appeared up ahead. It fronted the main palace building and was enclosed by what appeared to be administrative premises.

The throng of people navigating the piazza parted with a roar of startled murmurs when they landed in the middle of it. Guarded curiosity filled their eyes when they saw Cassius's white wings and Tisiphone's dark ones. From their refined garments, he guessed they were palace officials.

An elderly Potamos wearing regal robes and a scowl marched down a flight of steps to their right, his staff striking the ground with sharp clacks. A retinue of attendants with armloads of paperwork rushed after him, documents fluttering to the ground as they tried to keep up.

"What is the meaning of this, Captain?!" The male Nymph's irate gaze raked Cassius and Tisiphone dismissively before focusing on Nais. "How dare you bring these strangers to Her Majesty's palace without obtaining the Council's permission first?!"

"*Maybe you should do your thing again,*" Tisiphone whispered to Cassius out of the corner of her mouth.

"I really don't think a show of force is appropriate under the circumstances," he replied in a low voice after gauging the tense mood of the crowd. "We should let Nais deal with this."

Nais shot a contrite glance their way. Her expression hardened as she faced the elderly Potamos.

"I apologize for not being able to give the court forewarning, Minister Polyx," the Nereid told the

Potamos with a respectful bob of her head. "Our visitors' identities precluded it."

"Oh, really?" Polyx scoffed. "I doubt their station warranted you violating the palace's security rules." He turned to one of Nais's soldiers. "Arrest the captain and take these strangers prisoner! I shall decide what to do with them at a later date."

The sea Nymph he'd addressed didn't move from her spot.

"With all due respect, Minister, you should listen to what my captain has to say," she said in clipped tones.

Polyx's face reddened.

"That can't be good for his blood pressure," Cassius muttered worriedly to Tisiphone.

"Serves him right if he blows an aneurysm, the little tit."

Several of Nais's soldiers swallowed snorts. Cassius squinted at the Goddess.

Tisiphone shrugged. *"Hey, I'm a Fury. Being vengeful is kinda my default state."*

"Get me the commander of the Royal Knights!" Polyx finally screeched, spit flying from his mouth. "I want these fools apprehended and chained in the palace dungeons this very—!"

He choked on the rest of his words.

Shadows had exploded around Tisiphone. Her hair ends sprouted snake heads. Her features shifted into a deathly mask that caused several palace officials to faint.

Polyx paled.

Cassius had to admire the guy for still standing after witnessing the Fury's wrathful appearance.

Tisiphone leaned her face close to the councilor's. *"Look, you decrepit old fool! How about you pipe down and let Nais—!"*

"Tisiphone?!"

Cassius and Tisiphone turned at the sound of the crystal-clear, musical voice echoing around the quadrangle.

A breathtakingly beautiful, blonde sea Nymph wearing a crown of red coral and a white silk dress trimmed with gold had appeared from the direction of the palace, a handful of attendants at her side.

The darkness around Tisiphone abated. Her expression cleared. *"Dione."*

CHAPTER TWENTY-FOUR

A MEMORY SPARKED THROUGH CASSIUS'S MIND AT THE name Tisiphone had uttered. The Nymph crossing the quadrangle at a determined pace was a Goddess and sister to the queen of the Astrea Sea.

Clothes rustled and armor clinked as the Nymphs and Potamoi in the courtyard bowed to the deity.

"Your Highness," Polyx mumbled. "I beg your forgiveness. I shall deal with this matter—"

"*Shut up, Polyx,*" Dione snapped as she marched past him, her pupils flashing gold.

The sea Goddess ignored the spluttering minister and threw her arms around Tisiphone.

"*It's so good to see you!*" Dione pulled back, emotion bringing a flush of color to her cheeks. "*Where have you been all this time? What of your sis—?*" She froze when she registered Cassius's presence. Her eyes rounded. "*Awakener?!*"

Polyx looked like he wanted to disappear into the ground. Nais cast a derisive glance at the Potamos.

"Hmm, hi," Cassius said awkwardly, conscious of the battery of furtive stares being aimed at him.

Tears bloomed in Dione's eyes. Her gaze roamed his face, as if she were committing his every feature to memory.

She closed the distance to him and clasped his hands. *"We thought we'd lost you, Prince of Rain Vale."*

She pressed her forehead to their raised knuckles, wetness soaking her cheeks.

Cassius's chest tightened at the affection in Dione's trembling voice and touch. He hated that he couldn't easily reciprocate the feelings of the Goddess before him. Not for the first time, he cursed Elios for using Hypnos to erase his past and that of so many.

Still, the ties that had bound him to the ones who had cherished and supported him before the Fall had never broken. He'd sensed it with every forgotten ally who had appeared before him in the aftermath of the War in the Nether, just as he could feel his soul core acknowledging the deity holding his hands.

Determination filled Dione's face when she raised her head. *"Come, both of you. We must see my sisters!"*

She whirled around and led them toward the palace, her attendants in their wake.

They entered an immense hall of pale marble and navigated a veritable labyrinth of passages and staircases before finally reaching a set of impressive, gilded doors on the third floor. Just like the staff they'd encountered along the way, the Potamoi guarding the room bowed respectfully before stepping aside.

"Are my sisters here?" Dione asked tensely.

"Yes, Your Highness," one of the guards murmured. "They are having their morning meeting."

"*Good.*" Dione looked at one of her attendants. "*Prepare some tea.*" She grasped the door handle. "*And see that we are not disturbed.*"

One of the guards hesitated. "Prince Astrid wanted to see you, Your Highness."

Cassius startled. Prince Astrid was the demigod who wished to marry his sister Kalliste.

I forgot he's from this realm.

Dione frowned. "*My son will have to wait too.*"

Dazzling brightness greeted them when they crossed the threshold into the room on the other side. Cassius blinked.

It was an immense office bathed in sunlight that streamed through a pair of floor-to-ceiling, clear, leaded windows capped by sculptured arches. Bookcases lined the remaining walls, the cabinets stretching to the coffered ceiling and their highest shelves accessible by elegant, cast-iron, rolling ladders. The scent of the candles and bouquets atop various console tables filled the air with a pleasant aroma.

In complete contrast to the graceful surroundings, the large conference table to the right was covered with haphazard stacks of documents that made it look like it'd been hit by a storm. So was the coffee table to the left and the couches and chairs framing it.

A stylish oak desk similarly drowning in paperwork dominated the far side of the space. Seated behind it was a harassed-looking queen with hair that matched her crimson, coral crown. She was currently scowling at the folder in her hands through a monocle.

"I swear, I'm going to kick Menippe's ass when she comes back," she was in the midst of muttering. *"Why are her calculations so unnecessarily complicated?!"*

The blonde Goddess sitting on one of the couches leafed through the paperwork in her hands. She was clad in the same attire as Dione and wore an identical coral crown.

"I'll help you," she ground out.

"This stuff is giving me a headache." The brunette seated across from the blonde sighed, leaned back against the headrest, and dropped a document on her face. *"When did she say she was returning from her trip? I mean, it's been a hundred years already."*

"She didn't!" the monocled Goddess snarled. She finally clocked Dione's presence. *"Oh."* Her expression cleared a little. *"There you are, Di. We were wondering what was keeping—!"*

She gasped and jumped to her feet, her chair clattering noisily to the ground.

The brunette removed the paper draping her face and squinted at the doorway. *"What?"*

Her eyes rounded. Her crown slid askew on her head as she jerked upright.

"By the Gods," mumbled the blonde Goddess.

Paper fluttered to the ground as she rose, her face pale and the documents on the floor all but forgotten.

"Amphitrite," Tisiphone said with a grin. Her gaze shifted to the brunette closing and opening her mouth like a goldfish and hastily righting her crown.

"Panacea." Her expression turned dry as she looked at the stunned redhead behind the desk. *"A monocle? Really, Thetis?"*

"Tisiphone!"

The three Goddesses rushed over and hugged the laughing Fury. It was a moment before they stepped back and turned to Cassius. They studied him with expressions of pure reverence, as if they couldn't quite believe he was there, standing right before them.

"Awakener," Thetis breathed. *"No."* She shook her head. *"Prince Icarus."* Her eyes gleamed. *"We have missed you."*

Emotion tightened Cassius's throat. "I'm pleased to be back."

Dione surreptitiously wiped her eyes.

"Come, we have much to talk about," Thetis said.

A knock came at the door just as the queen and her sisters cleared the couches so they could all sit. An attendant wheeled in a cart filled with fragrant tea and cakes, served them their drinks, and bowed before leaving the room.

"Tell us what happened to you," Thetis ordered once the door closed.

Cassius met the sea Goddesses' tense stares.

"You should start," he told Tisiphone.

The Fury nodded, her expression grim.

The blood gradually drained from Thetis and her sisters' faces as Tisiphone recounted everything that had taken place from the time Elios captured them to their ill-fated escape from the Seventh Purgatory. She related how they had lived hidden in dozens of fractured realms through the past few hundred years, always on the run from Elios.

Cassius told them about Chester Moran and Loki, Lucille Hartman and Eden, and Elios subjugating Demetrius, the Reaper God, and Boreas with his corruption until he, Morgan, and Victor had freed the three deities.

"*What?!*" Thetis mumbled.

Cassius had just described Theo's awakening as the new South Star and wielder of the Spear of Light, and Nildar and Archon's intervention when part of London had ended up in the Hells.

"*Rohengar lives again?!*" Dione said hoarsely.

Panacea and Amphitrite choked back sobs.

"*The new South Star is devilishly handsome,*" Tisiphone stated.

Dione's shock shifted to disdain. "*None was more stunning than the first prince of Rain Vale.*" Her expression turned chagrined as she cast a sheepish look at Cassius. "*Present company excluded, of course.*"

Tisiphone grinned. "*Nice save, Di.*"

Some of the tension oozed out of Cassius. "Both Rohengar and Theo beat me hands down when it comes to looks." A sigh left him. "But I'm afraid their hearts belong to Coraos."

Thetis dropped her cake. "*Eh?*"

"*Huh?*" Amphitrite mumbled.

Panacea sucked in air. "*Coraos? Coraos is alive?!*"

Cassius nodded. He told them what Pan had revealed after the battle to save the Spirit Realm and how Victor had more than atoned for the sins he had committed under Hypnos's influence when he was known as Coraos.

"*Ivmir's brother was not of sound mind when he took Elios's side in the War?!*" Dione said, aghast.

"*No, he wasn't.*" Tisiphone's expression hardened. "*And there's more.*"

The Fury described how Elios had used Tenebra, Alecto, and Megaera to attack Earth and Ivory Peaks and how their ultimate target had been Morgan and the Sword of Wind.

Thetis swore. "*Tenebra's Rot is consuming Ivmir's soul?!*"

"*Elios has the sword?*" Dione said with a scowl.

"Yes." Cassius swallowed. "Atropos believes the Golden Apples guarded by the Nymphs of the West could counteract Tenebra's poison and save Morgan. But we do not know where the Hesperides ended up after the Nether tore."

"*That's why we're here,*" Tisiphone explained. "*We heard a rumor a while back. A Nereid saw Ladon fall through a crack between the realms when the Nether tore. The dragon ended up in the Astrea Sea, only briefly we believe. This Nereid has returned to your kingdom. We need to find her.*"

Dione's cup clattered on her saucer. "*Wait. Did you say Ladon?!*"

Tisiphone bobbed her head.

Dione and her sisters exchanged a strained look.

Tension quickened Cassius's pulse. "What's wrong?"

Thetis scratched her cheek. "*Our sister Menippe told us she saw what looked like a dragon appear in the Astrea*

Sea after the Nether tore. We thought she imagined it since we could find no trace of the beast."

Tisiphone blinked. *"Menippe? We were told this Nereid was some kind of noble who went by the name Meltem."*

"That's her alter ego," Thetis said sourly. *"Menippe is our finance minister. Except she keeps abandoning her duties so she can go gallivanting on one of her adventures!"*

The sea Goddess's burst of divine power rattled the windows and sent the paperwork around the office fluttering wildly into the air. Amphitrite and Panacea's faces fell as they watched the papers land in disarray.

"Sorry," Thetis muttered, contrite.

"Is that why you guys are poring over these documents?" Tisiphone asked sympathetically.

"Yes." Thetis pinched the bridge of her nose. *"She's the best of us at this stuff."*

"Wait a minute," Amphitrite interrupted dully as Tisiphone's words finally sank in. *"Did you say Menippe is back?"*

"That's what we heard," Tisiphone replied with a shrug.

Cassius winced as Thetis's cup cracked in her hand. This time, a veritable storm swept the room.

A vein throbbed in Amphitrite's temple. *"Why, that little—!"*

CHAPTER TWENTY-FIVE

CASSIUS SKIRTED AROUND A BANK OF CLOUDS AND navigated a slipstream with Tisiphone as they kept abreast of Thetis and Dione. The two Nereids rode their winged seahorses, their brows furrowed as they glared at the mountains looming in the distance.

The peaks formed the western end of the vast range that made up the backbone of the continent. It was where Thetis and Dione suspected their sister was hiding.

"Why those mountains?" Tisiphone had asked before they'd left the palace.

Thetis had sneered. *"She has a lair there."*

"It's more a love nest, really," Amphitrite had grumbled.

"She's a screamer in the bedroom," Panacea had explained bluntly at Cassius and Tisiphone's puzzled looks. *"Honestly, it used to scare the palace maids senseless. She decided it would be best if she indulged in her carnal desires elsewhere."*

"*Half her adventures are bedhopping ones too,*" Thetis had added darkly while Cassius flushed and Tisiphone smirked. "*I swear, I don't know where she gets her sexual appetite from.*"

Morgan's face had sprung to Cassius's mind at that.

"*Still, those mountains are quite far,*" Tisiphone had muttered. "*Why didn't she just get a place in the capital?*"

"*She did,*" Amphitrite had replied morosely. "*We received complaints from that district that a banshee had established her nest in a noble's mansion.*"

Panacea had sniggered before sobering in the face of Thetis's accusing stare. "*Sorry.*"

The mountains soon became towering, snow-capped peaks blanketed in thick, evergreen forests. Thetis landed her seahorse on a bluff some ten thousand feet in the air, jumped off her mount, and stormed toward a crack in the cliffside. Tisiphone, Dione, and Cassius followed.

The crack they entered quickly widened into a tunnel lit with ornate lanterns and filled with the heady fragrance of incense. A low murmur reached them. The words became clearer after they negotiated several twists and turns and finally came in sight of the exit.

It belonged to a female who was clearly enjoying herself.

"Oh! *Oh, yes! Right there!* Ah! *Deeper! Harder! Hmmm!*" the voice gasped and moaned. "*Don't stop!*"

Cassius slowed. Heat flooded his cheeks. Dione slapped a hand over her face. Thetis looked like she was about to explode.

A chuckle reached them. Tisiphone was grinning like this was the best thing that had happened to her in ages.

Thetis fisted her hands and stormed inside the cave from which the voice originated, only to stumble to an abrupt halt. Cassius studied the sumptuous furniture filling the space warily as he stopped a short distance behind her. His gaze finally landed on the large four-poster bed in the middle of the rug-strewn floor.

Visible through the gauzy canopy surrounding it were two figures in languid motion.

"By the Gods, that feels good," the one on the bottom grunted.

Thetis took a deep breath. "MENIPPE!"

Her roar made the cave tremble and sent something squeaking and flapping its wings agitatedly around the shadowy ceiling.

Dione grimaced and removed her fingers from her ears as the echoes faded.

The figures on the bed had frozen.

The one on the bottom yanked the closest veil aside and squinted at them. *"Thetis?!"*

Cassius breathed a sigh of relief.

The sea Goddess was lying on her front and having her back massaged by a sturdy Potamos in a loin cloth.

Her face brightened. *"Oh, hey! I brought souvenirs."*

Thetis ground her teeth.

Menippe gasped when she saw Cassius. She pushed up onto her hands and knees and scrambled off the bed stark naked, the healthy Potamos specimen behind her forgotten.

"*Icarus!*"

She flew across the room, jumped on him like a crab, and kissed him. Cassius's eyes rounded, hands rising aloft at his sides. Menippe squeezed her arms and legs tighter around him and pushed her tongue inside his mouth, passion glazing her face.

Tisiphone burst out laughing.

"*Why, you hussy!*" Thetis gasped, horrified.

It took both her and Dione to finally peel Menippe off Cassius.

Tisiphone wiped tears from her eyes. "*By the Gods, I wish I could have immortalized this moment and shown it to Ivmir.*"

Cassius grimaced. Thetis forced her recalcitrant younger sister into a peignoir and dismissed the bowing Potamos.

"*Where did you go this time?*" Dione asked wearily.

"*Not telling,*" Menippe pouted.

Her gaze darted to Cassius. Her expression grew unfocused.

"*His lips are the sweetest ambrosia I have ever tasted,*" she half mumbled to herself.

This sent Tisiphone into a fit of giggles and had Cassius swallowing a sigh.

It took several minutes for Thetis and Dione to apprise the rebellious sea Goddess of all they had learned in the past two hours. Menippe sobered as she listened.

Her frowning gaze swung between Tisiphone and Icarus. "*You're looking for Ladon?*"

"Yes," Cassius replied tensely. "Did you happen to see where the dragon you saw disappeared off to after the Nether tore?"

Menippe scratched the back of her head. *"It was a long time ago."* She flashed a sour look at Thetis and Dione. *"Besides,* some *people thought I made it all up."*

"This is important, Menippe," Thetis said in a hard voice.

The sea Goddess pursed her lips.

"His presence in our realm only lasted a few minutes," she finally muttered. *"By the time I reached the place where I'd seen him, he was gone. But I did catch a glimpse of the realm he fell to as the crack closed."*

Cassius's nails sank into his palms. "Where did he fall?"

Menippe hesitated. *"It was the kingdom of man."*

The Goddess sighed while the rest of them exchanged shocked looks, like she knew they wouldn't believe her.

"Wait." Tisiphone lowered her eyebrows. *"You're saying Ladon fell to* Earth?!*"*

Cassius studied the floor blindly. "I've never heard any accounts of a dragon being sighted during the Fall."

Dione rubbed her chin. *"Considering his size, he would have caused quite the splash."*

"And with the amount of divine power he carries, he would eventually have been detected, even if he wasn't at the time of the Fall," Thetis mused, puzzled.

Menippe grimaced. *"Well, he wasn't exactly in his original form when he was plummeting down there."*

Cassius stared. "What do you mean?"

IT WAS DAWN BY THE TIME THEY RETURNED TO EARTH through the portal Thetis had opened for them. Now that Theo had awakened as a Guardian of the Nether, all the realms had begun to realize that the once stable interdimensional doorways that had been destroyed during the Fall could be revived again.

Something soft and furry collided with Cassius the moment he stepped out onto his terrace. He staggered back a step before righting himself and holding on to the quivering imp in his arms.

Loki whimpered miserably against his chest. "Cassius."

Cassius hugged the imp back and ruffled his head with a tired smile. "We were only gone for a few hours."

He stiffened at what he sensed.

Tisiphone's eyes flashed gold.

"*Ivmir*," she mumbled.

The hairs rose on Cassius's flesh as he followed her gaze to his apartment. He could feel the darkness inside Morgan's soul core even from a distance.

Tenebra's Rot had spread in their absence.

Cassius pulled back and grasped Loki's shoulders, his touch rougher than he'd intended. "How bad is he?!"

Loki's ears and tail drooped. "He's...sleeping."

Cassius clenched his jaw. Loki wasn't meeting his eyes.

The sliding doors opened. Theo and Victor stepped out. They both looked pale.

Theo came over and wordlessly embraced Cassius. Cassius's throat tightened as he fought back tears. Theo and Victor's silence could only mean one thing.

"*Come,*" Tisiphone said somberly.

Cassius didn't know how he got to the bedroom. He could barely feel his legs, so deep was the fear twisting his insides. He hesitated for a moment before crossing the threshold.

An unearthly force throbbed across his skin.

Atropos, Kes, and Orena stood around the bed. Their eyes glowed brightly as they poured their divine energy into Morgan, their consciousness momentarily suppressed.

Horror drenched Cassius in a cold sweat. He swallowed a sob.

Morgan looked haggard where he lay lifeless in the bed. His once full cheeks were sunken and dark circles rimmed his eyes. His hair had gone gray in places and wrinkles furrowed the skin on the backs of his hands.

"His condition deteriorated three hours ago," Victor told Cassius in a flat voice.

Morgan's eyelids fluttered open. He turned his head slowly and peered sightlessly in Cassius's direction.

"Is that you, Cassius?" he croaked.

Cassius could tell that he'd gone blind. The agony that wrapped around his heart filled his ears with a loud buzz. He was barely aware of unleashing his full demigod form or the radiance that bathed the room as he approached the bed.

"Yes." He clasped Morgan's hand, climbed onto the mattress, and settled next to him, his soul leaden with grief. "I'm back."

Relief drained what little color remained in Morgan's face.

"Thank the Gods," he breathed. "Sorry, it looks like I might have something in my eye."

Cassius gently took him in his arms. "I can see that."

Movement at the side of the bed drew his gaze. Tisiphone had taken up position next to Atropos, her face wet with tears. Her brow furrowed as she focused her divine energy into the stream pouring into Morgan's body.

"Hmm." Morgan burrowed his face in Cassius's chest. "You smell nice."

Cassius bit his lip hard to stop the wretched sound that threatened to leave him. "So do you."

Morgan chuckled weakly. "Liar."

He grimaced in the next instant, the act seemingly causing him pain.

"Hush, my love." Cassius's silent tears soaked into Morgan's hair as he cradled his head. "You need to rest."

"'Kay," Morgan mumbled sleepily. "Stay with me?"

"Always." Cassius swallowed the lump in his throat. "I will never leave your side again."

He didn't know when they fell asleep. Nor did he care.

The only thing that mattered to him was the pulsing thread that connected his and Morgan's soul cores. It synchronized with their heartbeats as they entered a deep slumber, steady and bright and strong.

As long as it was still present, he would not lose hope.

CHAPTER TWENTY-SIX

Atropos closed the bedroom door gently behind her.

Theo rushed over from the direction of the kitchen. "Are they okay?"

His eyes were red from crying and his lips dry from chewing them.

"Yes. They're sleeping."

Victor turned from where he was standing in front of the glass wall overlooking the terrace. "Did you manage to stabilize Morgan's soul core?"

Though his tone was calm, Atropos didn't miss his clenched fists or the darkness dulling his eyes.

She hesitated. *"For now."*

Palpable misery filled the room, making the air heavy.

Loki slumped on the couch and hugged his knees even more tightly to his chest. Orena dropped her head forlornly on Kes's shoulder where they sat beside him. Tisiphone frowned heavily in the opposite chair.

It was mid-morning. Strickland and Morgan's team had visited a short while ago, along with Reuben and Jasper. They'd left with somber expressions and the promise that someone would call them if Morgan's condition worsened. Bailey and Julia had practically had to drag Adrianne out of the apartment. It wasn't until Orena had gently told the sorceress that Morgan and Cassius needed the peace and quiet that she'd finally relented.

Atropos took a seat beside Tisiphone. Though she was a Goddess, she felt drained and battered, her very soul bruised by everything that had happened in the last two days. It wasn't just the rollercoaster of emotions she'd lived through or the qualms that still haunted her.

The burden she'd carried on her shoulders had lightened when she'd met up with her brothers and the two Guardians of the Nether. With Morgan now out of action and Cassius incapacitated by grief, that load felt ten times heavier than before.

"Did you find anything in the Astrea Sea?" she asked Tisiphone tiredly, not expecting much of an answer.

"We found plenty," Tisiphone replied in clipped tones.

Atropos's breath caught.

Tisiphone grimaced when she registered her faintly accusing expression. *"I'm sorry. I thought this was more important."*

She glanced at the bedroom door.

Atropos sighed and sat back. She rubbed her temple. *"You're right. It is."*

"*What did you learn?*" Kes said, trying hard to mask the eagerness in her voice.

"*The Nereid who spotted Ladon was none other than Menippe.*"

Atropos's belly clenched. Kes and Orena traded an incredulous stare.

"Menippe?" Theo asked with a puzzled frown.

He'd gone over to Victor and wrapped an arm around his waist. Victor relaxed a little and kissed his lover's head.

He studied Tisiphone shrewdly. "If I'm not mistaken, that's one of the sea Goddesses who hails from that realm."

"*You're correct,*" the Fury muttered. "*You guys are not gonna believe this. Ladon is on Earth.*"

Kes flinched.

"*What?!*" Orena gasped, pale-faced.

A dizzy feeling swept over Atropos. Her powers of foresight flared.

Fate really does move in ways even us Goddesses meant to control her cannot foresee.

Victor's surprise turned to doubt. "I think we'd know if an eighty-ton dragon was roaming this planet."

Tisiphone heaved a heavy sigh, like she still couldn't believe what she was about to tell them. "*That's the thing. He's not in his dragon form. Menippe said she saw him shapeshift when he fell through the crack in the Astrea Sea to Earth. Apparently, it's one of his defense mechanisms when he crosses realms. He adopts a form better suited to the local environment.*"

"*What form did he take?*" Kes asked, horrified.

Tisiphone made a face. *"Some kind of reptile."*

Atropos gazed blindly at the floor, her heart racing. *He's been here all along?! But—we should have sensed his divine core the second we entered this realm!*

Suspicion bloomed. She took a deep breath, closed her eyes, and brought Ladon to mind. Heat flooded her veins as she focused her powers of divinity and her second sight on the current fortune of the three-headed beast.

Frustration churned her stomach after a moment.

Damnation! Clotho and Lachesis still blind my abilities. Otherwise, I'd surely be able to pick up a trail of Ladon's destiny. Even an echo of his divine soul where it resides in this realm would do.

"Anything?" Tisiphone said stiffly when Atropos opened her eyes.

She met her sisters' expectant gazes and shook her head, dejected. *"Clotho and Lache continue to muddy the waters. Besides, I suspect Ladon is masking his soul core so as to go undetected by Elios's agents and the otherworldly here, especially if he is in a weakened state."*

"So, how do we find him?" Bitterness underscored Kes's words. *"We don't even know what kind of reptile he is."*

A flare of light cast stark shadows across the room and sent a singular divine force dancing across Atropos's skin. Loki had removed the Eternity Key from within his body.

"Could this help?" the imp said doubtfully.

Atropos was about to shake her head when an idea blossomed at the forefront of her mind. She studied the imp's weapon, her heartbeat quickening once more.

"*Not on its own,*" she said slowly.

Confusion clouded Loki and the others' faces.

"*Ladon was created not just from the Hesperides' life forces but also from a rare kind of magic,*" Atropos explained, unable to contain the excitement in her voice. Her gut was telling her she was on the right track. "*A magic that is dark and dangerous. In fact, one that is identical to the potent magic possessed by the most powerful mage in this realm and her one-of-a-kind weapon.*"

"Wait." Loki's eyes bulged. "You mean, Eden and the devilwood staff?!"

Theo and Victor shared a dazed look.

Atropos nodded, hope bringing a flush of heat to her cheeks. "*I believe if the Eternity Key and the Bloodcursed Devilwood Summoning Staff work together, they might just be able to locate Ladon's soul core, wherever he may be hiding.*"

The front door opened, distracting them.

Eden trudged in with a truculent expression and a couple of takeout bags.

"I swear, I don't know why mom insists I continue to take lessons when the world is in danger and that bastard Elios could destroy the universe at any given moment," she was muttering to the pendant nestling against the base of her throat. She paused just inside the living room. "Oh, hey, mom sent lunch." She showed them the bags and stiffened at their stares. "What?"

CHAPTER TWENTY-SEVEN

THE BUSY CROWD BUSTLING AROUND THE PARK CAST curious looks their way where they stood in front of a glass and brick building. Eden could hardly blame the people slowing down to stare at them.

Out of her, Loki, and Kes, she was the only one dressed for a warm, sunny day.

Though he'd assumed his humanoid form, Loki had elected to wear thick, dark clothes that covered him from the neck down, a beanie hat that hid his horns, and sunglasses to mask his demonic eyes. Add to this his Doc Martens and he looked like he was about to raid a bank.

Kes, on the other hand, gave off the air of a rockstar diva with her enormous sunglasses, high-heel boots, a trench coat that showed tantalizing glimpses of her black dress and long, lithe legs, and a Bulgari scarf that almost swallowed her face.

"I should have brought Theo and Victor along," Eden mumbled under her breath.

The devilwood pendant quivered in agreement against her throat.

Kes shot a glance at her. *"What was that?"*

"Nothing." Eden squinted at the Goddess. "By the way, what made you decide on that outfit?"

Kes beamed like she was the cleverest person in the universe. *"I saw someone wearing the same thing on TV yesterday, back at Icarus and Ivmir's love nest."*

Eden suppressed a grimace.

"Can you please stop calling it a love nest?" Loki snapped. "I live there!"

Kes smirked. *"And aren't you the third wheel?"*

A kid stopped and stared as crimson light bloomed briefly around Loki's glasses. "Mommy, look!"

His parents' gazes followed the direction he'd indicated. Their faces glazed over when they saw Loki and Kes.

"Don't do that, Jordan!" the kid's mother berated in a fierce whisper. "It's not polite to point your finger at, er," her expression turned even more glassy as she cast another furtive stare at Loki and Kes, "— people."

The trio left hurriedly, little Jordan staring over his shoulder and pouting like he'd missed out on the show of his life.

Eden narrowed her eyes at the oblivious imp and Goddess glaring at one another. "Will you two stop it? This is meant to be a secret mission. You're attracting unnecessary attention!"

They ignored her. The air quivered red around Loki. Kes released a faint aura of shadows.

"I swear to God, I will tell on you to Attie!" Eden threatened.

The pair froze. They retracted their powers before fixing her with hurt stares.

Eden disregarded their aggrieved looks. "Now, how about we do what we came here to do?"

She frowned at the structure before them. It was where the devilwood staff and the Eternity Key had tracked Ladon's faint energy signature to.

Or, rather, his magic.

It was an hour ago that she'd listened in disbelief to Atropos's suggestion for how to locate the dragon who could guide them to the Hesperides.

"You want Woody to do what?" she'd asked the Goddess dully in Cassius and Morgan's living room.

"*I want him to eat the Eternity Key,*" Atropos had repeated steadily.

"Hell no!" Loki had clutched the artifact protectively against his chest. "The heck you want to do that for?!"

Atropos had sighed. "*Because I suspect it can dowse the magic inside the staff and trace Ladon. And it won't be permanent. As the Keeper, you will be able to eject the Eternity Key from the summoning staff.*"

"You're going to use the key and the staff as a dowsing pendant?" Victor had said skeptically.

Atropos had nodded. "*First, we'll need some maps of this realm.*"

Eden had hesitated for a moment, still uncertain about the Goddess's proposition. "Will a visualization do?"

They'd stared at her, puzzled.

Eden had sighed, focused her soul core and that of her summoning staff, and called forth her bloodcursed magic. The crimson sphere that had flared from her fingers had expanded into a detailed, three-dimensional globe representing the Earth.

"When did you learn how to do that?" Theo had asked, impressed.

"Woody and I were experimenting with our powers one day and he astral-projected my ass over to Atlanta," she'd muttered. The globe had expanded under her will. "That's when I realized he could map his environment."

The pendant had hummed happily, like she'd complimented it.

It had taken Atropos a while longer to convince Loki to let Woody ingest the Eternity Key as per her plan. The imp had watched on with a horrified expression while the summoning staff had swallowed his artifact in a single, giant gulp before shrinking back down to its pendant form.

Atropos had taken the medallion from Eden and held it above the slowly spinning globe. The Goddess's eyes had flared and filled the room with golden light as she'd invoked her powers.

"Divine the presence of the one who is like you."

The pendant had trembled briefly at the command before falling silent.

"Maybe it needs our powers too?" Eden had suggested.

Victor had frowned. "I think she's right."

Atropos had hesitated before dipping her chin. Eden and Loki had approached the Goddess and laid their fingers upon the pendant. Eden's heartbeat had quickened when the Moira's divine energy had brushed against the bloodcursed magic she was pouring into the summoning staff. She'd detected Loki and the Eternity Key's powers too, and marveled at how different they each were to her own.

"*With me,*" Atropos had instructed.

Eden and Loki had nodded, faces tense.

"*Divine the presence of the one who is like you!*" the three of them had barked as one.

The pendant had immediately jerked sideways.

Eden's mouth had gone dry. "Expand."

The projection had shifted at her order, giving them a closer view of where the devilwood pendant was pointing.

It was the Eastern seaboard of the United States.

Eden had frowned. "Focus."

The globe had blurred sickeningly before revealing details of a city.

Victor had straightened where he'd been leaning against the wall, surprise widening his eyes. "That's Philadelphia."

"*Can we get a more detailed location?*" Atropos had asked Eden stiffly.

Eden had nodded and furrowed her brow. The globe had blurred again and again until it got down to a two-hundred-foot-wide bird's eye view of the city.

Her eyes had rounded. "Is that—?!"

A voice interrupted Eden's recollection. "Excuse me."

She blinked. A young man in a safari outfit was peering awkwardly at them.

"Would you mind stepping aside?" he said politely. "You're blocking the entrance."

"Oh." Eden made a face. "Sorry. We were just admiring the architecture."

The guy looked at her strangely. Eden cleared her throat.

"Let's go," she murmured to Loki and Kes.

The Reptile and Amphibian House of the Philadelphia Zoo looked pretty innocuous in the bright sunlight as they headed inside it. They negotiated a short flight of steps, pushed through another pair of glass doors, and were greeted by a wave of heat and a cacophony of excited voices.

A class of eager sixth graders practically packed the interior of the building.

"What are these human children doing here?" Kes asked warily.

Eden spotted several harried teachers trying to herd the kids into some kind of orderly queue. "By the looks of things, they're on a field trip."

Kes observed the kids with a critical frown. *"They are very loud considering their size."*

"Look! A weird lady just came in!" someone said in a stage whisper.

Giggles broke out.

The Goddess's scowling gaze swept the room. *"Who said that?!"*

Her voice rattled the glass boxes lining the walls. Some of the children paled.

Eden wished the ground would swallow her. "Come here!"

She grabbed the irate Goddess by the arm and dragged her and a smirking Loki farther inside, to where the devilwood staff was urging her to go.

They passed dozens of brightly lit displays featuring exotic reptiles and reached an immense enclosure occupying an alcove at the far end of the building.

It featured a sleeping Komodo dragon.

Loki gulped. "Is—is that him?!"

Eden frowned. "Woody?"

Her staff spoke in her head. *It is not the big one.*

She looked around the enclosure, puzzled. "He says it's not the Komodo."

"There's nothing else in there," Kes said skeptically.

A flicker of movement drew Eden's eyes. Something had shifted under a cluster of twigs and leaves at her feet. She squinted. There was a creature hiding under the greenery.

Eden crouched and tapped the glass. Eerie stillness gripped the clump of branches and foliage.

"What is it?" Kes asked.

"There's something there."

Gold flashed around Kes's glasses. A gust of unearthly wind blew inside the enclosure. It swept away the twigs and leaves.

Eden stared.

An adorable, four-inch-long, pink-hued Texas

horned lizard was hugging the ground, eyes squeezed shut and claws over his head.

"Wait. Is that—?!"

Yes, Woody stated smugly. *That is the dragon.*

Brightness shimmered over Loki's belly. His jaw dropped open. His gaze locked on the lizard as he registered whatever he'd just sensed from the Eternity Key.

"La—*Ladon?!*"

The lizard lifted his head and blinked up at them. His pupils flared with recognition.

"*Fuck!*" he hissed.

Horror rounded Kes's eyes. "*What—what happened to you?!*"

"He's so cute," Eden mumbled.

Loki made a face. "He has zero presence."

The lizard froze. He puffed up his body, clearly incensed by the imp's words. "*Oh yeah, ugly?! I'll give you presssence!*"

He flipped a claw at Loki.

"*That's Ladon alright,*" Kes affirmed dully while the imp and the lizard traded glares.

Motion at the other end of the enclosure captured Eden's gaze. The Komodo dragon had opened a lazy eye.

"Uh-oh."

The Komodo dragon lifted its enormous head, yawned, and slowly waddled over.

Ladon followed her worried stare.

"*Don't mind Kujo. He's a big sssoftie,*" he said

dismissively. *"Hey, Kujo. Could you back off? I'm having a chat with some old friendsss. Kujo?"*

The Komodo dragon ignored him. To Eden's horror, it stuck out its long, forked tongue, licked him from his horned head to his tail, and picked him up gently in its jaws, mucus-covered scales and all.

"Look, for the lassst time, I'm not your mate, you dumb reptile!" Ladon screeched as the Komodo dragon took him back to its bed of straw. *"Hey, where'sss your tongue going? Noooo! Don't lick me there!"*

"Wow," Kes muttered, her voice laced with pity.

"Shouldn't we help him?" Eden said, a little aghast at what the lizard was being subjected to.

An evil smirk twisted Loki's mouth. "Let him suffer, the little shit."

CHAPTER TWENTY-EIGHT

Kes sighed. *"Look, for the tenth time, we're sorry, okay?"*

"No, you're not, you dessspicable Goddessss!" Ladon snarled. *"And I can hear you laughing, you damn imp!"*

He shook a claw at a sniggering Loki before clutching the banana Eden had given him.

"He's as rude as ever, I see," Tisiphone muttered.

"But also strangely kind of cute in this form," Orena observed with a hint of mixed feelings.

Ladon puffed up his cheeks. *"I am not cute! I am a fearsssome dragon!"*

Tisiphone picked him up by the scruff of his neck, banana and all. *"You're a lizard."*

Ladon hissed and spat at the frowning Goddess.

Atropos pinched the bridge of her nose. *"How about everyone calm down? Tis, release him."*

A bolt of sympathy shot through Victor at her brittle tone. Dealing with their sisters was like handling a bunch of kids on a sugar high. He was surprised she hadn't walloped one of them yet.

"Are we sure this is Ladon?" Theo murmured uncertainly.

Victor could understand his lover's wariness.

The lizard positively vibrating with indignation on Cassius's coffee table did not look in the least bit like a powerful divine guardian.

Ladon peeled his banana aggressively and munched on the fruit.

"*Five hundred yearsss of peace and quiet all gone,*" he grumbled under his breath. "*And I'd finally tamed Kujo too. Dumb imp and dumb Goddessss.*"

"*Hey, we can hear you,*" Kes said sharply.

"*Who's Kujo?*" Tisiphone asked Eden, nonplussed.

"A Komodo dragon." She made a face. "They were in the same enclosure, although I suspect the zookeepers didn't know Ladon was there too."

"Tamed?" Loki sneered at the lizard. "That didn't look like tamed. In fact, I'm pretty sure Kujo would have violated you had we not intervened."

"*Ssshut up!*" Ladon huffed out a trail of smoke and flicked his tail irritably. "*I had the sssituation under control!*"

Atropos watched the dragon for a moment. "*How long were you hiding there for?*"

Ladon did not meet her eyes. "*Twelve yearsss. I was elsssewhere before that.*"

Atropos exchanged a cautious glance with the rest of them. "*Menippe said she saw you in the Astrea Sea briefly before you ended up on Earth.*" She hesitated. "*Did *you not make your presence known to the otherworldly here because you were scared?"*

Ladon stiffened at Atropos's guarded question. For a second, Victor thought he would snap at the Goddess.

The dragon slumped despondently. *"I saw Erytheisss perish as I fell."* His voice quavered. *"Even though we had gone into hiding at your behessst, we were aware many of the alliesss we once trusssted had sssided with that evil God of Darknessss during the war. I...didn't know who to trusssst."*

Remorse tightened Victor's chest at his words.

Atropos gently lifted Ladon into her hand. *"I'm sorry about Erytheis, child."* She stroked his head gently, sorrow darkening her eyes. *"It is my fault you lost your mother."*

Ladon clutched her thumb and shook his head.

"I do not blame you, Goddessss," he mumbled forlornly. *"You were only acting for the good of everyone."*

"We need to locate the Garden of the West, Ladon. Can you help us?"

The dragon stared at the Moira, confused.

Atropos leaned her face close to him, her expression hardening and her pupils flaring gold. *"We have to find your mothers Hesperia and Arethusa and the Sacred Tree they guard. It is the only way to save Ivmir."*

Ladon tensed. *"Ivmir?"*

"Elios had Alecto poison Ivmir with Tenebra's Rot. He's dying as we speak. His only chance of survival may lie in a Golden Apple," Atropos explained.

"We've been looking for our sisters, but to no avail," Tisiphone said. *"Do you know where they are?"*

"*I—*"

Ladon stopped, his head and tail drooping. He froze a second later.

Cassius had stepped out of his and Morgan's bedroom. His shoulders sagged as he quietly closed the door behind him.

He ran his fingers through his hair before looking over at them.

"Hey."

Pain squeezed Victor's heart at his drained expression. He wished he could wipe away the shadows under Cassius's eyes. That he could tell him everything was going to be okay.

Victor clenched his jaw. Not only had he failed his best friend, he'd failed his brother too. He knew deep down inside that he couldn't have stopped Alecto and Megaera even if he had sacrificed his life to save Morgan. Nevertheless, he felt responsible for what had happened to the demigod in Ivory Peaks.

He'd promised his brother he would protect him, come what may.

He hadn't unburdened himself of the guilt he still carried, but that was the last thing Cassius needed to hear right now.

Theo's sorrow echoed across their soul bond. Victor met his lover's beautiful gaze. Theo's fingers tightened around his where he clasped his hand.

"I'm here," he whispered.

Victor knew he'd read his mind. He took a shuddering breath and fought back the tears choking his breath, forever grateful for the man beside him.

"*A—Awakener?!*" Ladon squeaked.

The dragon bolted from the table and shot across the room. He scaled Cassius's leg in the blink of an eye, startling him.

"*Awakener!*" Ladon cried. "*I—I thought you dead!*"

He shuddered where he clung to Cassius's chest.

Cassius's pupils widened. He gazed incredulously at Tisiphone. "Is this—?!"

The Fury bobbed her head. "*Eden and Loki found him.*" She frowned. "*Or rather, their weapons did.*"

The Goddess told him about the plan they'd come up with in his absence and Eden, Loki, and Kes's trip to Philadelphia. Cassius looked positively dazed at that. He patted the dragon awkwardly and came over to sit beside Atropos.

"I'm sorry," he said guiltily. "I didn't realize I'd slept for so long."

"*You needed the rest,*" Atropos said firmly.

"How's Morgan?" Eden asked hesitantly in the hush that followed.

"He's...the same." Cassius fisted his hands. "He hasn't gotten any worse, thanks to you." A weak smile curved his mouth as he studied the Goddesses in the room. It faded a little when he looked at the lizard sniveling and hanging on to him. "Ladon, I know a lot has happened today, but we need your help."

He picked the lizard up gently and raised him in his hand.

Ladon gazed dejectedly at Cassius when he brought him to eye level. "*I wasss going to asssk the sssame of you,*"

Awakener. You are the only one who can help me find my way back to my mothersss."

Dread tightened Cassius's face. "You do not know where they are?"

"They are in Argent Lake. But it will not be easssy to track them down."

Atropos and her sisters recoiled.

"Impossible!" Kes snapped. *"We scoured that realm for months and found no trace of them!"*

"They are in Argent Lake," Ladon insisted stubbornly. *"In a place no one can accessss."* He met Cassius's confused stare. *"None sssave the Awakener, I believe."*

"Why do you think this?" Atropos asked, stunned.

"Becaussse he isss the grandson of the Goddessss of all Nymphsss. He isss of Nephele'sss bloodline. Only he can sssing the Sssong of the Evening Ssstar."

"The Song of the Evening Star?" Victor repeated with a faint frown.

"It is the Hesperides' song," Atropos mumbled. *"Of course! Why didn't I think of this?!"*

Ladon swung his tail agitatedly. *"Only my mothersss and thossse of Nephele'sss dessscent can sssing the Sssong of the Evening Ssstar. It can reveal the Garden of the Wessst."*

CHAPTER TWENTY-NINE

THE WATERS OF ARGENT LAKE GLITTERED LIKE LIQUID silver beneath Cassius as he arrowed toward the pale wall filling the horizon. He glanced over his shoulder at the glimmering city fading on the dark shores behind them. His gut tightened.

Not for the first time, he wondered if he should have left Morgan in the capital.

"Do not worry, Awakener. He is in safe hands."

Cassius's gaze shifted to the figure easily keeping pace with him and Atropos.

The translucent, blue wings of the queen of the Naiads were almost invisible in the moonlight as she flew beside them, her breathtakingly beautiful face set in a serious expression.

"I wish we had more time to talk. Maybe after all this is over, we can do so." The Goddess met Cassius and Atropos's eyes guardedly before looking down to where four Naiads carefully carried Morgan in a net

woven from gossamer threads as strong as steel. *"But first, we must save Ivmir."*

"Thank you for agreeing so quickly to our request, Daphne," Atropos said gratefully. *"We have much to catch up on, like you say. And a war to prepare for."*

Daphne furrowed her brow. *"We have all been waiting for the call, Atropos. We will be ready when the time comes."*

Cassius and Atropos exchanged a guarded look.

It seems our allies have been biding their time too.

His heart throbbed as he studied Morgan's pale face where he slept huddled in a nest of blankets. He knew the slumber the demigod had fallen into was unnatural. Still, despite Atropos's misgivings on the matter, Cassius had insisted Morgan come with them to Argent Lake.

He didn't need to voice what he'd sensed with every passing hour since his return from the Astrea Sea. They could all see it in Morgan's rapidly aging body, just as he felt it in the dulling bond that connected their soul cores.

Time was running out. Tenebra's Rot had almost conquered the demigod's soul core.

Every second gained is vital. Cassius clenched his jaw. *Besides, I promised never to leave his side again.*

He felt movement inside his armor. Ladon popped his head out the top of his chest piece. The dragon clung grimly to the Stark Steel and squinted in the wind as he sniffed the air.

"We are getting close."

Cassius narrowed his eyes at the dense bank of fog they were approaching. It had arisen after the Nether had torn and split Argent Lake five hundred years ago. The extensive area it covered was forbidden to the Naiads, as per the decree passed by Daphne shortly after the disaster had struck their kingdom.

Though Atropos and her sisters had searched the banned region extensively during their secret visits to the realm, they had never found any evidence of Hesperia and Arethusa's presence. Same for Daphne and her soldiers. After the war had ended, the Naiads had tried in vain to locate the Hesperides they owed their lives to.

Daphne stared at Ladon. *"I still can't believe that's the dragon."*

A soft smile curved Atropos's mouth as she glanced at Ladon's lizard form. *"He grows on you."*

Guilt stabbed Cassius's chest as he recalled their hasty departure from Earth an hour ago. Theo and Victor were dismayed he'd insisted they stay back in San Francisco this time around, as was everyone else. Though there had been no sign of Elios, nor the Black Fate and Furies he controlled, Cassius couldn't take the risk of something happening in his and Atropos's absence. He'd finally convinced them of this, but hadn't been able to dispel their harried expressions.

Strickland and Morgan's team had insisted on being present before they'd set off through Theo's portal. Adrianne had cried openly while silent tears soaked the others' cheeks. Though no one had said the words out loud, they'd known this could be their last time seeing Morgan alive.

Cassius clenched his fists as they closed in on the mantle of mist covering the lake. He refused to believe he could not save Morgan.

They entered the fog and were rapidly swallowed by a silence that deafened all sounds and pale billows that obscured their vision. Bluish orbs bloomed above them, Daphne wielding her divine powers to create beacons so they would not lose sight of one another. The lake appeared in faint patches where the cloud cover broke below.

The tomb-like shroud started to thin after they'd travelled some three leagues. Cassius's breath caught as they shot out of the white mist and entered an open area some two miles wide.

Like the eye of a storm, the air here was clear and the sky above visible.

Dotting the silver waters beneath them were the remains of islands that had been decimated when the realm had ripped open, their residents forever lost to the depths of the lake.

Remorse constricted Cassius's throat at the sight of them. Though he realized Elios was ultimately at fault for the Nether tearing, it was his Awakener powers that had dealt the deadly blow to every realm connected to it.

"*Mother*," Ladon mumbled.

Atropos frowned. A muscle twitched in Daphne's cheek.

Cassius could tell from the sorrow radiating from the dragon and the Goddesses that this was where Erytheis had lost her life saving Argent Lake.

"*Where to, Ladon?*" Atropos asked in a hard voice.

"*There.*" Ladon indicated a dark dot drifting in and out of sight behind a low bank of clouds dead west. "*That was where we originally hid the Garden of the West.*"

The speck grew into an isle that soared out of the lake to form a plateau ringed by cliffs. It was carved in part by a jagged crevasse that split it all the way down to the dark waters below.

Cassius's stomach plummeted when they landed near the center of the island.

Bar a dead poplar tree, the landscape was barren, the soil still bearing the dark scars of the heavenly fires that had rained down upon it.

"Are you sure this is the right place?" he asked Ladon.

The dragon hopped out of his armor and landed on the ground with a soft plop. "*Yesss!*"

He darted ahead, his snout raised as he sought something only he could sense.

Cassius stiffened. His pulse quickened in the next instant. He could feel a faint energy close by. One that smelled strangely familiar. From Atropos's uncertain expression, she had not detected it.

He turned to Daphne. "Can you and your escort stay here and guard Morgan?"

The Naiad Goddess nodded graciously. "*Of course.*"

Cassius walked over to where Morgan lay under the poplar. He crouched on one knee and leaned down to kiss his lover's brow. Agony twisted his insides when his lips touched cold skin.

The fever that had afflicted Morgan since his return from Ivory Peaks had finally abated. Cassius wished he could interpret this as a positive sign. Except he knew it wasn't.

"I'll be back soon, my love," he whispered shakily. "Wait for me."

Morgan remained lifeless, eyes closed and face waxen. He was barely recognizable as the powerful demigod he had once been.

Cassius's nails bit into his palms as he rose and whirled away. *I swear on everything that I am. I will save you!*

He and Atropos found Ladon on a boulder a quarter of a mile from the poplar tree, close to the chasm that split the island. The dragon's tail twitched agitatedly as he gazed at the arid plain before them.

"*There's nothing here,*" Atropos said in a troubled voice.

Ladon looked beseechingly at Cassius. "*You can sense it, can you not?*"

Atropos looked between them, puzzled.

Cassius dipped his chin, the sound of the waves at the bottom of the gully faint in his ears. The strange force he'd picked up on when they'd landed on the island had gotten stronger.

Relief had Ladon drooping.

Recognition washed over Cassius like a warm summer breeze in the next moment. His eyes widened.

The power he was discerning smelled like Rain

Vale, his home and the place of his birth. It was the divine energy of the Nymphs.

"There is something here," Cassius murmured. "Something we cannot yet see."

His heart slammed heavily against his ribs. He hesitated before raising a hand, instinct guiding his movements. Heaven's Light flared on his fingertips.

It sparked when it made contact with an invisible wall some twenty feet away.

Atropos sucked in air. *"It's a barrier!"*

Cassius followed the path of the flashes fading above them, his chest lightening as hope surged inside him. "It's a dome. This is what the Hesperides erected to protect the location of the Garden of the West!"

"Yesss!" Ladon confirmed excitedly. *"I wasss ejected from it when the Nether tore!"*

"But why could my sisters and I not detect it?" Atropos mumbled. *"We should have been able to sense our sisters' souls through the bond that connects us, regardless of the presence of this shield."*

Cassius frowned. "I guess we're about to find out."

He walked over to the invisible wall, placed his hand upon it, and closed his eyes. Heat flooded his body as he drew on his divine powers. The words Ladon had taught him before they'd left Earth rose in his mind while he infused the barrier with the energy of the Nymph Goddess whose blood flowed in his veins.

Cassius opened his mouth and started chanting the Song of the Evening Star.

"Listen to the wind soughing through the branches of this most hallowed realm, Listen to the song of the Graceful Maidens born of Eos and Hesperus, They who guard the Garden of the West, the Sacred Tree, and its Golden Fruits, They who dance under the Setting Sun and above the Rising Moon, They who are Dazzling Light, Sunset Glow, Nymphs of Red and Gold."

Atropos's gasp had his eyes slamming open.

The shield was solidifying into a translucent wall. Shimmering in and out of view beyond it was a resplendent garden full of rich, fruit-laden greenery and gurgling brooks. Soaring in its midst atop a low hill in the distance, glowing as bright as a sun, was the Sacred Tree.

Ladon leaned forward, his pupils flaring gold as his soul core started absorbing the divine force it had long been deprived of. *"Don't ssstop, Awakener! You are almossst there!"*

Cassius focused on the rest of the song.

"Listen to the wind soughing through the branches of this most hallowed realm, Listen to the song of the Graceful Maidens born of Eos and Hesperus, Follow the Moonbeams to the Poplar, The Elm, and the Willow Tree, For it is there that the Daughters of the Evening Star await the dawn of a New Day, So they can dance under the Sunlight once more, until the Dragon swallows the Moon."

Arcane symbols flashed into life around his hand. They moved and merged, forming lines that demarcated an opening. The section of the wall they outlined faded to nothingness.

The heavenly scents of the Garden of the West

assailed Cassius's nostrils. Ladon darted through the revealed entrance.

"*Wait!*" Atropos warned.

A golden arrow hissed through the air and skewered Ladon's tail as he raced across the verdant ground. The dragon screeched and fell over.

CHAPTER THIRTY

Cassius and Atropos moved as one.

The Moira blocked the second arrow that would have pierced Ladon's head, the shaft clinking harmlessly off the armor now covering her from the neck down. Her eyes narrowed behind the winged helmet framing her face and covering her flowing, silver hair.

Cassius blasted away the hail of golden shafts raining down upon them with a powerful swing of his light-wreathed sword. His gaze found their attackers as the arrows stabbed the ground and shrubs around them.

Floating high above them, their wings blazing with the same dazzling light emanating from the Sacred Tree on the ridge to the west, were two armored Goddesses with golden bows and quivers loaded with arrows. They glared at Cassius and Atropos, their animosity palpable.

Dread sent a chill down his spine. "Are they under Elios's control?!"

Atropos shook her head, her expression growing perturbed. "*No. Now that we are inside the barrier, I can sense their soul cores. They are full of hatred and anger. That's what was obscuring our bond with them. They have,*" she paused and fisted her hands on her blades, "*—I'm afraid Hesperia and Arethusa have lost their minds to grief and rage!*" She turned, dropped to one knee, and gently removed the arrow from Ladon's tail, remorse tightening her face. "*Do not move from here, child. We shall handle this.*"

She hovered a hand above him. A translucent shield formed around the dragon.

Ladon lifted his head and peered forlornly at the angry deities above them. "*What is wrong with my mothersss? Why do they not recognize me?!*"

A wretched look darkened Atropos's eyes. "*They are not of sound reason, child. Hush now. We—*"

The hairs rose on Cassius's nape. A grunt left him as something powerful smashed into him.

"*Icarus!*" Atropos barked.

Arethusa plowed into the Moira and sent her flying into the barrier.

Wood and foliage exploded around Cassius. Hesperia was carving a path through the garden with his body as she carried him farther inside the dome, her fingers squeezing his throat and her golden eyes full of madness. Her bow shifted into a broadsword.

He cursed and blocked her strike with his gauntlet when she swung the blade.

We don't have time for this!

Cassius blinded the enraged Goddess with a burst of Heaven's Light, peeled her hand from his neck, and shot away from her.

"Come to your senses!" he shouted, Icarus's presence rising inside him. *"It is I, Icarus, grandson of Nephele! I am not your enemy!"*

Hesperia roared and charged him. Cassius gasped as she locked her arms around his chest and plummeted toward the chasm that split the island at inhuman speed.

The wind whistled coldly in his ears as gloom engulfed them. Cassius tried to free himself of the Goddess's tenacious hold as the walls of the gully soared around them at a vertiginous rate. The sound of crashing waves grew below. Then, he was in the water.

Hesperia rose and vanished swiftly as he sank beneath the cold surface of the lake.

An avalanche of boulders dropped toward him in the next instant. Hesperia had smashed the walls of the ravine to bury him in a tomb of water and stone.

Cassius swore, unleashed Heaven's Light, and ascended inside a dazzling sphere of power, debris bouncing harmlessly off his shield.

Surprise rounded Hesperia's eyes when he emerged from the lake. Her sword shifted back into a bow where she hovered above the gorge. She reached for a dozen arrows and aimed them squarely at him with a focused frown.

Her fingers froze on the string when the air suddenly shimmered gold.

Atropos had unleashed her full powers.

Cassius soared out of the chasm and spotted her where she clashed swords with Arethusa.

"*Snap out of it, Are!*" Atropos snarled at the Hesperis. "*We mean you no harm!*"

Arethusa blinked. Awareness flitted in her gaze for an instant as her sister's divine energy washed across her skin. It was replaced by incandescent wrath.

"*We shall not be so easily fooled, puppet of Elios!*" she growled. "*Tell your dark God he will not get his evil hands on the Sacred Tree!*"

Hesperia bared her teeth and attacked Cassius. Frustration churned his stomach as he deflected and parried her strikes. He dared not counter for fear of hurting her.

Arethusa's scream tore the air a moment later.

Hesperia jolted to a stop and whipped around. Terror drained the blood from her face.

Arethusa's blade was on the ground. Atropos had the Hesperis by the throat and had placed her hand upon her forehead.

"*REMEMBER!*" Atropos bellowed, her eyes bright. "*Remember who you are, sister!*"

Arethusa choked and convulsed, her pupils flaring as Atropos smashed through the rage clouding her judgement with her powers of divinity.

"*NOOOO!*" Hesperia howled.

The force that detonated around the Hesperis shoved Cassius back some dozen feet. She darted toward Atropos and Arethusa, the air around her vibrating with divine wrath. The arrows in her quiver rose so as to pierce her enemy at will even as she loaded her bow with a dozen others.

Cassius dove after her and prepared to unleash an attack.

"*Stop.*"

The word, though spoken quietly, made the dome tremble with its potent power and stilled the battle as effectively as a bucket of cold water. It bore echoes of three voices.

"*Please, mothers. I cannot bear to see you like this!*"

Cassius slowed and looked down. His eyes widened. Straining under the barrier that Atropos had erected to protect him was a giant, three-headed dragon.

With his soul core replenished, Ladon had assumed his original form once more. Golden tears slipped down his tortured faces as he gazed at Hesperia and Arethusa.

Hesperia's bow fell from her grasp. Her arrows tumbled to the ground.

Recognition flared in her pupils. "*La—Ladon?!*"

Atropos hesitated before slowly releasing Arethusa. Awareness was returning to the Hesperis's face once more.

"*Attie?*" Arethusa mumbled.

Shock replaced her blind fury. The Goddess gasped when she saw Ladon. She joined Hesperia as the latter winged her way rapidly toward the dragon.

"*Ladon! Ladon!*" the Goddesses cried as they hugged and kissed their child.

"*Mothers!*" Ladon whimpered. "*It is good to see you again!*"

His massive tail thumped the ground enthusiastically as he licked them with all three tongues.

Hesperia sobbed at the sight of his bleeding wound. *"I'm so sorry, my child!"*

She moved to his back and touched his injury lightly. Golden radiance flared around her hand.

Cassius drew a sharp breath when she lifted her fingers from the dragon. Ladon's wound had healed.

Is this the power they hold from living close to the Sacred Tree?!

His pulse raced as he headed toward them, Atropos converging on the two Goddesses and Ladon from the opposite direction. Hesperia and Arethusa looked around when they landed beside them.

Remorse darkened Hesperia's eyes as she stared at them, pale-faced. *"We could not see who you were in our rage."*

"Forgive us, Attie, Awakener," Arethusa mumbled, similarly repentant.

"It is alright, sisters," Atropos said briskly. *"You must pardon our haste. Though we have much to talk about, time is of the essence right now. Can you spare a Golden Apple for Ivmir?!"*

Hesperia and Arethusa startled.

"A Golden Apple?" Arethusa repeated.

"Yes." Cassius stepped forward, tension knotting his shoulders. "Ivmir is dying of Tenebra's Rot. Atropos believes the only thing that can save him is the fruit of the Sacred Tree."

Hesperia and Arethusa exchanged a troubled look.

"*Come*," Hesperia said in a flat voice.

Cassius's heart sank at her tone. He and Atropos followed the Hesperides as they flew toward the hill at the center of the garden and the bright tree crowning it, Ladon trailing ponderously in their wake.

It took a moment for him to discern the golden branches and leaves soughing in the wind when they landed beneath the Sacred Tree. Fear drained all the strength from his limbs.

"No," Cassius mumbled in denial.

He would have fallen to his knees had Atropos not grabbed his arm and steadied him.

The tree was empty but for its dazzling foliage.

Cassius barely heard Hesperia's despondent words above the loud buzzing in his ears.

"*It has been fifty years since the last crop of apples sprouted. Alas, it will be another one hundred and fifty before the next harvest.*"

"*Did you not use to keep them?*" Atropos asked, horrified.

"*We did. But with both Ladon and Erytheis gone, our ability to preserve them was severely reduced,*" Arethusa replied wretchedly.

She crouched and carefully parted the tall grass masking the base of the tree.

Carved into the trunk was a hollow chamber holding the last crop of Golden Apples. They were a dull yellow and had lost their sheen. Most had crumbled, their remains slowly returning to the hallowed source from which they had been born.

"No!" Cassius choked out. Tears blurred his vision.

The agony searing his heart was so deep he wished it would strike him down. "This cannot be!" His desperate gaze shifted to a pale-faced Atropos. "Does this mean there is no way to save Ivmir?!"

"I—"

Atropos paused, her features crunching up in a miserable expression. A fraught silence descended between them.

Something fell lightly on Cassius's head. He reached up and touched it distractedly.

It was a golden leaf.

Another spiraled down to his feet.

CHAPTER THIRTY-ONE

Hesperia startled. *"Ladon?!"*

The dragon had his faces buried in the Sacred Tree's tallest branches.

"There is still one," he said excitedly. *"I can smell it!"*

"You can?!" Arethusa gasped, stunned. *"But it's been so long since the last apple sprouted!"*

Hope burst into life inside Cassius, bringing with it a rush of adrenaline that quickened his pulse.

"A-ha!"

Ladon pushed his heads deeper inside the foliage. He straightened a moment later.

"Thank the Gods," Atropos whispered.

Cassius shuddered. Grasped gently in the jaws of the dragon's middle head was a glowing object.

Ladon lowered his neck and carefully dropped it in Cassius's hands. *"It is the last fruit of the Sacred Tree. Use it well, Awakener."*

Blood pounded heavily in Cassius's veins as he

beheld the dazzling apple. It was lighter than he'd thought it would be.

"*Well done, child.*" Hesperia patted the dragon's flank proudly. "*You were always the best at harvesting them.*"

Ladon made a pleased sound and puffed out some smoke.

"*Go!*" Atropos told Cassius urgently. "*We shall be right behind you.*"

Cassius nodded jerkily. He rose above the Sacred Tree and darted toward the dome's exit. He was outside the garden in a couple of heartbeats.

It took but a moment to reach the poplar tree.

But it was a moment too late.

The Naiads' abject cries reached him on the balmy wind blowing off Argent Lake just as the thin cord connecting his and Morgan's cores snapped.

No!

The denial ripped through his mind as the tree came into view.

Cassius's gaze skimmed the woeful Goddess and her distressed escort before settling fearfully on the figure swaddled in the blankets between them. He landed awkwardly under the tree, his eyes locked on the demigod who was everything to him.

Morgan lay deathly still in the moonlight streaming through the bare branches, his features devoid of the pain that had scored lines into his face in the past two days.

"*I am sorry, Icarus.*" Daphne's eyes gleamed wetly. "*He took his last breath but an instant ago.*"

Cassius fell numbly to his knees. The apple dropped

from his limp hand. It thudded onto the ground with a thump that seemed to mock him.

"You can't do this to me." He grasped Morgan's shoulders. Terror had him digging his fingers painfully into his dead lover's flesh. "Do you hear? *YOU CANNOT LEAVE ME, IVMIR!*"

His scream made the island tremble and tore the clouds asunder. Heaven's Light engulfed Argent Lake as his powers burst forth from his core.

"*Icarus!*" Daphne shouted, alarmed.

"*It's okay, Daphne,*" Atropos called out, her voice quaking with grief.

Cassius was barely aware of the Moira's presence as she and the Hesperides alighted next to him. The hot tears that fell from his eyes soaked into Morgan's cooling skin as they splashed upon his slack face. Rage flooded his heart. Elios's scornful expression rose before his mind's eye.

"*Awakener,*" Atropos warned when she sensed his bubbling wrath.

It took all of Cassius's willpower to dampen the incandescent force threatening to explode from his body. He took an unsteady breath, swallowed his anger, and stared blindly at the dazzling night sky above for a timeless moment before looking wretchedly upon Morgan's pallid features.

What would he do?

The answer came to him with a suddenness that made him curse himself.

"He wouldn't give up!" Cassius mumbled angrily.

He grasped the Golden Apple, tore away a chunk of

it with his teeth, and lifted Morgan into his arms. The sweet juices of the fruit of resurrection filled his mouth as he placed his lips over his lover's. Cassius pressed his hand upon Morgan's belly.

I believe! I believe in you, Ivmir! I believe in us!

Power poured from his fingertips and his lungs, his feelings for the demigod he held focusing the divine energy he possessed into a lance-like force that pierced the dead soul core that had been connected to his own. He fed Morgan the chunk of the Golden Apple and pushed it down his throat.

"I refuse to let you die!" Cassius growled. "Do you hear me?! *So, live, damn you!*"

He bit off another chunk of the Golden Apple and repeated the process, his fingers sinking ever deeper into Morgan's stomach.

"*Icarus,*" Atropos said miserably.

"He's not gone," Cassius insisted in a hard voice. "I did not give him permission to leave me. So, he isn't gone."

Regret. Hope. Fear.

They swamped his mind and his soul. But rising above them all, more powerful than anything he feared would drown him, was the absolute and irrevocable love he felt for Ivmir. It was a bond carved into their very history. One he himself had sealed, the night Ivmir first came to him and claimed his everything.

Memories flooded Cassius's consciousness as he fed Morgan another piece of the Golden Apple and imbued his cooling soul core with his own life force.

Of Ivmir's first touch.

His first kiss.

The first time he had merged their bodies together and taught Icarus such devastating physical pleasure he could only weep from it.

And he remembered what he'd done at first light, when he'd awoken in Ivmir's arms and gazed upon his hauntingly beautiful face in the pale dawn. The spell he'd whispered while Ivmir still slept. An enchantment that would bind their souls forever more. One born of his unique abilities.

One he knew remained alive to this day, deep within the body of the lifeless demigod.

"Awaken, Ivmir," Cassius whispered tremulously. *"Awaken, my beloved."*

Something sparked deep inside him. He felt the corresponding flash within the fresh corpse he held.

Thump.

Cassius froze, uncertain whether he'd imagined the pulse he'd just sensed.

Thump. Thump-thump. Thump-thump.

A sob fell from his lips when the rhythm steadied itself and grew in strength, the divine energy contained within the Golden Apple finally taking effect as he guided it to the revived soul it needed to mend. Heat flared under his fingertips. Morgan's core started repairing itself under the fruit's healing power of resurrection.

The demigod swallowed audibly.

Cassius unfroze, sank his teeth into what remained of the apple, and eagerly pushed another chunk past his lover's lips. Morgan slowly chewed and gulped.

"He—he lives!" Daphne gasped. *"By the Gods, Ivmir lives!"*

Atropos fell to her knees beside Cassius, silver tears coursing freely down her cheeks. Hesperia and Arethusa sobbed behind her. Ladon sniveled and wailed.

Color returned to Morgan's face. His chest shuddered into life, his ribcage rising and falling powerfully as he inhaled and exhaled. His hair darkened. His wrinkles vanished. His body swelled, his muscles and bones regaining their original mass and strength.

An incoherent sound left Cassius when Morgan's eyelids fluttered open. His irises shifted from the milky color that had rendered him blind to the deep cobalt of his demigod form before changing to the achingly bewitching turquoise he knew and loved.

"I...*carus*," Morgan mumbled.

He flashed Cassius a dazzling smile, grasped his face, and sealed their lips together, his touch so hot it seared Cassius's skin.

Cassius kissed him back just as ardently, his heart thundering painfully against his ribs. The wild beat was echoed by the strong one he felt against his chest when Morgan sat up and took him in his arms. He gasped, the world blurring around him.

Morgan had flipped him onto his back.

Cassius trembled with joy and pleasure as Morgan hitched his right leg around his hip and enthusiastically mated their tongues together, not a sliver of space left between their sweetly straining bodies. For a moment, he forgot all about the Goddesses, the Naiads, and even the dragon watching them.

"*Does Ivmir not see us?*" Daphne asked Atropos in a worried voice while the Naiads giggled.

Atropos sighed. "*I don't think he cares.*"

"*That poor Awakener is going to be ravished before our very eyes,*" Ladon murmured with all the avid curiosity of an eighty-ton dragon.

Cassius finally wrenched his mouth free from Morgan's, ears flaming and face flushed, the bond between their soul cores so strong and bright he was surprised no one could see it.

"Morgan! We have company!" he berated in a low hiss, his embarrassed gaze darting to their audience.

Morgan grumbled something indistinct before scowling at the group observing them with bated breath. The newly arisen demigod looked terribly annoyed by the presence of their eager onlookers.

"How about you ladies take a hike?" he told the four Goddesses and the smirking Naiads sullenly. He squinted at Ladon. "You too, lizard."

Ladon sucked in air before huffing smoke out of his snouts. "*How rude!*"

CHAPTER THIRTY-TWO

D AWN WAS BREAKING ACROSS S AN F RANCISCO WHEN they emerged from the portal that connected Earth to Argent Lake. Morgan inhaled deeply and closed his eyes for a moment as the first rays of the sun touched his face, a deep sense of relief coursing through him at the same time the crisp scent of the ocean filled his nostrils.

I never thought I'd see this city again.

To his everlasting surprise, the queen of the Naiads had kissed his cheek gently when they'd bidden each other goodbye in front of the gateway she'd opened in the gardens of her palace.

"Look after Icarus, will you?" Daphne had murmured. *"He...went through a lot tonight."*

"I know," Morgan had said quietly.

He'd looked over to where Cassius and Atropos were saying farewell to the red-eyed Hesperides and Ladon. Having accidentally crushed a fountain when he'd landed in the grounds of the palace, the dragon was looking sheepish and doing his best to keep still while a crowd of Naiad attendants hovered around him in awe, their blue wings shimmering under the starlight and their limpid eyes full of admiration for his majestic form.

Though the last two days had felt like a dream, one Morgan had been afraid he would never wake from, he was deeply conscious of the fact that Cassius had achieved the impossible, back on the island where the Hesperides had hidden the Garden of the West.

Though they were called fruits of resurrection, the Golden Apples didn't work on corpses.

It was Cassius who had sparked his soul into life once more, enough for the Golden Apple he had fed him to fully revive him.

Even Atropos appeared troubled by that fact, the furtive looks she kept stealing at Cassius full of questions. Though humans believed death was beyond Gods, deities were just as liable to meet their demise at the hands of a power greater than their own. Morgan knew Cassius would talk to him about what he'd done one day, when this was all over.

The terrace doors slid open behind them. Morgan turned. Victor came out. Shadows ringed the demigod's eyes. He looked like he hadn't slept in days.

He froze at the sight of them.

Morgan startled when he rushed over and closed his arms tightly around him.

"We'll give you some space," Cassius said with a soft smile.

He squeezed Morgan's hand and headed inside with Atropos. Cries of joy erupted in the apartment.

"You look like shit," Victor mumbled in Morgan's ear.

Morgan's insides twisted. Victor was trembling slightly.

"Oh yeah?" He hugged the demigod back just as hard before pulling away and studying his wan face critically. "Well, you don't look so hot either."

Victor smiled weakly. There was a darkness in the depths of his eyes. One Morgan knew was tied to the guilt he still carried from the recent fight in Ivory Peaks.

"You know you did everything you could, right?" he said in a low voice.

Victor stiffened. A muscle jumped in his jawline. He did not meet Morgan's questioning gaze.

Morgan blew out a sigh. "Sacrificing yourself would have achieved nothing, Victor." He made a face. "Besides, can you imagine how much grief Cassius and Theo would have given me if you'd died?"

A genuine smile tilted Victor's mouth at that.

They went inside and found Theo and Loki sobbing in Cassius's arms, having jumped on him and pushed him to the ground the second he'd entered the room. Eden was blubbering into a tissue next to them.

"This is turning into a goddamn soap opera," Morgan muttered.

The apartment door slammed open. Adrianne rushed in ahead of Strickland and the rest of Morgan's team.

"And it's about to get worse," Victor said wryly.

The sorceress froze when she saw him. "Mor—*Morgan?!*"

Her face crumpled. She burst into tears and bolted into his arms.

Morgan rocked back on his heels before straightening and patting her back awkwardly, his chest tight with emotion. He'd barely been aware of his surroundings after he'd returned from Ivory Peaks, Tenebra's Rot numbing most of his senses. Seeing how everyone was reacting to his miraculous recovery made him realize not just how much he'd missed out on, but how dearly he was cherished.

He felt Cassius's gaze on him. The luminous smile the demigod flashed at him as he climbed to his feet and pulled a red-faced Theo and Loki up made Morgan's belly clench with need.

All he wanted to do right now was take Cassius to bed and make love to him until he cried with pleasure. Morgan pursed his lips.

I wonder which deity I have to pray to to get that to happen?

Cassius's smile faded a little. He narrowed his eyes, like he'd just read Morgan's mind.

Morgan chuckled. Cassius blinked.

"I love you," Morgan mouthed silently.

Color stained Cassius's cheeks. His beautiful eyes sparkled with promise.

Morgan's soul core tingled. There was something different about the bond that connected them now. It felt more...sensitive. Stronger even.

He'd become more attuned to Cassius's emotions even before they'd left Argent Lake, just as Cassius had seemingly gotten more responsive to his. A thrill shot through Morgan as he contemplated the full implications of that observation. Would it mean sex between them would be even better than before? Though how that could even be possible he didn't know.

"Get your mind out of the gutter, brother," Kes scoffed. *"We can literally see you undressing Icarus with your eyes."*

Cassius blushed even harder.

Loki sniffed and squinted at Morgan. "I fear Cassius won't be able to walk for a week after he's done with him."

Cassius groaned.

"How about you shut it, you damn imp?" Morgan growled.

It was mid-morning when Strickland and Morgan's team finally left. Jasper, Reuben, and Brianna had dropped by before taking their leave too. Morgan and Cassius had promised to let them know their next course of action once they'd decided upon it.

"So, what *is* our next move?" Victor asked as Cassius handed him a fresh coffee.

"We rescue our sisters," Atropos replied in a hard voice from where she perched on a kitchen stool.

Tisiphone, Kes, and Orena exchanged a determined look.

The surviving Hesperides and Ladon had wanted to help them free Tenebra and the other Goddesses from the Seventh Purgatory. Atropos had insisted they remain in Argent Lake. Even though Cassius had used the last Golden Apple to revive Morgan, she didn't want to risk Elios finding the Sacred Tree. Cassius had concurred.

Daphne had promised to increase security in her realm so as to be able to pick up on any minute intrusion Elios might make into her kingdom.

"But how do we find the Seventh Purgatory?" Loki's tail snapped the air with fitful jerks. He addressed Atropos anxiously. "I tried to uncover the path to it with the Eternity Key in your absence, but you were right. Elios is hiding it from my eyes too."

"Even I cannot open a portal there," Theo confessed with a troubled frown.

"*There* is *a way to trace a path to where Elios is concealing the Seventh Purgatory.*" Atropos ran a hand through her hair and sighed. "*It won't be easy but it's about the only thing I can think of.*"

Eden leaned forward. "What is it?"

"*We can follow the echo of the Sword of Wind.*"

Morgan startled. Cassius's eyes rounded.

"*Remember I told you Morgan could manifest the sword at will?*" Atropos explained tensely. "*Now that his soul core is revived, he should be able to draw the weapon. He should also be able to sense where it is if it has already materialized elsewhere.*"

Theo drew a sharp breath. "He can track down the soul thread that connects him to it!"

Atropos dipped her head. "*Exactly.*"

Morgan pressed a hand to his belly. He could feel a

faint tug whenever he thought of the weapon bonded to him.

He furrowed his brow. "Won't Elios find out I'm alive and well again if I do that?"

"*He might suspect this already,*" Atropos confirmed. "*His ability to wield the Sword of Wind would have manifested the instant you died. Since Cassius revived you within minutes, Elios would only have been able to use the Sword of Wind for that brief moment in time. But we still have a problem.*"

Victor clenched his jaw. "Even if we find the Seventh Purgatory, we might not be able to get inside it."

"*Yes.*" Frustration tightened Atropos's face. "*Though Hypnos is no longer around, Elios's powers have grown so much from absorbing our divine energy over the centuries that he's made entrance to the Purgatory virtually impossible. And he is bound to have an even bigger army of war demons and Nephilim guarding the Goddesses imprisoned there.*"

Someone spoke in the gloomy silence that befell them. "*I can probably help with that.*"

Eden jumped. Morgan's pulse skittered. Loki whirled around and almost fell off his stool.

The Reaper God was standing by the terrace doors, his cowl of shadows shivering in an invisible wind.

"When did you get here?!" the imp squeaked.

"*Five minutes ago,*" the Reaper God replied in a hurt tone.

"*You should make some noise next time, Temir,*" Tisiphone advised, pale-faced.

Atropos rose from her seat, gold flaring in her pupils. *"You think you can get into the Seventh Purgatory, Temir?"*

The Reaper God bobbed his head. *"I do. But I shall need her assistance."*

He pointed a finger at Eden.

"M—me?!" Eden croaked, her eyes bulging.

"Your staff and my ring can open a doorway to that realm," the Reaper God told her solemnly.

Eden's expression turned glassy. "Oh. That's…nice. Ha-ha. You hear that, Woody?"

Her pendant vibrated with one hundred percent smugness and zero percent awareness of his mistress's dread.

"I know you helped us before, Temir, but don't Reapers usually take a neutral stand in the wars between Gods?" Kes asked with a worried frown.

Crimson and gold bloomed in the Reaper God's eyes. The shadows around him expanded, draining the light from the room.

"Let's just say I have a bone to pick with the God who would harm my mother," he said icily. *"I might as well make something clear now, Goddesses. We Reapers will fight in the war to come."*

Morgan's heart thumped heavily in his chest. He and Cassius traded a surprised glance.

Orena's eyes rounded. *"You will?!"*

"Is this because of what Icarus told us Elios did when he captured you?" Tisiphone asked, equally shocked.

"The God of Darkness interfered in our domain and killed hundreds of our brethren," the Reaper God stated in

a tone that would brook no argument. *"We cannot remain impartial under those circumstances, regardless of the rules that govern our interactions with the living."*

Atropos studied him for a timeless moment before dipping her chin gracefully. *"We appreciate the offer, Temir. Though it goes against the edict given to your kind by those that are supposed to govern us, I see no need to follow their decree when they have done nothing to stop Elios. We could use all the help we can get."*

The Reaper God positively beamed while keeping a somber face.

CHAPTER THIRTY-THREE

A SOUND DISTURBED THE EVER-LIVING DARKNESS FILLING the Goddess's mind. She ignored it, certain it would fade to nothingness, like everything else around her always did.

The sound came again. It was a woman's scream.

Her tortured cry jolted something inside the Goddess. Something she could barely recall. She frowned faintly where she stood chained to a dark boulder, barely aware of the shackles drinking her blood and the divine power that flowed through her veins.

Divine...power?

The thought fluttered through her consciousness, causing her frown to deepen. She did not know what it meant. But...she used to. Once upon a time.

The notion was rapidly swallowed by the wicked susurrations the chains made as they sank into her flesh and the numbness clouding her skull.

The Goddess blinked when the woman's scream came again. Her cry rose to a wail of pure agony. Something sparked within the Goddess's belly at the woman's suffering.

Something hot and bright and full of rage.

It caused a memory to drift through her mind for an infinitesimal moment.

Clo...tho?

The Goddess swallowed heavily. She clenched her jaw, lifted her head, and forced herself to scan her surroundings.

There were others bound to boulders around her. Women in tattered, golden dresses. Their faces swam in and out of view through the clouds of sulfur spouting from the jagged, lava-spitting crevasses carving red scars across the desolate crater she found herself in.

The women looked familiar, somehow.

One had been laid spread-eagled upon her prison of stone.

Giant, winged figures with bodies wreathed in shadows and crimson eyes were crushing her legs with stone maces. Bone and gristle poked out from the woman's shattered limbs before her flesh healed over, only to be split apart again and again by the weapons that smashed down upon her unblemished skin.

It was a cruel cycle, one meant to torment her into madness.

"*CLOTHO!*" someone bellowed.

The Goddess's gaze found the figure who was

straining against her chains. Silver tears dripped down the stranger's filthy face. Fury burned in her eyes as she glared at the dark entity hovering before her, the inky lines throbbing under her skin radiating from an ugly seed embedded within her chest.

"*Tell me what I need to know and I will make the Nephilim stop,*" the being hissed.

He held a blade of black currents that roared as it tried to escape his hold.

"*Go to Hell, Elios!*" the woman spat in his face.

The black cloak around the floating figure writhed agitatedly. He swelled in size.

That was when the Goddess realized he was made of darkness itself.

She shook her head and tried to focus on their conversation. It was important, for reasons she could not fathom yet.

"*I don't know why you lost control of the Sword of Wind!*" the woman snarled. Her distracted gaze darted from the weapon in his hand to the prisoner being tortured a short distance away. "*I saw Ivmir die, so you should be able to wield it!*"

The being before her fell silent.

"*I did, for a moment,*" he confessed. "*Could it be that Ivmir...still lives?*"

Something in his voice made the Goddess's skin prickle. It took her a moment to recognize the emotion he'd just revealed.

It was fear.

The fog clouding her brain lifted for an instant as

whatever control he wielded over her faded at this sign of weakness. Her eyes rounded.

My name is…Tenebra!

A gasp sounded on her left.

The woman chained to the stone beside her was staring wide-eyed at the figure opposite her. *"Alecto!"*

Gold blazed in the eyes of the woman she'd addressed. *"Megaera!"*

Horror drenched Tenebra in a cold sweat. She finally recognized them.

"Sisters?!" she mumbled.

The dam of darkness that had kept her memories suppressed for centuries finally burst open. Tears sprang to Tenebra's eyes as she recalled all that had come to pass. Their attempts at escaping Purgatory when the Nether tore. Elios and his army of war demons and Nephilim capturing her and her sisters. The ones who'd chosen to sacrifice themselves so that a few of them could get away. The evil deeds Elios had had his prisoners commit on his behalf. Her attack on Earth. What Alecto and Megaera had been forced to do to Ivmir.

Wrath stormed her soul with her next breath.

"You dare speak in my presence?!"

Tenebra choked. The fury rattling her bones scattered to nothingness under the wave of corrupt pressure saturating the sulfur-laden air.

Elios was glowering at them, the shadows around him bubbling with malevolence. He raised a hand and clenched his fist.

Pain squeezed Tenebra's chest. She wheezed, cold fire spreading through her heart and flooding her veins with ice. Her consciousness wavered as the black core he'd engraved within her won the battle to bend her mind and will.

No! Numbness swamped her senses once more. *I... must...remember...*

The Goddess slumped as she fell under the spell. The light faded from the eyes of the women whose identities she had briefly recalled, their faces growing slack.

Who...are they again?

The God of Darkness sneered. *"Good. You should know your place, sisters."*

He turned to the figure he'd been talking to, only to freeze. Brightness flared in the woman's pupils. She was staring unseeingly at the sky.

"What?!" the God of Darkness snapped.

A fierce expression distorted the prisoner's face. *"Icarus!"*

The name she uttered was a prayer full of hope.

The God of Darkness visibly startled. He followed her unblinking gaze and swore. The Goddess looked up, her skull creaking heavily upon her neck.

A point of light was growing in the amber clouds. They parted a moment later, revealing the portal being ripped open in the crimson sky.

The chains binding the Goddess clattered upon stone. She was dimly aware of the other two women being released from their shackles.

"*Kill them!*" the God of Darkness barked.

They spread their dark wings and rose, unable to disobey his command.

Troops of war demons and Nephilim lifted off from the cliffs surrounding the crater and followed in their wake.

"You're almost there!" Cassius shouted.

Eden gritted her teeth, her bloodcursed magic turning the gloom around them scarlet where she floated within a sphere that protected her human flesh from the interdimensional space that would have decimated her body.

The devilwood staff vibrated violently in her grip as it tore a hole into the Seventh Purgatory.

Sparks detonated against the weapon where the Ring of Death touched it, the scythe aiding the staff to breach the hellish realm. The Reaper God's pupils glowed red and gold where he levitated beside Eden in his skeletal form, the same focused expression tightening his bony face.

Dark wind pulsed faintly around Morgan. The currents throbbed in tandem with the weapon that lay trapped within Purgatory. It was the echo of this power that Loki had followed with the Eternity Key, the imp guiding them through the void between worlds with Theo's help.

A muscle jumped in Morgan's jawline as he observed the doorway Eden and the Reaper God were creating. Tension knotted Cassius's shoulders. He touched Morgan's arm.

"Be careful. He'll come after you."

"I'll be ready," Morgan said in a hard voice.

Cassius's pulse stuttered at his fierce expression. It reminded him of the undaunted look on Ivmir's face when he'd stood beside Icarus during the War in the Nether. His heart swelled with affection.

Every time I think I couldn't love this man any more than I already do, he goes ahead and surprises me.

Morgan startled when Cassius grasped him by the scruff of his armor and yanked him close. Heat bloomed inside Cassius's core as he sealed their mouths together and kissed Morgan with savage abandon. The demigod stiffened before kissing him back just as wildly.

The words Cassius had wanted to say to him for a while finally tumbled from his lips. It wasn't the right place. And it definitely wasn't the right time. But he sensed that if he didn't utter them now, he might swallow them forever more.

"If we defeat Elios," he breathed against Morgan's mouth, "if we win the war that is to come, I want us to have a baby."

Morgan blinked, stunned. Cassius's belly clenched.

Pleasure had brought a flush of color to the demigod's face.

"Yes!" Morgan gushed. "A thousand times, yes!"

He grasped Cassius's face and kissed him again, his eyes sparkling with delight and passion.

"*Wait. Are they planning to conceive right now?!*" Orena hissed to Kes.

"*But...they're both male,*" Tisiphone said, confused.

"*If I'm not mistaken, the Dryads have a fruit in their realm same-sex couples can consume so as to fuse a portion of their soul cores into a new being.*" Atropos smiled faintly. "*It possesses some of the properties of the Golden Apples.*"

Theo pressed his hands against his pinking cheeks. "I'm gonna be an uncle!"

Loki's face crumpled. "I'm gonna be a big brother!"

Victor rolled his eyes at the wailing imp.

Morgan wrenched his mouth from Cassius's and squinted at Loki. "Hey, who said you were our kid?!"

"Look, I'm pleased for you, but could you guys pipe down?" Eden groaned. "We're trying to concentrate here!"

"*Yes,*" the Reaper God grumbled. "*All this talk is making me want to return to my realm and ravish my sweet Mortis.*"

Eden almost dropped her staff.

"*Who's Mortis?*" Tisiphone asked blankly.

"The Khimer he loves," Victor muttered.

Kes stared. "*Temir is all grown up.*"

The portal finally stabilized. They tensed as they gazed into the Seventh Purgatory.

Atropos lowered her brows. "*Here they come.*"

Cassius narrowed his eyes. "Stick to the plan."

Atropos dipped her chin curtly. Power detonated around her in a haze of gold as she dove for the army rising toward them.

CHAPTER THIRTY-FOUR

MORGAN FINALLY CALLED UPON THE DIVINE ENERGY that lived inside his core. It emerged from the heart of him, bright and strong and full of the achingly familiar scent of the Dryad forests that were his true home. Heat filled his veins and warmed his flesh. His crown of oak and black wind materialized on his head. His wings and Stark Steel armor darkened.

A black tempest infused with dazzling, emerald magic detonated around him.

Morgan startled. The incandescent power thrumming from his body was making his very bones tremble.

I feel...stronger. He blinked, his pulse racing wildly. *Is it because I consumed a Golden Apple?!*

War cries below drew his gaze before he could make sense of why the godly force inside him seemed different. Atropos and Kes had engaged Tenebra while Tisiphone and Orena clashed with Alecto and

Megaera. To his surprise, he found he could keep up with their lightning-fast moves.

He gazed beyond them to the hellish landscape of the Seventh Purgatory and an immense basin cleaved by lava-spouting canyons, where two figures were chained to rock platforms.

Elios floated beside the captive Goddesses.

Morgan scowled. He reached for the humming string that tied his soul to the weapon he was born to wield.

"To me!" he roared.

The Sword of Wind exploded into life in his right hand, the weapon singing in delight as it bound itself to his arm with dark currents and green creepers.

The God of Darkness's shriek of rage echoed in the distance.

Morgan smiled savagely. *That pissed him off.*

He snapped his wings open and dropped through the sulfur-tainted air, fury focusing his vision. Black blood sprayed his face as he slashed effortlessly through the war demons who crossed his path.

Fiery cinders filled the air, Cassius decimating the horde heading for them from the right. He released a burst of Heaven's Light that blinded another troop of fiends approaching from the opposite direction and the Nephilim rising from below.

Loki drove the Eternity Key into the skull of the first Nephil, his pupils pulsing crimson with power in his Gargantua form.

"Suspend!" Theo barked.

He decapitated the Nephil he had frozen with his

time spell with the Spear of Light while the Reaper God sliced through the rest of the giants with the Ring of Death. Bloodcursed magic and dark flames swarmed the sky as Eden and Victor took rear guard.

"Go!" Cassius yelled at Morgan and the Reaper God. "We'll protect you!"

Morgan nodded grimly.

He and the Reaper God dove through burning ash and yellow clouds, the wind whistling shrilly around them making the black currents and shadows that wreathed their bodies shiver wildly. Cassius and the others surrounded them in a defensive circle that kept the war demons and Nephilim at bay.

A flash of movement captured Morgan's gaze as they neared the crater. Alecto had broken free of Tisiphone's hold and was shooting across the sky to intercept them.

"Dimensional Gate!" Theo snarled.

A portal bloomed in front of the Fury. She swore. It swallowed her whole and spat her out again close to Tisiphone, who confronted her once more.

Morgan's skin prickled. Corruption was imbuing the air.

He clenched his jaw against the powerful wave of evil energy drenching the Seventh Purgatory, so thick and vile it made it hard to breathe even though he was a demigod.

Elios was rising toward them.

Cassius and Theo dropped to cut him off while Victor and Loki faced the war demons and the Nephilim converging on them. The God of Darkness cursed, blinded by Cassius's radiance and the dazzling brightness throbbing from the Spear of Light.

Eden kept pace with Morgan and the Reaper God as they closed in on the basin where Clotho and Lachesis were trapped. They landed with thuds that shook the ground and headed briskly toward the Goddesses.

"*Iv—Ivmir!*" Lachesis gasped. Her stunned gaze shifted to the Reaper God. "*Tem?!*"

"Save your energy," Morgan said grimly.

Lachesis swallowed, raw anguish darkening her eyes. "*Please, help Clotho first!*"

Morgan stopped and looked over at the pale-faced, comatose figure a short distance away. His stomach twisted. He hadn't made out the full details of the youngest Moira's state from the distance.

Shadows exploded around the Reaper God, his eyes shrinking into gold-laced, crimson slits full of wrath.

Blood drenched Clotho's dress and the rock she was bound to. From the way it had caked the material and the gore clinging to the stone, it wasn't all fresh. The smell of iron scored Morgan's nostrils, the Goddess's ichor evaporating with hisses of steam from the mire it had created where it had soaked into the dirt. He ground his teeth.

He didn't have to ask Lachesis what Elios had done to their sister.

That monster!

"Morgan," Eden warned.

He followed her wary gaze. Tension knotted his shoulders.

Another army of war demons, Nephilim, and Cyclops had appeared on the rim of the crater.

"Shit!" Morgan cursed. He glanced at Eden, his hands fisting at his sides. "Think you can keep them occupied for a few minutes?!"

Eden scowled. "I'll try."

Crimson flared in her pupils. The magic she was born to wield silently expanded the sphere around her at the same time the blazing runes covering her staff spilled over onto her flesh. Static sparked the air above them. Lightning-charged clouds sprouted into existence where none had been before. They started spinning, bringing with them the smell of sulfur and ozone.

The power of the Nine Hells poured into Eden and the devilwood staff. It detonated around them in a violent blast that made the crater tremble and Morgan stumble.

Lachesis gaped at the bloodcursed mage.

"*She is strong,*" the Reaper God told an anxious Morgan. "*Do not worry. She will hold them at bay.*"

Morgan hesitated before nodding. Eden had proven more than capable of handling herself in battle.

Clotho's eyelids fluttered weakly when they reached her. A dry sound left her parched throat as she swallowed.

"*Te...mir?*" she mumbled through cracked lips.

"*Yes, Goddess.*" The Reaper God gently clasped her hand with his bony fingers. "*Conserve your strength. We shall soon set you free.*"

Morgan gazed at the sky and the savage battle that

still raged there. He could feel the fierce pulses of divine energy throbbing through Cassius's soul core.

Hang on a little bit longer!

He gripped the Sword of Wind and brought it down upon the shackles binding Clotho. Darkness flared around the Reaper God as he swung the Ring of Death at Elios's dark seed where it consumed the Goddess's powers.

Sparks exploded when their weapons made contact with the God of Darkness's corruption.

CHAPTER THIRTY-FIVE

CASSIUS'S PULSE RACED AS HE SLICED THROUGH THE INKY bands throttling Theo with his bright blade. The demigod gasped and shot out of Elios's reach. Cassius clenched his jaw.

Theo's skin was red where Elios's shackles had burned him.

The demigod glared at the God of Darkness, his fingers tightening on the Spear of Light as his wounds started to heal.

Elios sneered where he floated before them. *"You think you can defeat me so easily? You, who are barely demigods?! Your arrogance knows no—!"*

An explosion of black flames drowned the rest of his words and blinded his vision. Elios cried out as the Eternity Key carved a wound in his left flank. Inky blood dripped from his flesh.

He touched it gingerly, disbelief widening his eyes as he stared at the black ichor staining his fingers.

Loki scowled where he levitated behind him. "You talk too much, asshole."

A savage expression tightened Victor's face at the sight of Theo's injuries. He raised his sword of black fire and flashed toward Elios with a thunderous battle cry.

Darkness boomed around the deity.

It shoved them back some dozen feet.

Cassius narrowed his eyes as he used his wings to steady himself. *Damn it! Atropos was right! He's ten times stronger than before!*

A harsh shout reached him as they prepared to attack Elios. It came from Tisiphone.

"No, Tenebra! Stop!"

Cassius's head snapped up. Alarm twisted his gut.

Tenebra had Atropos by the throat and was slowly choking her. Tisiphone cursed as she attempted to get past Alecto to help the Moira.

"TENEBRA!" Orena bellowed from where she clashed with Megaera.

Kes screamed her eldest sister's name where she furiously engaged the war demons and Nephilim in her path.

Cassius cracked his wings and flashed toward Tenebra and Atropos. Bloodcursed magic washed across him from below. He slowed and looked down. His pulse stuttered.

Eden stood beneath a giant maelstrom that was swallowing the army attempting to reach her and the ones she protected, red sparks lighting the air around her body and undulating hair and her mouth open on a fierce roar. The devilwood staff vibrated violently in her grip as it nullified the Cyclops' lethal beams and shrieks. It was absorbing the energy of the Nine Hells at an exponential rate and expelling their enemy straight out of the Seventh Purgatory.

Shallow cuts bloomed on Eden's skin and her weapon as some of their foe made contact. The wounds closed up even as they formed, never deterring their formidable defense.

Golden light bloomed behind the mage.

Cassius's heart thumped heavily when he saw the figures in gold dresses and laurel crowns beside Morgan and the Reaper God. They blasted from the ground with expressions of pure fury, their white wings blazing with the same divine energy that Atropos projected, their clothes and crowns shifting into armor and winged helmets. A spinning staff and a rod appeared in their hands.

Now!

Cassius took a deep breath and reached for the source of his power.

"Ready yourself, Goddesses!" he yelled.

Confusion halted Elios in his tracks where he prepared to face off against Loki, Theo, and Victor. It turned to horror when Cassius unleashed the divine force contained within his core.

"NO!" the God of Darkness shrieked.

Whiteness flared across the Seventh Purgatory.

"AWAKEN!" Cassius bellowed.

AIR LOCKED IN ATROPOS'S THROAT.

She was barely aware of Tenebra letting her go, the Black Fate grimacing and moving jerkily backward as if in pain.

The incandescent force that held Atropos in its grip focused into a conflagration that overwhelmed her core. She raised her head and screamed, unable to contain her voice as her very being went supernova.

Tisiphone's harsh cry sounded dimly above the buzzing in her ears.

The flames blazed brighter and brighter inside Atropos, an inferno that blinded her vision at the same time it filled her to the brim with a strength that rattled her to the very marrow. Tears blossomed in her eyes. She blinked.

The divine energy that was flooding her veins was the purest form of power she had ever tasted.

So, this is what it feels like to be awakened!

Dazzling light radiated from Atropos on a balmy wave as her fully roused soul stabilized. It cleansed the air of corruption and sulfurous fumes.

Tenebra's hands dropped to her belly. A faint glow was throbbing inside her, the light superseding Elios's corruption. The glacial mask pasted across her face transformed into a dazed expression while the inky lines pulsing under her flesh started to fade.

"Fight it, Ten!" Atropos told the Black Fate. *"Fight Elios's hold on you!"*

Tenebra clenched her teeth and dipped her chin, determination filling her dark eyes.

Alecto and Megaera were similarly frozen where

they'd been confronting their sisters. Awareness was returning to their eyes, their newly awakened Goddess powers destroying the vile energy that had long pervaded their bodies.

It's working. Emotion choked Atropos's breath. *By the Gods, Icarus's plan is actually working!*

"Elios will force your sisters to fight us," Cassius had told Atropos steadily before they'd left Earth. "We may end up inadvertently hurting them. I think I have an idea how we can avoid that."

They'd exchanged stunned looks when he'd told them his suggestion.

"Will that work?" Victor had asked in a troubled voice. "You might actually be giving them the advantage if you do that."

"I agree," Theo had concurred uneasily. "This might backfire on us."

"It's a chance we're going to have to take," Cassius had said quietly. "It's the only way I can think of to end his hold on their minds so that we don't hurt them. But we have to do it at the right moment."

Atropos had exchanged a cautious look with the other Goddesses. What Cassius had proposed had never been done before.

She'd finally dipped her chin in agreement. *"Alright."*

Elios raged as Cassius moved to block his path alongside Loki, Theo, and Victor.

"Attie!"

Atropos froze at the sweet voices echoing in her ears. Clotho and Lachesis were rising toward her. They bolted into her arms with incoherent cries.

Their achingly familiar scent filled her senses at the same time she tasted the fresh energy throbbing from their roused soul cores. Atropos hugged them fiercely, their tears soaking into her hair just as her own dampened theirs. Remorse twisted her heart all over again.

"*I'm sorry I'm so late, sisters,*" she whispered wretchedly. "*I'm sorry I let him hurt you for so long!*"

Clotho swallowed a sob. Lachesis tightened her hold on Atropos.

"*Did Icarus really awaken us?*" Tenebra mumbled.

The Black Fate was staring at her glowing hands.

"*Yes,*" Atropos said with a shaky smile.

"*MOTHER!*"

Tenebra stiffened. "*Temir?!*"

Atropos followed her shocked gaze. Morgan and the Reaper God were soaring toward them, Eden floating alongside them within a scarlet sphere.

"*Mother,*" the Reaper God repeated solemnly as he slowed to a hover in front of Tenebra.

He'd regained his human appearance.

"*My child,*" Tenebra whispered. Silver tears tumbled from her eyes. She touched his face with trembling fingers. "*I am so sorry for what I did.*" She looked over at Morgan. "*You too, Ivmir.*"

Morgan shrugged. "Yeah, well, I've been told you all used to kick my ass regularly when I was a kid."

Atropos bit back a smile when she spotted his flushed ears.

"*You were not yourself, Mother,*" the Reaper God said adamantly. "*Bear with me a moment.*"

He wielded his scythe and destroyed the remnant of Elios's dark seed where it sat within Tenebra's chest. The Black Fate gasped, her pupils brightening as the last of the God of Darkness's corruption disappeared from her body.

He did the same to Alecto and Megaera.

Tisiphone, Orena, and Kes returned from where they'd disposed of the remaining war demons and Nephilim in the sky. Orena and Kes kissed and hugged Tenebra while Tisiphone took the sniveling Alecto and Megaera in her arms, her own face crumpling as she sobbed and wailed.

Clotho sniffed. *"I forgot how ugly a crier she could be."*

Atropos chuckled and wiped the tears dripping down her face. She stiffened in the next instant.

Shadows swamped the Seventh Purgatory as Elios unleashed his full powers of darkness.

"Cassius!" Morgan barked.

Theo, Victor, and Loki went flying as Elios charged through them.

Cassius grunted and blocked the God of Darkness's attack with his blade, white wings bracing. Their figures blurred.

"Shit!" Morgan closed his wings and dove inside a tempest of black wind and Dryad magic.

Atropos followed, her heart racing with dread.

Elios was driving Cassius toward the crater.

A violent boom shook the Seventh Purgatory when they smashed into it. Debris and ash clouded the air. The crevasses splitting the ground widened, lava spurting violently from the fresh fissures.

Morgan and Atropos darted around the rising jets of liquid fire and closed in on where Elios held Cassius down by his throat.

"*DIE!*" Elios roared.

Fear turned Atropos's blood to ice when she saw the orb of darkness solidifying in his hand.

"*NO!*" she screamed as Elios aimed it straight at Cassius's soul core.

Theo dropped down from the sky, his weapon blazing in his hands. "*SUSPEND!*"

Elios faltered for an infinitesimal moment.

It was enough for Cassius to counter his attack and for Theo and Morgan to make their move.

Dazzling radiance blinded Atropos. She slowed and squinted, hand rising to shield her eyes. Her breath stuttered at what she glimpsed through the gaps between her fingers.

Theo grabbed Elios by the throat and pierced his chest with the Spear of Light, his eyes radiating golden beams of fury. Cassius wrenched Elios's fingers from his flesh and immobilized the arm that sought to destroy his core, his brow furrowed in an almighty scowl.

Morgan cleaved Elios's hand from his body with the Sword of Wind and a sound of pure wrath.

Atropos blinked, stunned. *H—how?! Elios is made of darkness! Ivmir should not have been able to cut him!*

Elios froze. Incomprehension widened his inky eyes.

Atropos felt a moment's pity for the brother she could never love.

He flinched at the sound of his amputated appendage striking the ground. The pool of lava it had fallen into hissed and bubbled as it consumed his flesh.

"He's getting away!" Eden warned.

Theo cursed as Elios exploded into a million black strands in his grip.

"*I will kill you,*" the God of Darkness railed in a voice that shook with rage. "*I WILL KILL YOU ALL!*"

He vanished into nothingness, his words fading to an ominous whisper that would haunt Atropos for days to come.

CHAPTER THIRTY-SIX

Clotho remarked.

She dropped down on the couch in Cassius's living room, her hair still damp from the shower. The clothes he had loaned her hung loosely on her slender figure.

"That's exactly what I said!" Kes exclaimed.

"The door's right there," Morgan snapped as he came over from the kitchen.

"You tell them," Victor grumbled.

Cassius swallowed a smile. Morgan sat next to him and handed him a coffee, still muttering under his breath. Seeing Morgan and Victor interact with their sisters was proving to be more fun than he'd thought it would be. Judging by the amused expression Theo was struggling to mask, he thought the same.

Eden yawned where she sat on the floor. She leaned against Cedric, a contented expression on her face. The Dryad prince had been waiting for them at Cassius's place when they'd returned to Earth.

"How are things in Ivory Peaks?" Morgan had asked him worriedly.

"They're getting better by the day," Cedric had replied.

His gaze had darted apprehensively to the Goddesses exploring the apartment with open curiosity. Though he hadn't yet been formally introduced to them, he'd recognized Alecto and Megaera as the ones who'd attacked the Dryad realm despite their gracious appearance.

"*Eden is a powerful Magus,*" Lachesis had told Cassius quietly while Eden hugged her fiancé so hard she almost broke his ribs. "*She will be an incredible asset in the war to come.*"

"I know," Cassius had replied with a faint smile.

What Eden had achieved during the battle they had fought in the Seventh Purgatory was nothing short of a miracle, even more so since she was human.

The devilwood staff made the right choice in selecting her as its rightful wielder over Lucille Hartman. Cassius had glanced at Atropos at that thought. *Then again, she's the one who brought them together.*

Someone knocked on the door.

"I'll get it." Morgan rose and went over to the entrance. "Did someone order pizza?" he called suspiciously down the hallway a moment later.

Orena brightened. "*Yes.*"

The other Goddesses looked at her, visibly impressed.

Loki squinted at the Black Fate. "How did you pay for it?"

Orena smiled beatifically. *"That's for me to know and for you guys to never find out."*

"Theo saw her take Morgan's credit card out of his wallet earlier," Victor told the imp.

Loki smirked.

Orena's face fell. *"But I was as swift as the wind."*

"Theo's eyes are faster," Victor said smugly.

Morgan brought in fifteen boxes of extra-large pizza and dumped them on the kitchen bar before glaring at the youngest Black Fate. "How about you ask the owner of the premises next time you order something?"

"I'm sure Icarus doesn't mind," Orena said primly. *"Right, Carus?"*

She batted her eyelashes at Cassius.

"Don't give him a pet name!" Morgan snarled. "And stop flirting with him!"

Tisiphone tsk-tsked. *"Possessiveness is an ugly trait, Ivmir."*

Lachesis had lifted the cover of one of the boxes and was sniffing the contents with an inquisitive look. *"What did you call this thing again?"*

"It's pepperoni pizza," Morgan said sullenly. "It's a flat bread baked with tomato sauce and cheese and topped with meat and—"

"By the Gods, what is this magic?!" Lachesis mumbled around the mouthful she'd just stuffed in her mouth.

Gold flared in her pupils as she gobbled the remainder of the slice, her expression one of pure pleasure. She licked her fingers and stared at the pizza like it had been made in Heaven itself.

"It goes well with beer," Theo advised.

They ended up ordering another twenty boxes of pizza.

"I am stuffed," Eden groaned two hours later.

Kes belched discreetly behind her hand and patted her belly.

Cassius twisted his beer bottle distractedly where he sat next to Morgan. The disquiet he'd been experiencing since their return to Earth was now front and center in his mind.

"What is it?" Morgan said warily.

"There is so much I still don't understand." Cassius met his gaze, troubled. "Why did Elios want the Sword of Wind in the first place?" He waved a vague hand. "I get that it's one of the divine weapons that locked Chaos in the Abyss, but he can't do much without the remaining artifacts. Why go so far to get his hands on it?"

"He will likely not need the other keys," Clotho said somberly.

Shock reverberated around the room. Cassius's heart started a rapid tempo against his ribs as he stared at the youngest Moira. Loki studied the Goddess unblinkingly, crimson flaring in his pupils.

"What do you mean by that, sister?" Atropos asked in a hard voice.

Clotho and Lachesis traded a guarded glance.

Clotho bent her legs and tucked her knees under her chin, her expression grim. *"I think Elios is using the divine blood and energy he's been absorbing from us over the centuries to create demonic artifacts that can mimic the weapons used to seal Chaos."*

Horror widened Kes's eyes. Loki hissed.

Tisiphone jumped to her feet. *"WHAT?!"*

Power throbbed off her in a wave that rattled the windows and the bottles on the coffee table. Alecto touched her hand. The youngest Fury took a shuddering breath and sat back down next to her older sister, her divine rage abating.

Morgan's trepidation echoed across the soul bond that connected him to Cassius.

"Is that even possible?" the demigod asked, knuckles white where he rested his hands on his knees. "Making demonic keys identical to those original weapons?!"

Lachesis hesitated. *"The alchemists of the Shadow Empire are cunning enough to attempt it."*

Atropos dropped her head in her hands. *"So, all this time, when he was consuming our blood and our powers, it wasn't just to make himself stronger?!"* Her voice trembled with horror. *"Why could we not see this?!"*

Clotho swallowed, her face tight with regret and anger. *"Because he blinded us all, sister. I do not know whether it's because Elios still holds an element of Hypnos's power in his hands, but none of us could divine his plans."*

"And he did *use us to make himself stronger, Attie."* Lachesis clasped Atropos's hand. *"Our brother is a monster through and through."*

Victor lowered his brows in the fraught hush that followed. "So, why *does* he need the Sword of Wind?"

Cassius's stomach plummeted as sudden realization

blasted through him. He straightened, his eyes rounding. "Because it's Nyx's weapon!"

Tenebra nodded, her expression grim. *"Yes. Our mother bestowed her sword upon Ivmir and bound it to his soul. It is unique among the weapons of Heaven and cannot be imitated. Only Ivmir can wield it. But if he were to die..."*

Blood pounded heavily in Cassius's head as he stared at the Black Fate. "Then another son of Nyx could use the sword."

"Yes." A muscle jumped in Tenebra's jawline. *"It is likely one of the reasons he brainwashed Coraos into joining his ranks and gave him the order to kill Ivmir."*

Victor's eyes grew haunted at that.

Eden stiffened. Her pendant was vibrating against her neck, bloodcursed magic emanating from it in a red glow. She touched it and gasped.

"Woody says he can probably find those weapons!" she told them dazedly.

Cassius brightened. "He can?!"

Eden bobbed her head shakily. "Given time, yes."

Cedric gave his fiancée a worried look.

Tenebra straightened. *"What is it, Attie?"*

Cassius looked over at the eldest Moira. Atropos was staring at the floor, her expression distraught. Fear prickled Cassius's skin when she raised her chin and met their gazes.

"I saw another vision when we were in the Seventh Purgatory."

Her whisper filled the room with palpable tension.

"What did you see, Attie?" Clotho asked, her voice full of dread.

Atropos took a shuddering breath. She turned to Clotho and Lachesis, pressed her fingers to their foreheads, and closed her eyes. A focused frown marred her unblemished brow.

Gold brightened Clotho and Lachesis's pupils at whatever Atropos showed them. A horrified expression dawned on Clotho's face.

The blood drained from Lachesis's cheeks. *"By the Gods."*

"Tell us, sisters," Tenebra commanded in a steely voice.

Atropos opened her eyes and swallowed. *"Elios will succeed in opening the Abyss. Chaos will come to Earth."*

Bile flooded the back of Cassius's throat at her shaky words. He grabbed Morgan's hand. Morgan turned his palm over and clasped his fingers just as tightly, tension humming off his powerful frame.

"So, he will win?" Theo mumbled, his face pale. "He will win the war that will take place on Earth?!"

Victor took him in his arms.

Atropos paused, confusion warring with hesitation on her face. *"I...do not know for certain."*

Cassius recalled how she'd given them that very answer when Victor had asked her the same question the day she'd arrived on Earth.

"It's because I introduced three confounding factors to mitigate that risk," Atropos explained at their strained looks. *"Loki, Eden, and Theo."* Her voice hardened as Loki, Eden, and Theo startled. *"The outcome of this war is not set in stone. Even I cannot divine its ending right now. But, though I am unable to see the future beyond Chaos*

coming to Earth, it isn't because death awaits us and the universe will cease to exist. It's because the possibilities are still in flux."

Cassius swallowed, hope sending his pulse racing. "So, we still have a chance?"

Atropos nodded solemnly. *"Yes, we do."*

"It won't just be us against Elios," Tisiphone added, her expression growing determined. *"Just as the Naiads swore their allegiance to us, so did the Nereids. And they won't be the only allies who will stand by our side in the coming war."*

CHAPTER THIRTY-SEVEN

CASSIUS STARED OUT THROUGH THE GLASS WALL OF THE bedroom at the terrace and the city beyond. Golden rays pierced the sky to the east as the sun started to shine upon San Francisco. The first light of the new day danced across the waters of the bay, sending sparkles rippling across the dark surface.

Warm arms closed around him from behind. Cassius relaxed against Morgan's chest, the bond that connected their souls pulsing brightly in his belly.

"Are they all settled in?"

"For now." Morgan sighed and rubbed his nose in Cassius's hair. "I'll have to find them a permanent place to live. We can't have them camping out in your living room and my place forever."

Cassius smiled and turned in his hold. "It's not that bad."

Morgan grimaced. "I am not having my sisters stick around to eavesdrop when we're making out."

Cassius punched his chest lightly. "That's all you care about, isn't it? My body."

A low chuckle left Morgan. "Is that a trick question?"

Cassius's fake frown melted at his husky voice. He buried his face against Morgan. "No."

Morgan's hands found Cassius's back. He rubbed his flesh in slow, comforting strokes. "It's going to be okay."

Cassius tensed. "You don't know that."

His protest hung between them, a discordant tone that threatened to shatter the peaceful atmosphere.

Morgan tipped Cassius's chin up with a knuckle. "Do you trust me?"

Cassius gazed into the demigod's beautiful eyes. "Of course."

The smile that curved Morgan's mouth made his heart skip a beat.

"Then know that I will always protect you." Morgan rubbed a gentle thumb across Cassius's lips. "Wherever you go, whatever you need, I will always be there for you."

Cassius shuddered and closed his eyes, his chest tight with emotion.

Every time he felt down, every time the fears that plagued him weighed upon his heart, Morgan was always there to lift him back up. To dust him down, tend his wounds, and put a strong hand on his back to urge him forward once more.

It was a blessing he did not deserve. A salvation he

still felt he had no right to claim after all the suffering he had inadvertently visited upon so many realms.

I almost lost him twice. I don't think I could bear losing him a third time. And I'm afraid that might happen if Chaos does come to Earth, like Atropos divined.

Tender kisses rained on his eyelids, scattering his dark foreboding.

"Don't," Morgan whispered raggedly.

Cassius inhaled shakily. "Don't what?"

"Don't pull away from me. Don't hide your feelings. It breaks my heart when you do that."

Cassius swallowed and opened his eyes. The fierce light blazing in Morgan's pupils threatened to scorch him.

"I love you, Cassius. I will love you in this life and every life that may come after this one, in whatever form we may be reborn. So, be with me. Be mine, in every way possible. Let us make a child together, as we both wish."

The tears Cassius had been holding back finally sprang to his eyes. But they were of joy, not sorrow.

Morgan wiped them away gently before taking his mouth in a kiss full of promise.

Desire stirred Cassius's blood, slow and smoldering. Morgan deepened their kiss, passion painting red flags on his cheekbones. He guided Cassius to the bed and pushed him down. Cassius welcomed his weight with a moan as he climbed on the mattress.

Morgan stripped him of his clothes at a leisurely pace, his hands skimming Cassius's exposed skin with light touches that ignited his flesh, his mouth raining sweet kisses in the wake of his fingers.

Cassius trembled when Morgan pulled back so he could get undressed, the layers falling away to expose his powerful figure. A gasp left him as Morgan trailed a lazy knuckle along the length of his weeping cock. His ass twitched in anticipation of all that was to come.

He hadn't welcomed Morgan inside his body for days and his passage ached from his absence.

"You're so beautiful," Morgan murmured hotly. "Every inch of you is exquisite."

In the hour that followed, he showed Cassius exactly what he meant. Cassius shivered and moaned and writhed as Morgan worshipped his body with his lips and his tongue and his fingers, the slow burn between their soul cores making him dizzy with pleasure.

He relished everything about the way Morgan had sex with him.

But this? *This* right here?

When Morgan slowed it all down and took his time driving him out of his mind?

It wrecked Cassius in ways that seared his very soul.

"Ah!"

Cassius arched his back off the bed and bit his lip to muffle his cry. Morgan had just rubbed his hole with a lube-slicked finger.

He shuddered as Morgan parted his knees and settled in the cradle of his thighs. Cassius wrapped his legs around Morgan's waist and hugged his shoulders, Morgan's heart thrumming strongly against his cheek where he buried his face in the demigod's chest.

Instead of taking him, Morgan started a lazy dance, his hips rolling to stroke his erection against Cassius's turgid shaft while he played with the taut folds protecting his passage.

"Enter me!" Cassius begged brokenly, too far gone to bear this sweet torture.

He dropped a hand to his cock, eager for some kind of release.

"No." Morgan took his hand and kissed his palm before locking his wrists above his head with a firm grip. His eyes blazed as he nipped at Cassius's lip with his teeth. "Not yet."

It wasn't until he'd brought Cassius to a protracted orgasm that left him a hot, sweaty, breathless mess that Morgan finally guided his cock to Cassius's entrance.

Cassius shuddered as Morgan pushed inside him, so eager for this act that the sting and burn of penetration was but a fleeting ache. Morgan filled him to the brim inch by steady inch, hips rocking in steady nudges that threatened Cassius's very sanity. Morgan stilled when he was in to the hilt, his breaths coming heavily, sweat dripping from his chin into the crook of Cassius's neck.

Cassius clung on for dear life when Morgan started to move.

"Oh!" He whimpered, his hole spasming hungrily around Morgan's dick. "More! Harder!"

Morgan swallowed his cries with his lips and ignored his pleas. He swayed his hips at a measured pace as he thrust in and out, as if he had all the time in the world. And all the while he held Cassius's hands prisoner and fixed him with a torrid gaze full of passion and tenderness.

Cassius lost himself in their lovemaking, welcoming everything Morgan gave him, his body pliant and eager as he accepted the man who had chosen not to forsake him. Dizzying waves of ecstasy swelled from his sparking core as Morgan brought him to one devastating climax after another, his moans and soft cries lost in the space between their bodies before Morgan devoured them with his mouth.

His orgasms blinded him, just as the bond that linked their souls burned with a light that threatened to sear his body.

Every time Cassius floundered, every time his consciousness flickered, Morgan brought him right back to the moment with a sensuous roll of his hips.

They fell asleep to the sun blazing brightly in the sky, their arms wrapped around one another where they'd collapsed on the bed, Morgan buried deep inside Cassius.

EPILOGUE

SUZIE LEANED ACROSS THE BAR AND BECKONED CASSIUS closer.

"Who the hell are the hot chicks at your table?!" she asked in a conspiratorial tone.

Cassius glanced warily in the direction she indicated before peeking at Zach where he was helping the *Occulta* bartenders serve the busy Friday-night crowd.

"He didn't tell you?"

Suzie shot a suspicious look at her demon boyfriend. "No, he did not."

Zach sensed their stares and looked over.

"What?" he mouthed with a shrug.

"By the way, are you paying him?" Julia cocked a wary thumb at the Argonaut agent. "All he seems to do when he comes here is serve drinks."

Suzie arched an eyebrow. "Of course I pay him." A saucy smile stretched her lips. "With my body. I take him upstairs after we close up and I—"

Cedric cursed and clamped his hands over Eden's ears.

"Come, Eden," he growled.

He grabbed her soda and two bottles of ginger ale and dragged her away from the bar.

"What?" Eden said, confused. She looked over her shoulder at Suzie, her expression clearing. "She was talking about *sex*, wasn't she?"

She tilted her head at the scowling Dryad, her eyes sparkling with avid interest.

Suzie pursed her lips as she watched them leave. "Isn't it about time those two popped each other's cherry?"

Julia shuddered. "Don't let Brianna hear you say that. She'll ground Eden for life."

Cassius sighed. Julia was right. The road ahead for Cedric was not going to be easy.

Charlie came over and grabbed some of the cocktails they'd ordered.

"You better come back and save Theo," the enchanter told Cassius briskly.

Cassius straightened. "Why?"

Charlie made a face. "Victor went out to take a call and…well, just go over there."

Cassius and Julia headed after him once they'd collected the remaining drinks. It proved hard to get to their booth with the mob of *Occulta* onlookers openly ogling the nine drop-dead-gorgeous figures seated at the table.

The Goddesses' hair and skin practically glowed

under the muted lighting. They wore vivid sequin tops hinting at their voluptuous curves and skin-tight velour pants with matching stilettos that highlighted their long legs. The gems sparkling in their ears and at their throats and wrists looked like they averaged the gross domestic product of a small nation, while their perfect, make-up-free complexions made it seem like they had expensive cosmetics on.

Julia and Adrianne had taken them shopping the day before. By the looks of the Goddesses' clothes, the angel and the sorceress had gone to the top-end places in the city.

"I hope they didn't use Morgan's credit card," Cassius had muttered to Loki when he'd seen the labels on their shopping bags.

The imp had sniggered.

"*Come, drink, Theophile,*" Kes was telling Theo imperiously where she pressed up against his side.

Theo looked worriedly from the shot glass the second Black Fate kept trying to push into his hand to where Alecto was trailing a crimson nail down his chest. "Hmm."

The eldest Fury beamed at the demigod.

"*Why so shy, Theophile?*" Alecto breathed sultrily in his ear while she traced lazy circles on his shirt.

A shiver of apprehension shook Theo. He froze when Alecto dropped her fingers to his thigh and squeezed.

Atropos was sipping her drink glumly. From her resigned expression, Cassius gathered she'd given up trying to stop her sisters from seducing the young demigod.

"Jesus, get a room," Brianna murmured.

Her disapproving expression was matched by Cedric's. Eden, on the other hand, looked like she was taking notes from the Goddesses' book on seduction.

"How about you let him go before Victor comes back?" Cassius said lightly. He slipped in next to Theo and carefully lifted Alecto's hand from the demigod's leg. "Suzie will banish us if anything happens to her bar."

"Thanks," Theo whispered gratefully while Alecto pouted.

"Let's not tell Victor what happened," Cassius murmured.

Theo's eyes glazed over a little. "Yeah, let's not."

"I knew it would be you guys," someone said irritably.

Cassius looked up to find Jasper and Reuben standing by their booth.

The demon was frowning. "We were wondering why we couldn't get through the front door. We should have known it's because you brought *them* here."

He pointed an accusing finger at the Goddesses. Eyes narrowed around the table.

"*Why, if it isn't little Engrar,*" Tisiphone said acerbically.

Jasper lowered his brows further at the Fury. "I don't go by that title anymore. And there's nothing *little* about me."

Adrianne lifted a hand, her flushed cheeks a sign she was well on her way to getting stone drunk. "I can vouch for that. Charlie can barely walk some mornings." She squinted at Reuben. "Or maybe it's the angel who's got the bigger—"

Bailey muffled the rest of the sorceress's words with his hand while Orena cast a puzzled look at the scowling enchanter.

"Engrar?" Theo whispered to Cassius.

"It's Jasper's true name," Cassius murmured.

Julia blinked. "Oh, yeah. I'd forgotten."

Megaera's shrewd gaze shifted from Jasper to Reuben. "*I see you finally tamed the wild beast, Inias.*"

Reuben gave her a brittle smile.

Jasper looked suspiciously from the Goddess to his lover. "What does she mean by that?"

Reuben maintained a diplomatic silence and leaned down to drop a kiss on Charlie's head. "We'll see you later."

Charlie's frown vanished. He smiled warmly at the angel. "Okay."

Kes choked on her cocktail.

"*Wait! Those two and this kid are—?!*" she spluttered, her horrified gaze swinging from Jasper and Reuben's departing figures to Charlie.

"*Try to keep up, Kes,*" Tenebra murmured.

"By the way, it looks like you two have definitely kissed and made up," Julia drawled, her gaze pivoting between Bailey and Adrianne.

A goofy grin took over Bailey's face.

"He still has to make up for his mistake," Adrianne muttered belligerently.

Charlie rolled his eyes. "You never did tell us what he did that was so wrong you hardly spoke to him for a whole year."

Adrianne pouted.

Gold flared in Clotho's pupils. "*Oh. I must say, there was no way he could have avoided that situation.*" The Moira gave Bailey a look of pity and waved a hand vaguely. "*He's only human after all. Resisting both an incubus and a succubus's seduction would have been impossible.*"

Charlie's eyes rounded.

Julia sighed. The angel apparently already knew the reason Adrianne had been giving Bailey the cold shoulder.

Cassius scratched the tip of his nose and tried hard not to laugh. "So, er, that's why you were mad at him?"

Adrianne glowered. "They hired a hotel suite for an entire week. His dick was—"

Cedric cursed and clamped his hands over Eden's ears again.

"—bone dry by the time they finished with him!" the sorceress said in an aggrieved tone. "*And* they left hickeys all over his body. Those took months to fade!"

Bailey looked slightly abashed at that.

Tenebra was staring admiringly into her glass. "*What's this drink called again?*"

"It's absinthe," Brianna replied with a frown. "You shouldn't be drinking it neat."

The color drained a little from her face when she got a whiff of the strong alcohol.

Eden peeled her annoyed fiancé's hands from her head.

"You okay, mom?" she asked quizzically.

"Yeah." Brianna sipped her ginger ale. "I'm just a bit queasy."

Orena brightened. *"You know, the Nereids have a wonderful herbal tea that can cure pregnancy sickness."*

Eden's jaw dropped open. Cedric's eyes bulged. Atropos sighed.

A glass smashed close by. It was one of the Hexa agents who'd been eavesdropping on their conversation with a gang of Argonaut and Cabalista operatives.

Brianna narrowed her eyes at the wizard as he fumbled for the broken pieces on the floor. The guy flushed when he sensed her laser-like stare.

"That's great to know," she ground out at Orena.

The Goddess beamed. *"You're welcome."*

"I don't think she meant that as a compli—" Kes started with a grimace.

Clotho stabbed her elbow in the Black Fate's ribs. *"Read the room!"*

Eden closed her mouth. "You—*you're pregnant?!*"

Brianna winced at her squeal. "Keep your voice down, Eden." The witch's expression grew uncertain. "Are you upset?"

Eden shook her head, her eyes gleaming. "No! Not at all. I'm—I'm happy for you and Malik!"

She clasped her mother's hand and squeezed it, her lips curving in a dazzling smile.

Brianna relaxed a little.

"Does Malik know?" Julia asked.

"I'm going to tell him this weekend. It's his birthday."

Victor emerged from the crowd and took a seat next to Theo. "It's whose birthday?"

Theo brightened.

Surprise widened Victor's eyes when Brianna reluctantly told him about her pregnancy. "Congratulations."

"Thank you."

A loud sigh sounded opposite Cassius.

Tenebra was looking downcast.

"*Children,*" she mumbled. "*They sure get selfish when they grow older.*"

Julia leaned sideways toward Lachesis. "What happened to her?"

It was Atropos who replied. "*Temir kicked her and her sisters out of his domain.*"

Kes looked a little guilty at that. Tenebra narrowed her eyes at her.

"*All because you tried to seduce Mortis,*" she said accusingly.

"*I said he was cute,*" Kes protested.

"*You also touched his thigh, like Alecto just did to Theo,*" Orena said primly.

Victor froze. "What?!"

An aura of black flames shivered into life around him as he glared at the unrepentant Goddess in question.

"Great," Cassius mumbled, clocking Suzie's glower where she stood staring at them from behind the bar. "She'll definitely banish us this time."

Theo did his best to calm his bristling lover.

Warmth radiated through Cassius's soul core. His pulse quickened.

Morgan appeared at his side.

"Why does Victor look like he's about to commit murder?" he said in a puzzled voice.

He dropped a kiss on Cassius's cheek and sat next to him. Cassius handed him a beer.

"His boyfriend got groped by a couple of Goddesses," Julia explained.

"*A couple?!*" Victor snarled.

Morgan made a face. He removed three pairs of keys from inside his jacket and handed them to Atropos. "Here. These are for your apartments."

Atropos accepted them with a grateful smile. "*Thank you, Ivmir.*"

"*So, are we on the same floor as you and Cassius?*" Megaera asked brightly.

"Like hell I'd put you guys on the same floor as us." Morgan sneered. "You'd never leave our place."

Megaera's face fell. "*You know, I've been thinking this for a while now.*" Her brow furrowed as she looked from Morgan to Victor and back. "*You two sure have grown more impudent since we last saw you.*"

"That's because some of our sisters are giant pains in our asses," Morgan said sullenly.

Victor crossed his arms and nodded sagely.

"Exactly. At least they haven't tried to manhandle Cassius yet."

Cassius stiffened a little and avoided looking at Tisiphone. Tisiphone grinned and leaned toward him.

"*So, you still haven't told Ivmir what Menippe did to you?*" she asked in a stage whisper.

The atmosphere around the table turned glacial.

Cassius groaned. "I thought we'd decided never to mention that."

"What did Menippe do to you?" Morgan enunciated carefully between gritted teeth.

Atropos pinched the bridge of her nose. She looked ready to ding her siblings around the ear.

Cassius flashed a nervous smile at Morgan. "It was nothing, really."

"It was something if you're hiding it from me, Cassius," he growled, his knuckles whitening on his beer.

Victor touched Morgan's shoulder. "How about you calm—?"

"*She jumped on him naked and stuck her tongue down his throat,*" Tisiphone blurted out gleefully.

Gasps of shock and horrified delight echoed around the table. Atropos slumped in her seat like she wanted the ground to swallow her whole. Cassius dropped his head in his hands.

"*Go, Menippe,*" Alecto mumbled, her tone full of admiration.

The bottle in Morgan's hand cracked. He jumped to his feet.

"Theo, open a portal to the Astrea Sea right *now!*"

THE END

Follow Cassius and Morgan's final adventures in the epic conclusion to the Fallen Messengers series in Crimson Skies.

AFTERWORD

I hope you enjoyed Harbinger, the fifth book in the Fallen Messengers series. I'm pretty sure those Goddesses came as a surprise to all of you! I loved writing about them and I am so pleased with how Cassius and Morgan's family keeps growing. I would be grateful if you could leave a review of Harbinger on Goodreads or on the store where you purchased it. Reviews help readers like you find my books and I truly appreciate your honest opinions about my stories.

Make sure to sign up to my store newsletter for special deals on my books and new release alerts.

Or you can sign up to my author newsletter instead to get upcoming release notifications, sneak peeks, and giveaways.

ABOUT THE AUTHOR

Ava Marie Salinger is the pen name of an Amazon bestselling urban fantasy author who has always wanted to write MM urban fantasy romance. When she's not dreaming up hotties to write about, you'll find Ava creating kickass music playlists to write to, spying on the wildlife in her garden, drooling over gadgets, and eating Chinese food. She also writes contemporary MM romance as A.M. Salinger.

Visit Shop AD Starrling and buy all of Ava's ebooks, paperbacks, hardbacks, and exclusive special edition print books direct.